e-llegal code

e-llegal code

C. V. Alba

All rights reserved. The moral rights of the author have been asserted.

No part of this book may be reproduced in any form or by any electronic or mechanical means, including information storage and retrieval systems, without permission in writing from the publisher and copyright holder, except in the case of brief quotations embodied in critical articles and reviews.

The story, all names, characters, and incidents portrayed in this production are fictitious. No identification with actual persons (living or deceased), places, buildings, and products is intended or should be inferred.

Copyright © 2024 by C.V. Alba

ISBN 979-8-9884814-1-6

Cover Design by Humble Nations

www.cvalba.com

FREE SHORT STORY!

Sign up for the author's mailing list and get a free copy of ***Johnny and Jake***.

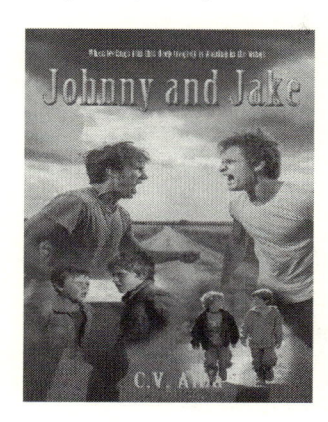

A chance encounter ramps up a long-standing feud between two brothers.

In Johnny's mind, his life seems to careen down a one-way street of lost opportunities, ones that favor his brother Jake.

How long can one endure a life spent watching your brother have it all?

When feelings run this deep, tragedy is waiting in the wings.

Start here: cvalba.com

Table of Contents

Chapter 1 1
Chapter 2 16
Chapter 3 35
Chapter 4 46
Chapter 5 62
Chapter 6 73
Chapter 7 80
Chapter 8 90
Chapter 9 106
Chapter 10 117
Chapter 11 126
Chapter 12 132
Chapter 13 140
Chapter 14 147
Chapter 15 161
Chapter 16 167
Chapter 17 183
Chapter 18 199
Chapter 19 206
Chapter 20 213
Chapter 21 222
Chapter 22 230
Chapter 23 237
Chapter 24 249
Chapter 25 259
Chapter 26 264

Chapter 27	270
Chapter 28	277
Chapter 29	281
Chapter 30	291

e-llegal code

Chapter 1

Fall 1993

Sweat rolled down the young man's forehead, stinging his eyes. He blinked, desperately searching for a way out. The second-floor stairwell on his left! He hit the door, pushing it open with the full force of his running body, almost falling through. After careening down the stairs, he found himself in an alley between the building and its neighbor. His eyes darted right and left. Which way? The alcove for the building's trash cans! He squeezed down behind the bins and into the corner.

The words from his last conversation with Rosa haunted him.

"He told you to do what?!"

"Just a little fun, a joke," the young man said.

"But it's against the law!" she replied.

"Not really, but even if it is, that's what makes it fun." His reply, with his impish grin under dark sparkling eyes, drove her crazy. *"I'm not hurting anyone. Anyway, if I can program it and no one finds it before they install the updates, we've proved their security is flawed. We'll tell them and they'll fix it. We'll have done them a favor."*

"But if you don't tell them ahead of time that you're doing this it makes you a bad guy. Kim, I don't like it." Her voice was laced with fear and urgency.

"Don't worry so much, anything happens to me, I left a message about this."

"Where did you leave it? Who did you tell what is going on?"

"I said, don't worry. Everything's going to be fine." He knew he hadn't convinced her, but she'd see. Everything was going to be just fine.

Kim started hearing soft, muffled footsteps in the distance. The footsteps resumed their progress, stopping from time to time, it seemed, to think. The hair on the back of his neck rose. Gulping back bile from his stomach, he cursed anew. Silence. Where were the footsteps? The trash bin moved in front of him, and he stood, starting to run. A blow bent him double, knocking his breath out in a swoosh and his feet from under him. Powerful knees locked around his waist, squeezing out the little breath he had. He gulped for air and felt a thin wire settle into his neck. Breathless, terrorized, and overwhelmed by a raw, screaming will to live, all his energy was focused on clawing at the steel knees, the thin wire around his neck. He searched for the wire that bit into his skin, sinew, and muscle; choking him. Expert knees held him; expert hands twisted the wire until Kim's eyes bulged and his tongue thrust out of his mouth as if there were no longer room for it in his head, until there was no longer a need to breathe. Black-gloved hands straightened the rumpled shirt and tied the lace on one tennis shoe. With a smooth motion, they hoisted Kim over one shoulder. These same black-gloved hands stuffed the thin wire of the garrote into a pocket, stroking the cool metal as if to calm a hawk after a successful hunt.

***

"Strangled?" Greene's gruff voice mixed fascination and repulsion in equal amounts. Mat turned in time to watch the detective trace a line around his neck with a pudgy index finger. He stood behind the beat-up desk inches from Mat's chair and met her gaze, the end of an unlit cigar protruding from the right corner of his mouth. As he listened, his bushy eyebrows rose in astonishment. With his free hand, he hitched his pants to a more secure position under his dough-boy stomach. Mat turned back to the screen but continued listening to the conversation. She tried to make something out of the occasional "uh, huh" and "yeah, gotcha" Greene contributed from his end of the wire. She punched a few keys and sent a test page to the printer to assure him she was working.

"No kidding?" His handlebar moustache beat the rhythm of his words. "Naw. You say a motorcycle cop saw him sticking out of a ditch out on Route 50? College kid? Why do you think that?" He returned to flipping a cheap ballpoint pen as he talked, hands and eyes unconnected from the conversation occupying his ears and mouth. Mat's curiosity was getting the better of her. She turned to look at Greene.

"Yeah, okay," Greene continued. "Maybe he was drunk and got all tangled up in something . . .

What's that? Dragged from somewhere else? Yeah, you do that. Run all those tests."

He turned to Mat, and she whipped her eyes back to the screen, feeling his gaze on the back of her head.

"Well, well. Uh huh." Greene's voice brought her attention back to the one-sided conversation. "Tell you what, I got something better than that. I got someone here who knows all about that stuff." He slammed the phone into its cradle and Mat cringed.

Matilda Briscoe had met Detective Greene when she helped uncover a pornography ring at her last company. She was fired by her boss, the ringleader, when she started getting too close. After the case was solved, jobless and close to broke, she decided to go into business for herself as an IT consultant. She was surprised to get a call from Detective Greene asking for general maintenance support to keep the antiquated machines in his office going. It was a challenge. Still, it paid the bills. Greene was a curmudgeon, irascible and not the brightest cop she'd ever met. In spite of that, she had developed a tolerance, if not a fondness, for his boorish manners and rough edges. *Okay, I can be bought, but I do a good job, it keeps the rent paid, and I'm not digging ditches.*

"Done yet?" he addressed the back of her head.

"After the backup." Mat didn't turn around.

"Don't you do stuff like that at night? I hear people like you are always working at night."

"Double my rate and I'll consider it."

"Tell it to the captain." Greene's voice was curt. "Turn that thing off and come on. I want to show you something." He grabbed his jacket from a pile of papers stacked by the desk and stalked off. Folders dislodged by his abrupt departure fluttered to the floor. He maneuvered his bulk between the rows of desks with surprising agility. The old, green metal desks, an arm's length from each other, shuddered under his weight when he turned a corner too sharply. His colleagues lifted coffee cups when he came their way or risked working on damp, brown-stained case files.

Mat's fingers flew through the shutdown cycle for the PC while she gathered up her sweater and knapsack from the floor. Glancing over her shoulder, she watched his rumpled gray pants with fraying cuffs and navy dress socks in scuffed tennis shoes disappear down the row of desks. She pushed the chair aside and raced to catch up, grabbing her cell phone lying beside the computer. It was a necessary acquisition once she went into business for herself and found she was never in one place for very long. Trying to keep track of phone messages and be responsive without one had proven impossible.

Mat caught up just as he stepped onto an elevator filled with office workers returning from a late lunch. She slipped in beside him and asked, "What's going on?"

"I plan on you tellin' me," he said, staring straight ahead. "Ever been in a morgue?"

"No." Mat felt her stomach drop.

"First time I saw a dead body, I tossed my guts all over the body."

"Tossed your guts?"

"Yeah. Got sick, threw up. Kid had been beat up bad and left out in a field. It was a few days before we found him. Heat was bad that year. He was all bloated and the flies were all over him. They give you some kind of cream to help with the smell, but it don't do much."

Mat glanced at the other passengers. Most appeared uninterested in Greene's sordid tale except for one pale young woman standing near the button panel who bolted out as soon as the doors opened at the next floor. Greene, oblivious, launched into a colorful description of the state of a human body after days of exposure to heat and humidity. *Enough already.* Mat thought about the reaction of her housemate, an effervescent artist given to séances and incantations to diminish the effects of Mat's encounters with the quick and the dead. *My God, what'll Zorah do about a morgue?*

Further thoughts were cut off by the sudden lurch of the elevator as it stopped on the lower level. Mat hesitated, then stepped in behind Greene who strode off down a concrete corridor, continuing his soliloquy on murder, motives, and the insidious wickedness of computers and other machines.

"Well?" Greene stopped in his tracks and turned, nearly enveloping Mat's nose in the zipper of his warm-up jacket.

"What?" she managed to mumble, mentally scrambling to recall what he'd been saying.

"I said, ever seen a dead body?"

"Oh. No. Closest I've been was that reporter's body in the back of the car at Zorah's studio but I didn't really see him. Just smelled him."

"Well, don't worry, kid," he said. "They won't let you see the body. I just wanna show you something." He was silent for the rest of the trip down the tunnel to a door at the other end.

Behind the door was a small anteroom. The walls were beige, the floor covered in nondescript linoleum that Mat was sure she'd seen in more than one kitchen years ago. Several chairs, plastic covers over metal frames, took up the little space in a rather haphazard manner. A soiled metal ashtray sat on a small table next to rings likely left by various cans, ceramic mugs, and paper cups. *Sad,* Mat thought, a sad room, forlorn and somehow without hope. The door provided the entrance to a room on the opposite side.

"Not much to look at, huh?" Greene said. "Places like this aren't at the top of the list for fixing up."

"What's this one used for." Mat avoided his eyes and continued her methodical examination of the room and its sparse contents.

"Sort of a waiting room, I guess."

"Waiting room?" Mat caught his eyes with hers. "What would you wait for in here?"

"Coroner or medical examiner. Folks gotta have someplace to wait 'til they go see the body." Greene looked away first. "Sure hard on folks. Seen some bad times here. It's the kids, though. Don't seem fair to see 'em here or back there." He jerked his head toward the door on the other side of the room.

"C'mon." He shoved aside a chair and headed for the opposite door. Grasping the knob, he pushed it open and yelled, "Hector!"

"Yeah?" came a distant reply.

"Got that kid here."

Mat stared at Greene. *Kid?*

"What kid?"

"Kid who can tell you about what you found on the dead guy."

Kid?

"Kid?" The puzzled voice was followed into the room by a small, thin woman with salt-and-pepper hair, a prominent nose and chin, and singularly small ears. Mat's mind clothed her in a pointed cap and gave her a broomstick to ride.

"Sweetheart!" Hector's face lit up at the sight of Greene. She cocked her head to one side. "What brings you here? I thought you'd forgotten all about me."

"Naw, I wouldn't do that." A pale, but unmistakable, blush peeked from Greene's collar. "This here's Matilda Briscoe." He nodded back toward Mat. "Bet she knows what you found on that body. Remember?" As he spoke, he stepped back and pushed Mat into view.

"Mat, please call me Mat," said Mat, extending her hand toward the diminutive woman. She looked Mat over and ignored the outstretched hand. Mat felt like she'd been judged and came up short, though of what, she couldn't have said.

"Hector," said Greene gruffly. "Just show her what you found."

Hector shrugged and retreated through the door behind her. Greene fell into step, and Mat

e-llegal code

brought up the rear. As she crossed the threshold, Mat gazed in disbelief at the parts of the room she could see around Greene's corpulent form. All the flat surfaces were covered with files, sheets of paper, forms, and unopened mail. Even the extra chair beside the desk was piled with tattered, letter-sized envelopes and manila folders. A large plate-glass window provided a view into the working center of the morgue.

"You need to clean this up," stated Greene who had stopped two steps into the room. "This ain't right, you being the medical examiner. How do you know you got all the papers on those dead folks?"

"If it doesn't get done, either I get a call or it doesn't matter. I get the important things done." Hector disappeared behind the mound of papers on her desk, and they could hear drawers opening and closing.

Like a magnet, Mat found her gaze drawn to the window behind Hector, revealing the examination room beyond. Part of a gurney was visible, surrounded by stainless steel sinks and work surfaces. A single bare forearm and hand extended below the sheet covering the form on the gurney. Above the arm, Mat followed the outline of a head and chest lying motionless under the sheet. She closed her eyes against the image, against the destruction of the promises and hopes life brought that now would never be.

"It's here, I put it where I'd know where to find it," Hector said, continuing her search.

"Oh brother." Greene bowed his head in disgust, and concern mixed into his voice.

"They're going to get you for this someday, Hector. Then what'll you do?"

"I'm too small a fish and I've been here too long. If they wanted me out, it'd have happened long ago. Got it!" Hector reappeared holding two plastic evidence bags. Inside one was what looked like a business card. The other contained a flat square object.

"These were in an inner pocket. If we hadn't been searching his clothes, we'd never have found them. He had a couple of layers on with those big patch pockets. Couldn't tell he had anything in them unless you checked every one."

She shouldered Mat aside and pushed the papers on one corner toward the center of the desk. Mat watched in fascination as the huge pile shuddered and regained a precarious equilibrium.

"Looks like the business card is yours." She looked at Mat then thrust the plastic bag with the business card at Greene. "This other thing, not sure, but it looks like it belongs with a computer." She held up the bag with the square object.

"Poor kid," Hector continued, nodding toward the body that could be seen on the gurney through the window. "Been dead a couple of days when we found him. No ID, but a pocket protector, remember those? Didn't know anyone used those things anymore. Had a pencil in it with the logo of one of the local universities, forget which one. That's not all. He had a scrap of paper with letterhead from some local politician, name of Dan Collins. Just found that." She handed the bagged scrap of paper and the square object to Greene. "Figured you'd want to check that out."

"Thanks," grunted Greene, who took the bags and studied the paper through the plastic before shoving it into his pocket. He handed the square object to Mat.

Mat looked at the flat object with interest. *I do love a puzzle, especially the computer kind.*

"So?" Hector asked, impatience in her voice. "What is it?" She turned her attention to Greene, crossed her arms, and leaned against the desk. "Maybe your kid genius here isn't so smart, huh, Greene?"

Greene grunted for a reply.

Mat looked up at the short woman, trying hard to keep the irritation from her expression. *This office could be a source of valuable information if bodies keep turning up in my line of work. I really don't want to make an enemy of Hector.*

"On the face of it, there's nothing unusual about it. It's a floppy disk used to store computer data and programs." Mat looked from Hector to Greene while she fingered the square object through the plastic bag, her fingers itching for a keyboard. "I assume you'd like to see what's on it. Can I keep it for a few days?

"Er, well, it's not done regular," Greene began. When Mat didn't respond, he looked at Hector, who shrugged.

"Guess I can sign it out to you. It's been dusted for prints so it's okay as far as that goes. Only for a few days. It's police property, so don't go losing it," he growled. "Gotta sign for it. We'll stop by the office on our way out."

"I'll have it back within the week," Mat said, slipping the disk into her shirt pocket. Greene retreated toward the door they had entered. Unable to stop herself, Mat stared once more at the body behind Hector. He had been young and bright, and now he was dead. She swallowed the lump in her throat. Hector followed her gaze and lowered the window shade, her small face overtaken by a disapproving frown.

There was little else to say, and she and Greene soon left. They made a brief stop at his office where Mat signed a form acknowledging receipt of the computer disk. It was a relief when they emerged into the afternoon sun slanting down the narrow street beside the morgue entrance. The warmer air of the afternoon was fading into the cool brisk tonic of early fall. Mat slipped on a sweater jacket while listening to Greene.

"Ambulances and hearses go around the corner. There's another entrance in back," Greene was saying. "It's marked better so you know where you are. Guess that helps, but I use this one if I can, don't seem so, I don't know . . ."

"Like you just left a morgue?" Mat finished for him.

"Yeah, I guess." He straightened his jacket and turned away, dismissing the topic. "You need a lift? I got a car around the corner."

"Thanks, but mine's not far. I'd just as soon walk."

"Suit yourself." Greene shrugged and stalked off, leaving her standing in the receding light of the afternoon.

The sharp screech of tires grabbed their attention, and Mat's heart leapt to her throat. A black Lincoln limousine dug into the gutter in front of them. The rear passenger window rolled down and a man's face emerged from the dark interior and looked out at them.

"Hey!" he commanded. "Are you Greene? Detective Greene? I need to talk to you."

Greene stiffened, and Mat saw the muscles of his jaw clench.

"You're Greene, aren't you?" the voice demanded, a voice used to being obeyed without challenge.

Greene moved forward one step. The man's face was lightly tanned under wavy hair cut to show off its thickness and gold highlights. It matched a perfectly trimmed moustache. His topcoat was unbuttoned, and she could see a white linen shirt under his navy suit. As Greene drew closer, Mat noted a diamond earring in his ear and the scent of a cigar. He smiled. Mat disliked him at once.

Greene stopped five feet from the car. Mat sensed the tension in his stance, so at odds with the authoritative bonhomie of the man in the limousine.

"Hey, how're you doing?" he asked, waving the cigar in the air. "Name's Dan, Dan Collins. Remember? You helped with security at one of my rallies. Say, who's that pretty thing hiding behind you?"

Greene didn't move. "What can I do for you?" the detective asked in a neutral tone.

"I'm looking for someone. Didn't show up where he was supposed to. Been gone a couple of days. No one seems to know where he is. College kid. Asian. He has something of mine that I can't find. He might have kept it with him. I've been to the drunk tank over at the jail. Don't like the thought, but wanted to ask if there's anyone in the morgue that might fit that description."

"You kin?" Greene asked from his spot several feet from the car.

Dan hesitated, shrugged, and said, "Not really. The kid I'm looking for was doing some work for me."

"What kind of work?" Greene asked.

"This and that. Office work. Nice kid but doesn't speak English that well."

"Well, I'd need a name and I can't really give out specifics unless you're kin anyway. It's too late today, but come in tomorrow morning and we'll take a statement and I'll see what I can do for you."

His words chased the smile from Dan's face. He leaned out the window of the limousine, reaching out to Greene with his voice. In low tones he asked, "Coming in is a waste of my time. Do I have to talk to your supervisor?"

"That's another way," Greene replied. He relaxed into the bent knee, hand-pocketed stance of one prepared to wait.

"Listen, you—" Dan leaned further out the window until he seemed to stretch his torso beyond its limits. "If you find anything that belongs to me I want to know about it immediately."

"How will I know it's yours?"

"I'll tell you. Just let me know if you find anything."

His eyes seemed to snap at Greene as he disappeared into the limousine. They caught a glimpse of a silver-headed cane jabbing at the glass partition behind the driver. The car sped off and Mat watched the dust from the street swirling in its wake. She felt as if a small tornado had passed by—malevolent, violent, and capable of much more damage than had been inflicted this time. Her hand wrapped around the sharp edges of the computer disk in her pocket. She wondered what Greene was thinking.

Chapter 2

"But Zorah, I only saw part of the body and I didn't touch it!" Mat declared from the depths of a worn beanbag chair. She was sitting to Zorah's right, behind the oversized canvas that held the artist's attention. Greg McCawley leaned against an old sofa on the other side of Zorah's easel. He was an attorney and Mat's frequent companion. They had met when Mat moved to the area and was looking for a place to stay. He owned the old Victorian house Mat and Zorah shared. Restoring it had been a labor of love.

Over time, he'd revealed a little of his story to Mat, how his prison guard father had been arrested for taking bribes and he'd been left in a foster home. The rest was a classic story of a determined, self-made man who'd succeeded via hard work and Harvard on grants and awards. She'd assured him their stories weren't that different but had yet to find the courage to fill him in.

Earlier that evening, he and Mat had met for dinner, then decided to go see what Zorah was up to. It was close to midnight, the time when Zorah did her best work. The cool night air of early fall wafted into the vast reaches of the warehouse that was now known as Candlewick and used as an artists' studio. The broken windows and skylights gave an uninterrupted view of stars twinkling above, providing a ceiling of black velvet studded with diamonds.

"It doesn't matter, Mat," Zorah replied. "That aura of death will hover. You can't escape it." The artist underscored her words with wide sweeping motions of her brush, ignoring the blobs and bits of paint that flew off in all directions. "It'll affect your moods, you won't be able to work." She leaned forward, drawing paint across the canvas as if to emphasize the words. "And I, for one, don't need an evil aura around. I need to get this painting finished in time for the mural competition. It could be my big break. I'm almost at the end of my savings and I do not want to go back to being a busboy at that diner down the street."

Mat twisted in the worn beanbag chair and turned frustrated eyes on Greg. His answer was an amused twinkle in his eye and an impish grin. Mat was struck again by the strength in his lean features, emphasized by hazel eyes that could look deep into her soul. She looked away, self-conscious as though found out.

"Just what do you propose?" he asked the artist.

Zorah paused mid-brush stroke. "A consultation with Salee," she stated without hesitation.

"Sally?" asked Greg.

"S-a-l-e-e," spelled Zorah with a touch of impatience in her voice. "Ask Mat. She'll know what to do." Zorah sat back with a satisfied sigh, whether with the painting or her advice, Mat couldn't tell.

Greg raised an eyebrow and Mat shrugged. Before she could disavow any knowledge of

Salee, they heard the urgent, muted thud of footsteps hurrying across the old wooden floor beyond their view. The spotlight at the end of the room illuminated a figure with flaming-orange hair perched on top of a floor-length caftan. It hurried toward them.

"Minnie!" Zorah called out in greeting. She sprang up to greet the brightly colored caftan, pushing Mat off the beanbag in her haste to envelop Minnie with a hug and a smile. At the last minute, she was held off by the urgent pleas of the figure within.

"Zorah, you've got to help me," Minnie demanded. "It's Lilah. She's sick and I don't know what to do."

"Who's Lilah?" asked Zorah.

"My friend. You know. We've been friends for ever so long. She's the one dating that rich guy."

"What's wrong with her?" asked Zorah.

"I don't know. She won't wake up. I shook her and shook her, but she won't wake up." Minnie wrung her hands while she talked, brows knit together, eyes darting from her hands to Zorah and back. With Greg's help, Mat picked herself up from the floor and brushed away the dust and debris that rose with her. Greg chuckled silently at her efforts while ignoring the withering expression she sent his way.

"Is she sick? I mean, has she got a fever? Did she eat something funny?" Zorah lobbed one comment after another at Minnie.

"Yes, no, I mean, I don't think so. I don't know."

"Which?" Zorah demanded. "Which don't you know?"

"Any of it. Zorah, I don't even know if she has a fever, I didn't check. I thought I'd go see her. She told me she'd be back by midnight and Dan was away. Please, just come help me. I don't know what to do," Minnie pleaded, grabbing Zorah's arm and pulling her toward the door.

Zorah looked back at Mat and Greg. She ignored the expressions of irritation and amusement on their respective faces.

"C'mon," she urged. "You two can help."

"They're friends," she assured Minnie who stopped in her tracks, appearing to see Mat and Greg for the first time.

"Oh, I don't know," she said, backing away a step or two.

"Well, I do," Zorah declared and grabbed Minnie's arm.

"Where are we going?" asked Mat.

Minnie looked with uncertainty at Mat. "Not far. I rode my bike. Don't have a car."

Mat pushed aside her irritation and smiled at her. "Good, sounds like we should get there as soon as possible."

Minnie heard her without smiling in return. She turned and let Zorah pull her toward the door. They trouped out in an awkward single file. Once they reached the sidewalk, Zorah and Minnie led the way with Mat and Greg close behind.

Four blocks away, Minnie entered an ancient but stately four-story building. She led them up two flights of stairs explaining it was faster than the elevator. Mat ran her fingers over the polished wood banister worn with age and the caress of thousands of hands. The wide stairs and high ceilings were faintly illuminated by the glow from a single globe on each landing. The building exuded a decrepit dignity that Mat found appealing and sad at the same time.

As they climbed the stairs, Minnie continued a nervous monologue describing her friendship with Lilah. "We met five years ago at a women's health clinic. We've been friends since then. But she changed when she met Dan. Honestly, I try to like him. But I know he's just using her like he does everyone else. Pays the rent for her apartment, stuff like that. I told her, but she won't listen. Thinks he hung the moon." Minnie giggled. "My mom used to say that. Anyway, he rides around in this big black limousine. Name's Dan something. Collins, that's it. Think he's in politics."

Dan Collins. That's the name of that guy in the limo and on the letterhead Hector found on the kid's body. Mat turned in surprise to Greg, who responded with a puzzled expression. Before she could explain, Minnie stopped in front of the third door and searched her pocket for the key. The door swung open on a short hall leading into a spacious living room. A three-panel bay window looked out on the tree-lined street below. Oak paneling and worn wood floors could be seen in the half-light. A modern sofa and chair shared space with an antique china cabinet. Near the window, a bouquet of tired flowers hung over the rim of a glass vase, their drooping hues a reminder of the careless rush of life that left them unwatered. Somehow, the space had an air of elegance blended with an easy lived-in feeling.

"This way," said Minnie. She crossed the room and pushed open a door, beckoning them to follow.

Mat caught up and peered over Zorah's shoulder. Both stared in disbelief. The overwhelming wash of red made objects indistinguishable at first, then the bedroom took shape in bits and pieces. A huge canopy bed was draped and blanketed in red satin. Red carpet ran wall to wall. The window was topped by red balloon shades and surrounded by red-on-red paper that covered all four walls. On the bed lay a young woman, her back to them, wrapped in a pink negligee that was twisted under arms and legs bathed in perspiration. She glistened in the light and shadows cast by their bodies in the door. Rumpled sheets had been tossed aside, pillows scattered across the bed.

"Lilah?" said Minnie, rushing to her side. "Honey, I brought help." In the silence, she looked back at the three faces, searching their features one at a time, her flaming-orange hair a striking complement to the red tones of the room. The intense colors lent an exotic air to the room that seemed a retreat for the sins of the flesh, a bordello. *What sort of person is this Lilah?*

Greg stepped forward. He approached the bed and lifted one wrist, then put a hand on her forehead. "How long has she been like this?"

"I don't know. I got home half an hour ago. She said she'd be up late. And I found her there on the bed."

Minnie turned to Greg. "Are you a doctor? Do you know what's wrong?"

"I'm not a doctor. But I do know she's got a high fever and rapid pulse. You need to call 911."

Minnie gasped, her hand at her throat. "She's that bad?"

"A high fever and rapid pulse by themselves might not be that serious, but she's unconscious and has been for at least half an hour. I don't want to guess what that's all about. Go call 911."

Minnie turned and retreated to the living room, where Mat heard her punching in the number. Zorah hung back by the bedroom door.

"Mat"—Greg beckoned her toward the bed—"can you place that odor?"

Mat inhaled, taking in the faint pungent, coppery smell.

"Blood." She looked at Greg who held a hand up in caution. "Where's it from?" Mat asked. "She's alive isn't she?"

"Yes. Don't touch her or the bed. Let the medics do it."

"They'll be here right away," Minnie said, returning from the outer room to stand beside Zorah in the doorway. Mat looked from Zorah to Minnie who attempted a crooked smile in return. A few minutes later a siren's wail broke the silence.

***

"How did you get mixed up with them?" Mat asked. She was sitting on the top porch step outside the kitchen of the old Victorian house she shared with Zorah. It was late the next evening, a peaceful time that they found to be a natural pause in the day, a point when they could catch up before Zorah left for the studio. The floppy disk Detective Greene had given Mat lay on the porch step, teasing her with the mystery of its purpose. She picked it up and turned it over, examining the small device for the hundredth time.

"With who?" Zorah asked in return, wrapping a broomstick skirt around her ankles as she squatted on the weathered boards and rested her head against the back door frame.

"Minnie. This Lilah person."

"Yeah. Weird, huh?" Zorah shrugged.

"Have she and Minnie been friends long?"

"Don't know. They were friends when I met her. Met Minnie, I mean. It was Lilah who suggested she try art lessons. Something about finding herself. So Minnie came by the studio a couple of years ago to learn how to draw. I guess we stayed in touch. Didn't realize how long it'd been. Anyway, I think they were both volunteering at a women's clinic at the time. I always thought Lilah was strange. Still do." She brushed a wisp of brown hair from her face.

"Strange? In what way?"

Zorah was silent for a few minutes, then breathed a long sigh and answered, "I've never met someone who was so lost in someone else. I mean, she didn't seem to have a life without this

Dan person. Everything is about him. Irritating, you know. I mean, I could never give up my painting for anyone like that."

The phone rang in sharp bursts, demanding their attention.

"I'll get it." Zorah jumped up, grabbed the screen door, and reached for the phone, bracelets jangling. Mat watched her disappear into the bright light of the kitchen and continued to turn the diskette over in her hand. Her first attempts to read it had been fruitless. Whatever was on it had been encrypted, and she needed a code to unlock the contents. *What to do?* Just because that kid had it on him when he died didn't mean anything. Then again, maybe it did. She looked up as Zorah emerged, a stricken expression on her face.

"What's wrong?" Mat asked, rising from her seat on the porch.

"She's dead."

"Who's dead?"

"Lilah."

"Lilah? But she wasn't that sick, was she? How could she be dead?" Mat sat up, surprise and disbelief evident in her wrinkled brow and round eyes.

"I don't know. That was Minnie on the phone. She's pretty upset. I couldn't get much out of her."

"Was she at the hospital?"

"Maybe. She said she called a couple of friends from the women's clinic, but they weren't home. She doesn't want to go home by herself. So I invited her to come over."

"I'm glad you did," Mat assured her with a smile. "She can stay overnight if she wants." Most of the time she enjoyed Zorah's impetuous generosity and felt more human by association. Except for the time they found one of her artist friends sleeping in his car and Zorah invited him to stay with them temporarily. He had quit a carpentry job because the sanding was ruining his hands. It took them two months to get him out of the drawing room.

The phone rang again, jarring them again with its insistent tone. Mat looked down and realized it was her new cell phone. *When am I going to get used to having this thing right beside me?* She grabbed the phone and answered on the fourth ring.

"Thought you weren't home," Greene's voice growled at the other end.

"Sorry . . ." Mat floundered for words. "Uh, I had my hands in dishwater." For some reason she didn't want to tell him about Lilah. He was a client now. She needed to remember that. "What can I do for you?"

"Thought you'd want to know about a conversation I had this afternoon. Got a call from a guy name of Dan Collins."

"Dan Collins?" Mat said in astonishment.

"Yeah. What's it to you?"

"Nothing, really." Mat thought quickly. "Isn't that the guy who showed up at the morgue? He's some kind of politician, right?"

"That's what he says," Greene replied. "Gets college students to volunteer to help with his campaign. Seems our body was one of them."

"*Our* body?"

"Yeah."

"How did this Dan Collins know one of his volunteers was in the morgue?"

"Don't know. Wanted to know, again, if we'd found anything that belonged to him on the body."

"Like what?"

"Didn't say. Guess I forgot to tell him about the disk thing." Mat heard Greene's smile. "What'd you find?"

"I'm working on it."

"I figured that." His impatience crawled down the wire to Mat's ear. "You've had a whole day. It can't take that long to figure it out. You're supposed to be smart that way."

Greene kept his fear of computers hidden behind disrespect and oversimplification of the issues they entailed. Most of the time, Mat let it roll off her back, but on top of Zorah's news, it was hard to do.

"Yeah, well, I'm working on it. I'll call you when I find out something. It's encrypted."

"It's what? That contagious?"

Mat chuckled in spite of herself. "No. It means the information on it is protected. I need to get around that."

"Oh. Well, you got a week. Something else," Greene was on a roll, "that girl you and your friends called the ambulance about. Doc said she was hemorrhaging from a miscarriage when you got to her. 'Course it could just be Mother Nature, but these days we check for other stuff. We want to know what drugs she may have taken. There are some that induce abortions, you know.

She regained consciousness long enough to say she didn't take any drugs, but we'll let the test results show us that. She's unconscious. Critical condition." He hung up without another word.

Mat stared at the receiver. *So you don't know that she's dead.* The image of the shrouded body beyond Hector's door, and then Lilah's limp form, filled her mind.

For the third time, the sharp sounds of a bell intruded into her thoughts. This time, the sound was accompanied by loud knocking on the front door. She looked around as Zorah strode by on her way to answer it. She winked at Mat as she passed, her long brown hair drifting behind her, shifting in waves to her sides as she walked by. Mat heard the low murmur of solicitous tones, the front door shutting, and soft footsteps moving away from the door. Curiosity led her to the front sitting room where she saw Minnie on the love seat, wiping her eyes with a delicate, lace-edged handkerchief. Zorah was perched beside her. They looked up at Mat's entrance.

"I'm so sorry about your friend," said Mat, sitting in the overstuffed armchair opposite Minnie. "I had no idea she was that sick."

At that, Minnie broke out in a fresh round of sobs. Mat raised an eyebrow and caught her friend's eye over Minnie's bowed head. Zorah stroked the bowed head and, after more dabs at her eyes, Minnie said, "I just can't believe it. Lilah was on the verge of something so wonderful. It's just not fair she had to die now."

"What do you mean, 'she was on the verge of something wonderful'?" asked Mat.

"I guess she wouldn't mind if I told you. Not now." Minnie's lips quivered but she maintained her tenuous composure. "She was going to have his baby. Oh, we were so excited." The dam of tears broke again, and Minnie gave in to fresh sobs.

Mat looked at Zorah who shrugged in reply and said, "Did Dan know? Surely she told him. Were they going to get married?"

Minnie sat up, withdrawing from the soothing warmth of Zorah's hand. "Doesn't matter now does it? Anyway, I don't think so. She was going to nurture a life without all the burden and repression of marriage. If she'd married him, it would have been ruined. He understood that."

"Different strokes I guess," replied Zorah. "I have lots of married friends who don't find it ruinous. They seem to like it."

"Whose baby was it?"

Minnie's wild wet eyes flashed over to Mat and she seemed confused. Mat didn't know if she couldn't decide whether to answer the question or wasn't sure what she'd heard. Before she could repeat the question, Minnie blurted out, "Why Dan's, of course."

"Why 'of course'?" Mat persisted. Zorah's eyes widened, then scrunched shut. Her face took on a pained expression. Mat held Minnie's gaze, ignoring Zorah's visual cue to drop the topic.

"Well, of course it's his. She wasn't seeing anyone else. She loved him so much." The tears began again, and anger followed the tears. "How can you ask me that?"

"Did they tell you they are checking to see if she took an abortion drug?" *Well, Greene didn't actually tell me I couldn't pass that along.* "I was just thinking that if she had taken something to induce an abortion and it was intentional, maybe it was because the baby wasn't Dan's."

"She wouldn't have done that, and it had to be Dan's. There was no one else and I should know." Minnie tossed the words at Mat as she gathered her shawl and headed out the door. "Anyway, it's none of your business. I'll find somewhere else to stay."

Mat and Zorah winced at the slamming of the door. It didn't latch and drifted slowly back into the room. Zorah turned to Mat.

"Well, you did it this time. What's it to you anyway if it was or wasn't Dan's?"

Mat looked at her friend in surprise. They rarely fought and never over someone else's problem. "Whoa, I was just trying to understand what happened."

"Like she said, what's it matter? They'd probably been dating a long time is all. So, of course he'd be the father."

Mat considered her words. "Guess you're right." She rose from the chair and faced her friend. "Zorah, I didn't mean to run her off. Does she have anyplace else to go?"

"It's a little late to worry about that, isn't it?" Zorah raised her hands at her own words. "Sorry, Mat. It just seems you never get caught up like most of us do. I mean, nothing seems to upset you."

Before she could answer, the front door crept open even further and a head of wavy black hair appeared.

"Hey, anybody home?" Greg asked as he stepped into the room. "Having an open house?" Seeing their expressions, he added, "Just joking. The door was standing open and . . ." He looked from Mat to Zorah, then said, "Why don't I go out and come back in?" He turned around as if to put the thought into action.

"No, wait. Greg, hello, come on in." Mat stepped across to him and gave him a playful kiss on the cheek. "Sorry, we were in the middle of a conversation."

"Must have been pretty intense." Greg relaxed at her welcome. "Did it start outside?"

"Huh?" Mat was caught off guard again.

"The door," said Greg. "Didn't you know it was standing open?"

"Oh," Zorah said. "Minnie came by and left in a hurry. Guess she didn't close the door."

"Minnie? Oh, that interesting girl with the sick friend," Greg said.

"She's dead," Mat added.

"Who's dead? Minnie?" Greg looked confused.

"No, she was just here. Lilah is dead," said Zorah.

"Lilah from the red bordello bedroom?" Greg looked from Mat to Zorah for confirmation.

"You got it. The doctors are trying to find out if she took some kind of abortion drug, although it's not clear that's what killed her."

"Whoa. You mean she was pregnant?"

"Yeah. Minnie said she was dating some rich guy."

Zorah gathered herself together and moved toward the door. "I'm going to work on my mural. I don't want to talk about this anymore." She left the room, broomstick skirt waving in bright colors behind her.

"What's with her?" Greg asked Mat.

"Beats me." Mat avoided his eyes. She breathed deeply and smiled at him. "Greg, did you tell me once that you follow local politics?" A quizzical expression floated over his face at the change of topic. He sat back, and she felt his eyes on her.

"Probably, but my knowledge of the day-to-day depends on the time I have. What's up?"

"Did you ever hear of a Dan Collins?"

"I know one who's a politician. There are plenty more with that name I'm sure."

"The politician will do for now."

"Fastest-rising son-of-a-bitch I've ever met. Why?"

"Why do you say that?" Mat asked.

"Fastest-rising or son-of-a-bitch?"

"Start with fastest-rising and go on to son-of-a-bitch."

"He's an ambitious man and the word is he's got what it takes. He's moved up the party ladder faster than anyone in recent history. It would seem he's got the ruthlessness and thick skin those ambitions require. He has a permanent arrangement with an agency for secretaries and chauffeurs. Seems he goes through them almost as often as he changes clothes. I've been backstage and seen how he treats them, so I'm not surprised."

"How come you know him so well?"

"Curiosity, I guess."

"Got those kind of ambitions yourself?" she asked, a faint smile at the corners of her mouth. She wondered how many other surprises he would have for her. The ones already revealed were enough for most relationships to absorb in a lifetime. Of course, she had made her contributions as well, with more to come.

He smiled in return and sat back against the lush pile of clipped velvet covering the overstuffed armchair.

"Can't say exactly." He cocked an eyebrow and looked at his hands, the long fingers tip to tip. "Can't make a commitment and can't stay away."

"Sounds familiar," Mat said with more bitterness than she expected. Greg glanced up, the smile fading fast. "Never mind," she said. Then added, "So how do you know this guy?"

Greg shifted in his seat and took a minute to answer. Mat kicked herself. *What do I sound like? A bitter woman unable to let go and get on with it?*

"Went to a rally once and he was there. Introduced the speaker as I recall. I was standing by the stage when he came down and we met. He invited me to sit at his table and we had a drink later."

"So he singled you out. Why would he do that?" Mat asked.

"He had the idea I was an attorney with an influential law firm on the Hill. I didn't set him

e-llegal code

straight once I figured out what was going on in his mind. Wanted to see where it would take me."

"Where did it?"

"Not far," Greg said, chagrin in his voice. "Someone must have straightened him out later because I've gotten the cold shoulder ever since. Guess that's part of his game."

"Until you're really with an influential law firm on the Hill."

"Yeah. Forgiving and forgetting, at least on the surface, is also part of the game. Why all this interest?"

"He's the guy Minnie's friend was dating."

"The one who's dead? The pregnant one who's dead?"

"That's the one."

Greg loosed a long, low whistle. "He'll want to keep that little escapade under wraps."

"Dan . . . I want to meet him. Can you arrange it?"

"Why? And I don't know if I can. Like I said, I'm persona non grata these days."

"He's interested in a body Greene and I saw at the morgue the other day and, if Lilah took an abortion drug, I'm interested in who gave it to her. He seems a likely candidate."

"Mat, maybe she took it herself. Anyway, none of that is any of your business."

"The body of that strangled student may be. Greene wants me to find out what's on a storage device he found on the body. I'm wondering if it's connected to Dan in some way. He told Greene the kid was doing some work for him and

33

has something of his. I wonder if it's the computer disk we found on his body."

"That's a stretch, Mat."

"I don't think so," Mat replied stubbornly. "Can you introduce us?"

"Well, I don't like it. Anyway, I'm not sure I'd be the best one to introduce you. Remember I'm not a favorite of his at the moment."

"But you know the territory and the players. Come on, Greg. This isn't cops and robbers. You're right, it's none of my business and there's probably nothing there but it'll satisfy my curiosity. Anyway, I'd like to know what fascinates you about politics." Mat tried to smile in her most beguiling way, knowing he would see right through her.

He studied her for a moment, then returned her smile. "It's against my better judgment, but there's a rally next weekend in Sterling. I'll check to see if he's scheduled to be there, and we'll take it from there."

Mat grinned and enfolded him in an enthusiastic bear hug.

"Hey," he said, hugging her close in return and speaking to the top of her head, "your hunches have gotten me in a lot of trouble in the past. I have a feeling this time will be no different."

Chapter 3

"Unconscious? Who?" Mat flailed her way through a fog of deep slumber. "Hector?" A kaleidoscope of images and thoughts came rushing at her as she surfaced to impenetrable darkness split here and there by dim shafts of light. *Who the hell is Hector?*

"Slow down. Start at the beginning." Mat pushed herself to a sitting position while trying to keep the cell phone at her ear. She glanced at the clock: 4:00 a.m. *God.*

"What's going on?" Greg stirred beside her.

"Shhh," Mat hissed in his direction. *Why is Greene calling at 4:00 a.m.? And who the hell is Hector?*

"Slow down," Mat demanded, "and start over. Please. Who did what to . . . did you say Hector?" *OMG, the medical examiner!*

"What happened? When did you say you found her?" Mat asked, blinking sleep out of her eyes. She listened and winced at the anguish in Greene's voice.

"Unconscious? Really? Who? Why do you think he did it?"

Greg struggled to a sitting position and switched on the bedside light. He ran fingers through tousled black curls. Mat's heart skipped a beat as she followed the outline of his neck to the slope of his broad, muscular shoulders, past the curve at the small of his back and . . . She jerked her mind back to the phone and murmured comforting noises. She looked at the clock and felt irritation pushing aside all other emotions.

"I know, I know," she said, trying not to sound annoyed, "but there's not much you can do at the moment. Do you realize it's 4:00 a.m.? Okay, I'll meet you. Yes, at Elie's Café. At 7:30." She hung up and crashed back on the pillow, shutting her eyes against the glare of the lamp.

"So, what gives? Who was that?" asked Greg, sitting up, knees bent lotus style, arms stretched out behind him on either side. He sounded tired, as if anticipating the blare of the alarm in two hours, and resigned to the drag in the day this lack of sleep would bring. She worried again that her lifestyle was a bad fit for a pin-striped lawyer. If it was, she knew it was better he see it now and move on. *But please, if you see it, make the moving on come later, much later if at all.* She grabbed his hand and put it to her lips, throwing him off balance so that he fell out of his lotus, legs akimbo.

"Whoa, let me get untangled," he said, laughing and pulling his hand free to right himself on the bed.

"That was Greene."

"I figured. Couldn't think of anyone else who'd call you at 4:00 a.m. to discuss unconscious persons." Mat saw his droll smile buried in her shoulder.

"Sorry. Someone broke into the morgue. Whoever it was found Hector, the medical examiner, working late and knocked her out. Seems she's in intensive care, they don't know when she'll regain consciousness."

Greg commented with a long low whistle. "Why would anyone break into a medical examiner's office?" he asked.

"Greene thinks robbery was the motive. Hector was there, finishing up some paperwork." She remembered the mountain of paper on the diminutive doctor's desk. "Yeah. Good luck with that!" she said with a raised eyebrow. She felt Greg's hands stroke her hair. *How can he be so much better at this sympathy thing than I am?*

"Okay. But why would anyone break into the medical examiner's office to steal anything? The only things they have in there are dead people, right?"

"Apparently, that's what they were after, one of the dead people. Remember the kid they found out on the highway? The one I told you had been strangled?" The picture of the cloth-shrouded figure with a single visible arm appeared in her mind.

"Sure."

"Well, whoever broke in pulled his body out of the locker and left it in the middle of the lab. Greene thinks they figured his clothes were stored with him."

"They aren't, are they?"

"No. Greene's guessing they found the storage unit where the kid's clothes were stored and ransacked it. The body was just left out in the lab, not disturbed in any way."

"So Greene thinks that once the thieves realized the kid's things weren't kept with the body, they left it alone while they searched the rest of the lab."

"He said that Hector heard them. She called 911, then must have tried to stop them."

"Sounds like Greene already has someone in mind, a suspect."

"Dan Collins, or his henchmen. He showed up when we were leaving the morgue. And Greene told me he called again after I left and wanted to see the kid's body. Greene stalled him."

"Dan Collins again. Still, I can see why Greene thinks it was him."

"Well, they may not have gotten what they were after." She felt Greg turn in her direction and saw his curiosity in the dim light, guarded and insistent. His emotions flickered across his face in her imagination, scrunching his brow, a smile tugging at the corners of his mouth. He rolled away from her and straightened out, stretching long legs into the darkness. She saw his arms rise briefly, then slip into the darkness under his head.

"Because . . .?" he asked in a tone another would have heard as disinterested, even bored. Mat replied, knowing he would hear the smile in her words.

"I still have the floppy disk they found on the kid's body."

"Who else knows you have it?"

"Just Greene. And . . ." Mat's voice trailed off.

"And who?" Greg insisted, up on his elbow, facing Mat.

"Hector." Mat slipped down on her pillow. *Damn. Did Hector remember my name?*

"Did she know your name?" asked Greg.

"I don't know. I can't remember if Greene introduced us. Even if he did, maybe she didn't remember it."

"That's thin, Mat. We won't know what Hector told them until she regains consciousness." He sat up. "If they got it out of her, your name's in the phone book and it won't take them long to get here. In any case, you'll be safer if you get out of here."

"Zorah will have to leave too. They'll have no way to tell she's not me."

"Oh, I think they'll know she's not you."

Mat heard Greg's sardonic tone and replied, "Really? You think they won't equate her bohemian dress, caftans, and smudges of paint with my left-brain skills?"

"But they could use her to get to you, like before."

Mat cringed. *How much of that could our friendship withstand? How much of that could I stand?*

"You could move in with me." Greg switched on the light and gathered his clothes from the various parts of the room where they'd been dumped. Mat watched him moving around, her own mind working in slow motion, piecing together her choices, trying to fit them into a scenario she could accept. *Whoa, wait a minute!*

"That won't work either. They'll head straight for you," Mat said, glad of a logical reason to avoid that topic. "Lots of people know we're together. Same for Zorah." She stopped in mid-thought, aware that Greg heard it too. The sound of a metal latch sliding open grabbed them at the same time.

"The front door?" whispered Mat. She turned toward Greg, searching for the glint of his eyes in the dim light.

"You locked the front door, didn't you?" he whispered back in her direction.

"Of course I did," hissed Mat. They paused as the soft pad of footsteps on the stairs reached their ears. Mat slid out of bed and crossed to the door. She stood with her back to the wall, searching for the outline of the brass knob. Greg slipped into position beside her.

"What's the plan?" Greg hissed.

"Don't know, but he ought to be surprised when there's no one in bed—enough to give us a chance to jump him."

"What if there's more than one?" Before Mat could answer, they heard the footsteps pause outside the door, then continue down the hall. Mat exhaled, aware for the first time of holding her breath. Ignoring Greg's hand on her arm, she inched the door ajar and peered into the charcoal-gray light of the hall. A darker form moved forward to the room beyond. The figure paused at the door and stepped inside. At the same moment, Mat jerked open the door and yelled:

"Zorah!"

Instantly light enveloped them from the end of the hall. Zorah reappeared from around the door. She stared at Mat and Greg, eyes wide with fright.

"Omigod, you scared me to death!" the artist scolded them. She stepped into the hall holding a pair of sandals. "I was afraid I'd wake you. Guess I needn't have worried about that."

"We thought you were breaking in," Mat said.

"Why would I do that? I have a key," Zorah replied, confusion replacing the fear on her face.

"I mean, we thought you were someone else."

"Who?"

"I don't know. Listen, Zorah, we need to talk."

"Now?"

"Yes."

"Okay. But let's go get some tea. I skipped that to keep from waking you guys, but if you want to talk I need something to lubricate my vocal cords. Want some?" Zorah had dropped her sandals and was halfway down the hall. Mat and Greg hurried after her.

***

At 7:30 a.m. Mat met Greene at Elie's Café. Greene ordered coffee and a large cheese Danish. Mat opted for coffee and yogurt.

"You start," Mat said, pouring milk into her coffee.

"*Humpf.*" Greene tried speaking around a mouthful of Danish, then gave up until he had swallowed most of it. "Way I see it, Dan wants that computer thing we found."

"The disk."

"Yeah. Dan asked about something the kid had when he stopped to talk on the street. Remember?"

"Of course."

"Then he called to see if he could come in and see the body."

"Right."

"Makes sense that if someone broke into the morgue and pulled the kid's body out, it'd be connected to Collins."

"One and one does seem to add up to two in this case."

"They had to go and beat up a woman too." Greene's attention was on his hands as they turned his coffee cup around in circles. "Don't know why they had to do that."

"I've heard Dan's a son-of-a-bitch. Maybe this is one of the reasons why. Not that I think he was there himself."

Greene nodded his head in agreement and looked up at Mat.

"If Hector mentioned your name," he continued, "it won't take them long to find you. Actually, they should have done that already if she did."

"Maybe they need to get directions from someone higher up. Or maybe she didn't tell them."

"Until we know, probably better if you lay low."

"*Hmm*. I'm willing to bet they don't know what I look like. What if I moved temporarily? Zorah, too, because they might go after her if they find my address."

"Where would you go?"

"Well, it occurs to me that the last place they'd think to look would be Lilah's apartment. It's empty now. Maybe the owner could be convinced by a certain authority to allow someone else to live there temporarily, especially if it would help an ongoing investigation. What do you think?"

"Could work." Greene tapped his coffee cup with beefy fingers, then lifted it up to drain the last drops. His expression had become increasingly morose as they talked. "It's probably as safe as any place else."

"And, depending on how much rent has been paid, it's free, at least for a while. Here's hoping we won't be there too long."

"Ok," Greene summarized, "you and Zorah move into Lilah's apartment. I'll talk to the landlord and tell him we need to hold it for a possible criminal investigation."

"With any luck, it will be the last place they'll look for me, assuming they were after the disk and know who took it."

"I'll get surveillance on your house," Greene added. "If someone breaks in, we might get a lead on who attacked Hector."

"And how they figured out I have the disk."

"Oh, yeah, that too." His usual take-charge attitude had retreated behind a melancholy that was unfamiliar. Mat found it both endearing and irritating. *What is going on?* Remembering Zorah's words, she forced herself to make sympathetic noises. *Just need more practice.* Greene didn't notice.

"Hector's important to you, isn't she?"

"What? Oh. Well, we been pals a long time."

"Since she came to the morgue?"

"Before that. Born in the same small town." Greene turned to Mat with a wry smile. "Bet you didn't know that."

"No, I didn't." She digested this bit of information. When he didn't elaborate, she asked, "Did you go to school together?"

"Yeah. Well, not really together. I mean same school but she's older. Smartest girl there. 'Course I knew who she was. Everyone did." He shrugged, started to take another sip of coffee, and set down the empty mug. "She was *that* kind, the kind that had it all, know what I mean?" He glanced at her, and she nodded.

"Yeah, we had a couple like that too."

"Yeah, smarts, cute, even did okay at sports. Knew where she was going too. Always said she'd be a doc." Greene stared at his empty mug wistfully, remembering.

I'll be damned! He had a crush on her. Maybe still does. Explains a lot. Not sure I'd call her cute, but he's clearly looking through rose-colored glasses.

"Got there in spite of her dad." Greene paused to wipe his plate with his index finger and lick it free of crumbs.

"Her dad?" Mat prompted.

"Oh, yeah. Well, he always wanted a boy. Didn't care if everyone knew. Named her Hector. After his kid brother who got killed in the war. Made her wear her hair short, go out for sports."

"Really?"

"Girl like that, I'd a been right proud of her. Wouldn't have had to be a boy. Some people get ideas you can't shake 'em out of. Had boyfriends too," Greene said, the sadness of unrequited love mixing with a crooked smile. "Two of them were brothers, Johnny and Jake. Lost their parents young. Seemed real close, you know? Then one of them shot the other dead over a woman. Don't recall who shot the other. Never can tell about folks."

Greene abruptly slid his chair back with a screech and stood, threatening to slosh any remaining liquid in Mat's coffee mug over the rim. "Time to go," he announced, shaking off the memories.

Blinking in surprise, Mat stood, then put a hand on Greene's sleeve.

"Wait, I have another idea."

"Yeah, what is it?" Greene continued to put on his jacket.

"I think it would be interesting to get closer to Dan Collins," Mat said.

"Yeah?" He paused, intrigued. "How's that gonna happen?"

"I'll volunteer to work on his campaign."

"You're crazy. Once he figures out who you are and what you got, if he hasn't already, you're dead."

"I would be already if they had. I'm betting Hector didn't say a word about me."

"Maybe. You're nuts." Mat heard the words and the hint of excitement in his voice and saw the slow smile tugging at the corners of his mouth.

Chapter 4

"I don't know," Zorah said again. "It's *so* red, so red, Red, RED. What was she into, that's what I want to know. I mean red is all about getting attention, making you hungry, you know. That's why so many restaurants have red walls. A color that means 'come here, screw me, and while you're doing it, look at my lips, nails, hair, cheeks.'" Zorah wagged her butt, pursed her lips, and waved her hands through her hair.

"You're only sleeping here. And not at the same time I am. Besides, it's temporary.." Mat laughed from her side of the four-poster. She picked at the red coverlet and patted the red satin pillow. "We could get different sheets if you want."

"Wouldn't help," stated the artist. "It'd just be a cover-up. I'll just have to get Salee over here. I can't work until she's been here, that's all."

"We don't want to attract attention, Zorah." Mat was beginning to feel irritated.

"I'm not going to sleep here for the next who-knows-how-many weeks then try to work with red all around me. It'll be in my dreams and get into my work. I can block it out if Salee's been here. But I have to get my mural done, or I won't get it into the show. If I don't get it into the show, I won't even have a chance at first place. Mat, my options aren't that many, and I don't want to have to go back to work at some restaurant or typing job. I just couldn't stand it unless I knew I'd tried everything."

Mat groaned in exasperation. "Zorah, I'm sorry I got us into this, but I didn't know what else to do."

The artist stopped pacing around the room and turned her attention to Mat as if seeing her for the first time.

"Oh, Mat. I'm not mad at you. The excitement of this is going to energize my work. I just need to deal with the red. Sleeping in red is very disruptive."

Mat shrugged one shoulder in a "what next" gesture at Zorah's mercurial shift in mood. Zorah responded with a wink and resumed her pacing.

"Well, you figure that out and I'll work on this." Mat raised the diskette in a salute. She left Zorah and crossed into the living room where she'd set up her computer in a corner near the bay window. At the punch of a button, it hummed to life, welcoming Mat to a world devoid of physical flesh but replete with character, personality, challenges, and emotions as well as logic. She experienced the familiar sense of security and control, deceptive though she knew it to be. At the log-on she tapped in her user ID and password and watched the characters and symbols reform into familiar patterns.

"Mat?" Zorah leaned out of the bedroom. "Mat!"

"What?" Mat replied, not taking her eyes off the screen.

"That scratching sound. I think it's the door."

"No, it's just the keys."

"It is not. It's the door."

"What door?"

"The front door. Can you get it? I'm working something out here." Zorah withdrew.

"And I'm not?" Mat bit her tongue. The scratching started again, louder and more insistent. With a sigh, she closed the window on her screen and rose to open the door.

"Minnie?" Mat stared at the orange hair and haunted eyes above the deep-purple caftan. "Come on in."

Minnie stared back, unmoving, her hand raised to insert another key into the lock. "What are you doing here?" she demanded, anger and confusion in her voice as she punctuated her words with the keys she still held in her hands.

"Please, come in," Mat repeated. *How are we going to explain this one?*

Minnie hesitated, then swept across the threshold, her caftan brushing everything within two feet. Mat felt like she'd passed an air vent.

"Zorah," she called. "We have company."

"Really? Who?" Zorah's voice preceded her entry from the bedroom.

"Minnie!" She hesitated a moment, then swept into the room, arms outstretched. "What a surprise." The two caftans merged as Zorah enveloped Minnie in a hug and escorted her to a seat. "I was just telling Mat how helpful it would be if you showed up."

Mat blinked and swallowed her protest.

"After all, I can get just so much out of a person's environment. Friends add a dimension that is so important."

Minnie stared blankly at Zorah and Mat in turn. Mat smiled gamely. *Okay, Zorah, where are you going with this?*

"Didn't Mat tell you? I guess she didn't have time. Well, I was so upset about Lilah, even though I didn't know her that well, it just seems to me she represents all of us young women struggling to find ourselves and be independent. And I was inspired." Zorah waved her arms in a lavish circle. "Inspired to create a mural in her honor. Isn't that exciting?"

Without giving Minnie a chance to respond, she continued, "I just knew I needed to get closer to Lilah. I mean you can only get so much of a feeling from a few encounters don't you think? So I asked the nice man who owns this apartment if I could stay here for a couple of weeks to absorb her karma, get into her colors, her style, feel her in my bones." Zorah hugged herself in a tight clasp. "After all, you're not here, and since the rent's been paid to the end of the month, he said he didn't care. Of course, I offered to clean out all her things that no one else wanted when I left. I think he liked that. And Mat said she'd stay with me. Well, what do you think?"

"Zorah, it's brilliant!" Mat assured her. "Absolutely brilliant." *How do you do that?* she thought with a hint of jealousy. *How do you come up with something like that on the spur of the moment?* She applauded her friend, who dipped her head in acknowledgment. "Tell Minnie what your outline is for the mural," Mat added with a mischievous glint in her eye.

Zorah glared at Mat over the smile she held for Minnie. "Still working on that." She dismissed the topic with a wave of her hand and said, "Now, I'm going to meditate on the colors to use. Red, of course, will be central to the entire piece." With a flourish of silk, Zorah turned like a dervish beginning his dance and swept back into the bedroom, shutting the door behind her.

To Minnie, Mat said, "Well?"

"I don't know what to say," the young woman replied, her eyes darting from Mat to the bedroom door to various objects in the room. She appeared dazed by the proposal or perhaps unable to conceive of such a tribute to her friend. In spite of her apparent confusion, she gazed at Mat with clear eyes, gold flecks in a brown field brought out by the deep-purple caftan.

"That's all right," Mat reassured her. "She has that effect on a lot of people." Mat sat down next to Minnie and leaned forward.

"Minnie, I'd like to help Zorah as much as possible. Since you're here, maybe you can help too. Maybe you could tell me about some of Lilah's friends. I can pass that along to Zorah. She keeps talking about the external auras of people and I think knowing a little about Lilah's friends would be helpful." She sat back and took a deep breath. "Why don't we start with that fellow she was dating?"

"You really think that would help?" Minnie asked, her interest baited. She had a corner of the caftan in her hands and was methodically twisting it into a tight ball. Mat wondered if the material would ever recover.

"Absolutely," Mat replied. *Might as well kill two birds with one stone. Zorah's mural idea could be the thing to entice Minnie to tell what she knows about Dan Collins.*

"I guess it couldn't hurt. Not now." Minnie screwed up her eyes in an attempt to hang on to her composure but lost the battle in a paroxysm of tears and gulps of air. Mat grabbed a box of tissues from the sofa table, handed it to Minnie. She waited for the worst to be over.

"I'm sorry," blubbered Minnie, blowing her nose in a huge wad of tissue. "It's just that I miss her so much."

"There's not much worse than losing someone close," replied Mat, wincing at the trite words. *Well, it's true. I sure felt that way.*

Minnie nodded her head and wiped her eyes. "There's not a lot to tell really. Lilah worshipped the ground Dan walked on, that's for sure."

"How do you know that? I mean, in what way?" asked Mat.

"She talked about him all the time, it seemed whenever any subject came up, she had a way of bringing him into it. Like, we might be talking about the flowers in a garden shop, and she'd say which ones were his favorite or how many he'd sent her the day before. When I showed her a painting, she'd talk about his favorite artist or what style he liked. And she could talk about his clothes and how much he knew about everything all day if I let her."

"Did you resent that?"

"Of course not." Minnie's protest could not erase the jealousy in her voice. She sat up and smoothed the caftan around her knees, picking at the fabric in a nervous attempt at calming herself.

"I mean he's educated, sophisticated, has such important things to do every day. He always knew what places to go to, shows, restaurants, things like that. I never got tired of hearing about him."

And you wish with all your being that he was dating you, Mat thought. Aloud she said, "Sounds like Lilah must not have had much time for you."

"But she did. Dan traveled a lot, so it wasn't like she was with him *all* the time. But when she was, it must have been wonderful." Her voice had taken on a dreamy quality and Mat felt her slipping into a fantasy world of her own.

"He took her to see an opera once." Minnie glanced at Mat, awe in her voice. "In New York. They flew up in his jet and stayed at a grand hotel. Lilah wore this lovely gown he bought for her. They went to a fancy restaurant before the show. They had a box to sit in at the opera and everything. It was in Italian and he understood every word." Minnie continued to smooth the fabric of her caftan absent-mindedly.

Two lonely young women living on the fantasy of one's existence as a concubine. Mat nodded her head in understanding.

"Did Lilah work?" she asked.

"Dan didn't want her to." Minnie looked up at Mat. "He wanted her to be free to go with him whenever he was ready."

"He must have given her money. This place isn't free, and I expect it's not cheap."

"Sure he gave her money. He loved her."

"Why didn't he marry her?"

"They weren't ready for marriage." Minnie turned her head away and searched around for another tissue. "Anyway, that's none of your business! Why do you have to keep bringing that up?!" Minnie stood, sending the tissue box tumbling to the carpet. She began to gather up her shoulder bag and shawl.

"I'm sorry, Minnie. Please don't go," Mat pleaded and jumped up to follow her to the door. If she left angry, she might not come back. "I'd really like to hear more about Dan, and Zorah needs you to help with the mural."

Minnie stopped and turned back to Mat, eyes flashing in self-righteous anger. "Alright I'll stay, but only because Zorah needs me. And I'm not going to discuss Lilah's baby with you, not with someone who just can't understand."

"I'm sorry, Minnie." Mat bit her tongue. "You're right, perhaps you can help me to understand. She must have had a beautiful relationship, maybe I'm just jealous."

Minnie sniffled and looked for the tissue box. Mat picked it up and handed it over as Minnie sat down and said, "Yeah. Jealousy makes you do such horrid things." She was quiet for a time, which Mat chose not to interrupt. Emotions flickered over her small, elf-like features. Sadness and what appeared to be deep sorrow, perhaps regret, then her face relaxed into resignation. She gulped once as if stifling a sob and asked, "So, what do you want to know about Dan?"

"What's he like, where does he work? Stuff like that." Mat managed a conversational tone.

She smiled in what she hoped was an apologetic manner. Minnie settled back in her chair.

"He's a businessman, I guess. He buys them, businesses. He's got a lot of them, travels around to them, inspecting them. He took Lilah sometimes."

"On his business trips?"

"Sure. Anyway, he was funny, at least Lilah thought he was. He always dressed so nice. She said he liked excitement. Maybe that's why he wants to get into politics." Minnie's face grew animated as she continued, "She said he wanted to be a brain surgeon when he was little."

"A brain surgeon?"

"Yes. Lilah said when he was a student he spent a summer on one of those hospital ships. They went to the most interesting places."

Really, thought Mat. *Doesn't sound to me like someone whose second choice would be politics.* Mat rubbed the back of her neck and tried to keep the skepticism out of her voice. "Sounds like quite the story and quite a guy."

"Oh, he is," Minnie continued with enthusiasm. Her expression had brightened around eyes wide with childlike wonder.

"What didn't she like about him?" asked Mat, fascinated by the uncensored adoration she saw on Minnie's face. *When did I last feel that way? Have I ever felt that way about anyone?* The first days with Curt, her most recent ex, were as close as she'd come. Inevitably, reality and balance followed, accompanied by crushing disappointment.

In some ways, she was glad she hadn't felt that with Greg. Unencumbered by that heady, out-of-control feeling, she found the small pleasures and surprises in her relationship with Greg to be full of wonder. He was a quilt of bold, contradictory hues that should never have come together. Yet they blended in patterns that softened the harsh colors and reflected a solidarity and strength she found she could admire and trust. *And love?* Mat started at the thought, unvoiced but strong, insistent.

"Anything wrong?" asked Minnie, her voice filled with the nurturing concern Mat often found smothering.

"No. No, nothing's wrong. Listen, it's not fair of me to ask you so many questions all at once. Why don't we plan to get together later, and I'll think about what I'd like to know that we can talk about."

"Oh, thanks." Minnie smiled in relief. "I do so want to help, but it would be better if I could come back another time." She gathered her knapsack and Mat watched the swath of purple move away. She followed Minnie to the door and shut it. For long minutes, she stood with her forehead against the cool wood, gathering her thoughts.

***

Outside the school, campaign party flags hung from poles set in attractive concrete basins that resembled copper tubs. The grass was newly mowed. Preprinted and laminated signs provided directions to parking. Inside, everything looked scrubbed and polished.

"Does he always set up like this?" Mat asked Greg as they left the parking lot and headed toward the beacon of light emanating from the red-bricked gym. Strains of a John Philip Sousa march grew louder as they approached.

"It's a sort of trademark," he answered. "He has an entire crew that comes in the night before and sets this stuff up. If they need signs that aren't already in their stock, they send someone the information and get it here before the rally. You should see his web page."

"I have. Are campaign donations that good?"

"I expect he's using some of his own funds. He's worth a lot of money, but it won't be enough if he doesn't attract the voters."

"That's all about his platform and how it appeals to the voters, isn't it?"

"Yes, and while his team has done a lot of canvassing to determine what's important to his constituents, there's some strategy involved too."

"Like what?"

"Well, he wants to start in a small precinct to test his methods and candidacy. He needs to win impressively enough to get deep-pocket donors to give to his campaign."

At the door, enthusiastic staffers wearing campaign buttons and hats greeted them. They accepted the party flags and literature thrust at them as they entered the cavernous expanse of the gym. A table set up near the bleachers held copies of past speeches, newsletters, brochures, policy statements, and a pile of buttons, pens, pencils, and other collectibles for the faithful. Across the floor, at the far end of the gym, a band, lights, microphones, and a podium held center stage. A young woman wailed a rock song. Hundreds of supporters greeted each other and talked at the same time, moving about in a kaleidoscope of colors and sounds. The excitement was palpable. Mat saw Greg speaking and leaned toward him in an effort to hear his words.

"I'm glad we could get here tonight," he was saying. "It's the kick-off of the last leg of his campaign."

"How long before he comes out?" Mat asked.

"Probably about an hour. After the singer, some of his supporters and key party officials will have their moment in the spotlight. Dan speaks for about half an hour, more or less. Depends on how much applause he gets."

For the next half hour, Mat and Greg mingled with the crowd. Several knew Greg and stopped to chat. The topics were inconsequential, the tone upbeat and jovial. At the same time, Mat felt watched and judged, especially by those few whom Greg did not know, but who made it a point to introduce themselves. She felt they were being assessed, although for what she couldn't say.

"It's time," Greg said and began to maneuver them closer to the stage. "Let's get up on the bleachers if we can. If we go to that spot just above the door we'll see Dan come in. They've stopped the band. The campaign song is next."

The crowd roared, standing and waving small flags, and started singing the campaign song. They sang it by heart over the clamor and shouts of support. As the last notes faded, the house lights dimmed and a single spotlight lit the center of the stage. Mat waited in anticipation, shared with a hundred others, for the main event.

Several officials in Dan's political party extolled the virtues of the candidate. Then Dan's campaign chairman took the stage. He glorified Dan, his goals, and everyone in the chain of command from the district to the state party chief. At last, Dan was introduced to loud hurrahs and applause. The crowd stood as he strode on stage, hands waving above a face that seemed to glow from the stage lights.

With half an ear, Mat heard his opening phrases, her attention held by brilliant, undulating colors and the restless throbbing of the crowd. She felt Greg's hand on hers and turned to look at his face. He nodded in the direction of the stage then whispered, "Notice anything unusual?"

Mat turned back to the stage and scanned the crowd. "Well, he certainly has a lot of stage presence. And he's eloquent and mesmerizing. This crowd is spellbound," she whispered. "I haven't attended many of these things but is it just me, or does he have some kind of power over this crowd?"

"It's not just you," replied Greg. "He's getting a reputation for being able to manipulate a crowd to an astonishing degree. It's one reason he's risen so high so fast in the party."

"Makes me understand how he could throw a spell on an impressionable, naïve girl like Lilah."

They watched the crowd and listened as Dan promised change, new policies and a different

e-llegal code

level of integrity, weaving in stories that underlined his points. Mat found lumps in her throat more than once, and she sneaked a glance at Greg to see how he was doing. He had a thoughtful expression on his face but seemed unmoved by Dan's words. *You are such a mystery to me.* She could hear him say she might as well get used to it since there would always be something about him she wouldn't understand. *But I'll never be satisfied with that.* She knew she would always be trying to put every piece of his personality in a nice, neat category.

Thunderous applause and shouts broke into her reverie. She stood with the crowd as Dan waved and exited the stage. She wondered if political speeches included encores and was relieved when he did not reappear.

"He's got another stop to make before the night is over," explained Greg. "Let's see if we can catch him before he gets out of the building."

They slipped through the crowd; dodging groups of three or four; waving off enthusiasts with flyers, banners, hats, and pins on their way to the back of the gymnasium. Outside the men's locker room, several men and women had congregated, looking as if they were waiting for someone. Mat noticed several reporters, identifiable from the badges, microphones, and cameras shouldered by their entourage.

"He's inside, probably getting a minute to relax before taking on the next engagement," Greg said. "Let me see if I can get a word with him." He disappeared into the locker room and Mat tried to fade into the concrete wall beside a cameraman. She watched reporters trying to get into position and Dan's staff eyeing the locker room door. Ambition and a hunger for power pulsated on both sides. *Whatever would Zorah think of all this?*

The door to the locker room squeaked open and all eyes turned as one. Greg blinked in the glare of the camera lights. He beckoned to Mat who slipped behind a reporter and cameraman in baggy jeans and made her way to the locker room entrance. Mat heard the murmurs of disappointment as the door shut behind her.

"Should I be in here?" she asked, pointing to the sign indicating Men Only Beyond This Point.

"The only difference is this time the guys have clothes on," Greg said, grinning at her and propelling her into the area filled with lockers and wooden benches. "I'm not sure why I got this close, but he's in the mood to meet you, so here goes."

A hint of anxiety crept through her chest as she followed Greg. *What am I thinking? What did Greg say to him?*

She saw the hand first, tipped by groomed nails, then the hint of an expensive watch beneath tailored fine linen held together by pearl cuff links. Her eyes followed the white-on-white stripe up his arm, across to the gold bar beneath a red, white, and blue patterned tie, and up to where they were met by intense blue eyes under wavy hair flecked with gold. He smiled and she felt a force as powerful as any magnet. Lilah would have been toast. Mat forced a smile in return and shook the warm, firm grasp. Dan covered her hand with his left and continued to caress it in a gentle motion.

"My good friend here"—Dan nodded in Greg's direction—"tells me you've got quite a crush on me." Mat darted a look at Greg, who shrugged his shoulders and grinned. "I'm always glad to meet constituents, especially such attractive ones, who feel I have something to offer. Is there anything in particular I can explain or help you with?"

"Uh . . ." Mat felt hot waves roll up her neck and her shirt grew damp. "I'm, uh, I was wondering if you needed any help, uh, maybe on the campaign." She swallowed a huge lump in her throat and was rewarded with a chuckle from Dan. He leaned over and spoke in a conspiratorial manner under twinkling eyes, "Stop by my office tomorrow morning and we'll find something for you to do." He straightened up, gave her hand one last squeeze, slipped into the suit jacket offered by a smirking staffer, and swept out of her sight.

"I'll kill you," Mat hissed at Greg.

"Why?" he asked, raised eyebrows feigning hurt and confusion. "You got what you wanted, didn't you? And your reaction was perfect. He thinks you're another star-struck groupie he's given the thrill of her life. What more do you want?"

Mat couldn't think of a thing except not to feel like such a fool.

Chapter 5

"So, what's the story?" Greene demanded, his voice sounding hard against her ear.

"Not sure," Mat replied.

"What's that supposed to mean? You've had that thing long enough. Maybe I should find someone else to look at it."

Mat took a deep breath, fighting irritation. She struggled to not let him get to her. "It's only been a couple of days, so go ahead if you want," she said more sharply than she intended, "but they'll take just as long to get as far as I already have."

There was silence while Greene digested this. He said, "So, you got something or not?"

"I do have something. It has code that reads something from an external source and an algorithm that involves a tally of something."

"That's a lot of somethings. What does all that mean?"

"I'm not sure. I'm working on it."

"Maybe this Dan fellow knows. He sure wanted a look at the body. Maybe that's what he was looking for." Mat could see him twirling a pencil as he talked. "Hey, you're working for him now, right?"

"Yes, but I don't expect him to volunteer that information out of the blue. After all, he didn't tell you what he was looking for, so he probably doesn't want just anyone knowing about this."

"So how you gonna get him to tell you?"

"I'm not going to get him to tell me. He is almost certainly not the only one who knows what this is all about. I need a couple more days to work my way in, you know, to figure out who knows what, stuff like that. Then maybe I can figure out who would know and start working on them."

"How long is that going to take?"

"I have no idea. Look, this kind of exploring doesn't come with a roadmap."

"Yeah, but something less than forever would be great," growled Greene.

"I'm working as fast as I can. I don't want to make them suspicious before I've even started. It won't help if I get thrown out on my ear." Mat struggled to keep the impatience out of her voice. *How can people who don't know anything about computers be so sure they do?*

Greene snorted. "Well, get a move on!" He hung up.

Mat set the telephone down as if handling a very hot potato.

Zorah was in the bedroom meditating and wouldn't come out for at least another hour. Mat had interrupted her once before. She vowed never to do it again. *I'd sure like a dose of her offbeat thinking. Guess I'll have to wait. I hate waiting.* The shrill blast of the telephone sent a shot of adrenaline coursing through her veins. She grabbed it before a second ring could double the quicksilver chill that spread through her chest.

"Hector was doing something with an abortion clinic."

"What?!" Mat felt her hair stand on end. She thought fast. *God, Greene. Again.*

"I found some notes on her desk," he continued. "She was working with an abortion clinic, sending them stuff. Thought you ought to know."

"Why do you think I ought to know this?"

"Maybe she was involved in doing abortions. Even though they are legal, some folks just can't abide them or those who do them. Maybe some clown found out and decided to let her know how they felt."

"You mean broke in, pulled that kid's body out of the freezer, searched the place, and hit Hector in the head when she found them because they don't like her work with an abortion clinic?"

"Uh, yeah, guess it doesn't make sense when you put it that way. Anyway, I thought you ought to know. Oh, something else too. You know that pregnant friend of yours who died?"

"Lilah? She's not my friend. Anyway, how do you know about her?"

"Doctor at the hospital called. The one who's standing in for Hector. They think it's suspicious. They want a postmortem to find out what killed her. Says it was something in her system, something that caused the miscarriage. You know, caused the infection that killed her. I'm guessing she either didn't really want this baby or someone else didn't want her to have it. Could be suicide, could be homicide."

"My God!"

"Didn't expect that, did you?"

"Uh, no." Mat sat back, trying to absorb this new information. "Uh, by the way, how did you even know I know her? Lilah, I mean?"

"Read the reports when they brought her in. Mentioned Greg somebody, a lawyer who also restores old houses. Said he called the ambulance. Sounded like your friend. I got it right didn't I?"

"Yeah, you did."

He hung up without another word.

"Hell's bells. What's next?"

"What's next?"

Mat whirled in her seat to find Greg standing inside the front door.

"You left the door unlocked and no one answered my knock," he said by way of explanation, shutting the door behind him and crossing the living room to sit in the chair opposite Mat. "Who was that?"

"Greene. Apparently, Hector is mixed up with an abortion clinic and they think Lilah's death could be a suicide, or maybe even homicide."

"Whoa!" Greg whistled in response. "This is really turning into tragedy on top of a tragedy."

"If it turns out to be suicide, it sure doesn't match Minnie's description of how excited Lilah was about the baby."

"Maybe Dan wasn't as excited as she was . . ."

"Frankly, I expect he wasn't. I'm sure his publicity team wouldn't have been excited about it either, especially if this race is close. Which could make it a homicide."

"Let's not get carried away." Greg reached for her hand. "But let's do go get dinner. You can tell me what happened at campaign headquarters today."

***

It was still early when Greg dropped Mat off at the apartment. She had begged off a nightcap and whatever else might follow. Once inside, she turned on the computer, idly watching the opening credits and sign-on screen pop up. She felt jittery, as if she'd had too much caffeine, even though her last cup of coffee was hours ago. Maybe it was the shotgun image she had of this case. Or cases. There seemed to be at least two or three. A dead boy in a morgue. A break-in at the morgue. A computer disk that might have interesting information on it, emphasis on *might*. A candidate for political office who pushed his weight around, according to Greene. A candidate who had just hired her to work on his campaign. Oh, and a mistress. A dead, pregnant mistress. And don't forget a medical examiner who had information about an abortion clinic on her desk. And a cop who almost certainly had a crush on the medical examiner. She felt like a voyeur. *Beyond the dead boy, none of this, one could argue, is my business. Anyway, what is wrong with any of this, other than being morally suspect?*

The phone shrilled. She jumped and clutched her chest with the first ring, unbelieving. Calls this late were obscene because of content or timing. By the third ring, she'd moved to the phone and stretched her hand toward it as if to a familiar, but untrustworthy, object.

"Hello?" she said in a whisper.

"I knew you'd still be up," the smooth voice was vaguely familiar.

"I'm sorry, but you've got the wrong number," Mat said, and prepared to slam the receiver into its cradle.

"No, I don't, Mat," the voice continued. "Am I so forgettable? I thought I'd made quite an impression."

It came to her in a rush.

"Dan! I'm, uh, I'm sorry. I wasn't expecting you, or anyone, actually, to call this late. I mean I didn't expect you to call me, well, at least not so soon. Actually, I didn't expect you to call at all." *Shit.* "How did you get my number?" The initial cold wave faded in the wake of a sudden cold sweat. *How does he know my new phone number? Does he also know I'm in Lilah's apartment?*

"You didn't fill it out on your volunteer application, so I had one of my aides find it. You must have just moved in."

"Yeah, that's right. Last week." They'd gotten a new telephone number. *So you don't know where I am.*

"Hey, I have an idea. If it's not too late, why don't I pick you up for a drink? I know a great place that never closes. We could get to know each other away from all the craziness at the campaign headquarters."

"Um, okay." Mat considered the wisdom of agreeing to this. "Why don't I meet you there? I have a very protective dog who would raise the roof if a stranger came to my door at this hour and the neighbors would call the police."

"Not well trained is he?" chided Dan.

"A failing of mine," admitted Mat.

"Well, I'll have to meet him sometime. He'll see there's nothing to fear. In the meantime, how about Dusty's near Tysons Corners?"

"Sure, about half an hour?"

Dan's answer was a dial tone. *Why am I surprised? He has serial sexual predator written all over him. Add that to 'fastest-rising son-of-a-bitch'* . . . Mat slipped on jeans, black flats, and a white shirt tied at the waist. With a black sweatshirt jacket over her shoulders, she left the apartment and headed toward Dusty's. *This is so not part of the plan, at least not my plan. So, what is my plan?* She spent the drive trying to come up with one, half convinced she'd arrive to find she'd imagined the call.

He was sitting on the other side of the room behind a cold, dark ale, condensation darkening the cocktail napkin under it. He rose when she appeared. With a wave, he beckoned her over and pulled out a chair. A sky-blue cashmere pullover intensified the hue of his eyes and set off the pale-yellow shirt collar standing against his tan neck. His sleeves had been pushed up to reveal a thick gold chain around one wrist, an expensive watch surrounded the other. She'd seen wealth and taste before, but not like this.

"Sorry to keep you waiting," Mat said, easing into her seat.

"Not at all. I'd wait a lot longer for you," Dan said, running his blue eyes over her face and neck, down her white shirt. Once at her waist, he smiled and lifted his eyes in a slow retreat to her chest. Mat felt like a sideshow, on display for cheap thrills. She crossed her arms and said, "You done looking me over?"

Dan laughed out loud, throwing his head back and slapping the table with the palm of one hand. "I'll be damned! Cool as well as beautiful. What will you have?"

"Coffee." Mat wondered what was behind the show. It seemed forced, as if he were testing her somehow.

"One coffee," he said, and motioned to a waiter. "Irish or Cappuccino, perhaps?"

"No. Thanks."

Dan nodded to the waiter and settled back in his chair. "Jim tells me you're quite the computer whiz."

"Jim tells me you're quite the skirt chaser."

"Did he?" Dan's smile faded and his eyes hardened.

"No, actually he didn't," Mat backed off. "But others do."

Dan chuckled. "Don't believe everything you hear. Politicians and successful businessmen are as susceptible as celebrities to the press's need to contort and enhance reality to sell copy."

Mat collected her thoughts in an effort to catch up. Everything since she'd sat down had come out of left field. She'd expected a sophisticated pass or perhaps a confrontation about the reason she'd joined his campaign. Keeping up with this verbal foreplay was exhausting, especially at this hour.

"Did you think I was the press?"

"Everyone who joins my campaign gets checked out, you should know that. I can't take any risks with the people I hire."

"What kind of risks would those be?" Mat asked, playing for time.

"Moles, people trying to get dirt on me, perverts, trash like that." Mat watched Dan's eyes dim as he seemed to look inward, and his knuckles turned white around the dark ale like snow caps at the top of a mountain. He smiled as if to cover his tracks.

"Anyway, you're clean and I need someone like you."

"Like me?"

"Yes, someone who knows computers. Besides, I think I can trust you."

"Why are you so sure?" Either someone had taken her story at face value, or she was being set up. She hoped she could find out which before this went much further.

"I trust Jim and he makes sure I'm never disappointed."

"Who's Jim and why do you need a computer expert? Don't you have plenty of those in your business?" Mat turned her attention to the coffee that had just arrived. She tried to speed up her brain to stay ahead of or, at least, even with him.

"They have full-time jobs." Dan smiled in his disarming way. "I only get part of their time and part of their expertise. I tried one of the students at the university, but they're undependable. No real-world experience. Got interns at my business, but for this I need someone who isn't always running off to class or leaving to study for an exam. What do you say?"

Mat wondered if he knew what he was asking for. *Someone with more experience than a student might be a liability rather than a help. Unless he's sure of his control over that person. This could get very interesting.*

"Tell you what," she replied. "Why don't I do a security audit on your system. I'm sure you don't want your opponents hacking in and getting at your policy statements, not to mention your contributor lists. I can find out how vulnerable you are." She took a sip of the hot, dusky brew and continued, "If you like my work we can discuss a more permanent arrangement." *If he bites, this will allow me to find the back doors to his system.* She felt the pushback from her conscience but reasoned she would tell him everything eventually. At least she would when she was satisfied he was clean. Dan smiled and she felt a chill. He wasn't the least bit worried about what she would do with whatever she found.

"And I'll tell you what I'll do," Dan replied.

Mat fought waves of flight-or-fight impulses. She shifted in her seat and tried to smile invitingly. "What's that?" her voice a little higher than she wanted.

"I'll take you on a plane ride."

"A what?" Her eyes widened in surprise.

Dan's smile broadened into a Cheshire cat grin and he chuckled. "I can see that's not what you expected. Let me explain. I have a couple of short stops the day after tomorrow to begin the last leg of my campaign. We could drive, but it's so much easier if we fly. I like to take one or two of my volunteers along as a little benefit of working on my campaign. If you're not busy, you can join us. I was thinking of taking Sheila too. You can meet her tomorrow. I think the two of you will hit it off." He stood up and motioned to the waiter for the check. "This is on me." As they left the diner, he walked her to her car and held the door for her. "We'll have a great time, trust me." He waved her off with a few last words, "You'll see."

Mat drove off wondering how she'd fallen into his trap just like every other Collins groupie she'd ever met.

Chapter 6

The next day, she found a minute to share coffee with Sheila, the talkative middle-aged woman who was part of the volunteer team at Dan's headquarters. They were sitting at a little bistro table near the coffee setup.

"Guess we're going to be going on a plane ride together tomorrow."

"I know!" Sheila's enthusiasm boomed in her voice. "I was so surprised when he invited me. I know others have gone, but I didn't think I'd ever get chosen."

"Why not?"

"Well . . ." She looked around, her shoulders sagging a little. "I mean, in the past the ones he's taken are all much younger than me. Like you. I just figured he wanted to leave the impression that he appealed to a young, hip crowd. Know what I mean." She looked down at her coffee cup and continued, "Maybe I'm going because voters in these places are older. I don't know." Sheila shrugged, attempting to shake off the implication that he was using her to appeal to an aging group of senior citizens. "Anyway, I'm going!" She smiled, her loyalty insisting on an enthusiasm she clearly did not feel. "That's the important thing. It'll be fun." Her determined cheeriness dissolved into a rueful half smile as she looked down, her hands gripped tightly around the Styrofoam cup. She stroked the side with one thumb. They sipped their coffee in silence for a moment.

Mat finally broke the silence. "Well, one thing's for sure. There is a lot going on here. Is everyone here a volunteer?"

"No, not all." Sheila looked up. "The volunteers come and go. After a while you get to know who the staff are partially because they stick around. I ask when I'm not sure, but mostly it's pretty obvious."

"How long have you been with him?"

"Oh, since the early days," Sheila confided. "I was here when he tried this seat before. Didn't go so well. I guess he learned a lot. I sure did. Anyway, when I heard he wanted to do it again, I got involved right away."

Mat feigned fascination with the story Sheila spun. On the one hand, she seemed the epitome of a bored suburban housewife needing to be part of a younger, fast-moving crowd. The vibrant, frenetic atmosphere of Dan's campaign headquarters must appeal to many like her. But alongside the cheerleader words, she had shown she was alert to the activities and subtle ways Dan controlled voters' impressions of him and the campaign.

"There are only two or three staff. Most of us are volunteers," Sheila continued. "I got to know him a little when he lost the first time. He was so upset. Swore it would never happen again. I guess when you're that good, it's hard to accept others don't see it too. I mean he is so intelligent and good with people." Sheila's voice grew more animated as she listed Dan's abilities. "I don't understand why everyone doesn't see he's the perfect person for the job. Anyway, I swore I'd work on his campaign if he ran again and here I am."

I bet a lot of these volunteers share that opinion of Dan. Maybe some, like Lilah, share more than that.

"I wonder what he'd be like as a boss, you know, if you worked for him at his company? What's his business anyway, do you know?"

Shelia answered her first question, "Oh, I'd think he'd be a great boss. You might get a lot of good information about that from some of the interns he hired over the summer. They'll probably tell you exactly what they think too." Sheila paused. "Of course, I'm sure they hope he'll hire them full-time. I mean he has to make sure people do what they're supposed to, right? Sometimes students think they don't have to follow the rules."

"What do you mean about students not following the rules?"

"I didn't mean that in a bad way," Sheila hastened to explain. "I mean he can be firm, I guess you'd say, if you don't do what he says. Not that he doesn't give us a chance to say what we think. He does. But after he makes a decision, you should do what he says. Don't you think?"

"I guess." Mat hesitated for a second, then asked, "What did you say his company did?"

"Oh, I don't think I said," Sheila replied, "but it's something to do with buying and selling companies. I forget what the name is. He owns businesses, all kinds. Anyway, I'm sure it's successful if Dan is running it." She looked at Mat and smiled.

"I'm sure it is. Well, time to get back to it. Thanks for filling me in."

"Sure thing, anytime." Sheila drank the last of her coffee and got up from the table, heading for the door. "See you tomorrow."

Mat followed close behind.

***

"Get ready everyone! We have things to do." Dan looked back from his seat in the six-seater bush plane to the passengers behind him. They'd left the small Manassas airfield at 7:00 a.m. and headed south with three stops to make before sundown. Dan explained that a lot of these trips were to places away from regular airports. The short takeoff and landing plane could set down in off-airport locations such as fallow crop fields. Dan had not provided headsets for the passengers and noise from the engine's roar made conversation impossible. Mat watched the scenery pass by. She tried to meditate on the events of the last few days, enjoying the companionable silence necessitated by the engine's roar. After about half an hour, they approached a field in a graceful arc, landed with a small bounce, slowed, then turned and taxied several feet to an area next to a large circus-style tent. It was an Indian summer kind of day with above-average temperatures, clear skies, and a gentle breeze. The kind of day that would bring out the crowds, and associate Dan with fresh air, bright sunshine, and the promise of good times. Mat couldn't help thinking he could manipulate the weather—as well as people—to his advantage.

The day passed quickly, with each stop a carbon copy of the one before. They deplaned with Dan exiting last to enthusiastic applause and cheers from his entourage. They surrounded him as he entered the tent, strode up to the podium, and met the local officials. Mat and Sheila passed out souvenirs and brochures to the audience. Both were tasked with identifying how many attendees were there with notes on the demographics.

"You were right," Mat whispered to Sheila. "Most of these voters are older. Mostly women too."

Sheila nodded in agreement. "It's a workday too. I get the impression most of the men are retired or out of a job. Maybe they're hoping for some free food."

The second stop at a larger venue did, indeed, include a barbecue with coleslaw and cornbread, followed by a selection of cakes and pies. Stuffed to the gills, Mat wandered over to a row of chairs alongside a small partitioned area used to store extra handouts. The crowd was still milling around the food and display of souvenirs. She welcomed a chance to sit apart and observe Dan's team working the crowd. Slowly voices behind her intruded on her thoughts, low at first and muffled by the fabric of the partition behind her, then louder and increasingly strident.

"Frankly, I don't care how you do it." Dan's voice was unmistakable. "I'm not losing again!"

"I'm getting the vote out the best way I know how," a second male voice insisted. "I don't know what else you expect me to do."

"I expect you to make sure I win this time," Dan growled. "If I win, it'll be worth your while. If I don't, I'll make sure you never work on another campaign in this town, or anywhere else for that matter."

"Shall I stuff the ballot boxes?" the second voice sneered. "I don't know of another way to guarantee a win."

"Why not?" Dan's cold voice replied.

"What do you mean?"

"I mean I expect my campaign managers to be ready to go the whole nine yards. I need you to help finish what I started. Your hands are already dirty with that intern. This piece just finishes the picture. Here's what you have to do."

Mat strained to listen as the voices moved away until they were mumbles that merged with the din from the crowd on the other side of the tent. *What the hell?* She got up and, moving as quickly as possible without attracting attention, reached the end of the partition opposite where she sat. She peered around, but whoever had been there was gone. She turned to look around. An area of the crowd that was reassembling after moving aside for someone to pass caught her eye. She hurried in that direction and saw that beyond it was one of the openings in the tent. Beyond it, stood several groups of people caught up in lively chatter. She looked rapidly at each one for signs someone had just joined in. Dan stood close by in a group that seemed absorbed in an ongoing discussion. Mat caught a glimpse of several people at the perimeter of the crowd walking away toward the makeshift parking lot. *Is one of them the second man?* She took a deep breath, then turned and re-entered the tent, going over and over the conversation she'd heard.

She finished the trip in a daze, smiling automatically and doing her part as needed. The last thing she needed was for Dan to suspect she'd overheard his conversation. At the same time, what she'd heard kept replaying in her mind. The whole idea of stuffing ballot boxes clashed with her sense of integrity and fair play, not to mention the illegality of it. *Was the body at the morgue 'that intern'? Is the campaign manager the man Dan referred to as Jim?*

Chapter 7

The next day, Mat dialed the number she'd found under the university listing in the phone book. It was answered at once with a burst of information about the office she'd called, its hours, and who else to contact for related information. The campus was twenty minutes away in the countryside, where trees were beginning to turn startling shades of red, gold, and orange. On impulse, Mat stopped at a coffee shop and picked up a blueberry bagel and a latte. Halfway to the campus, she pulled onto the wide shoulder, killed the engine, and moved the bucket seat as far back as it would go.

The panorama of color stretched ahead along the road, providing a stark contrast to the monotonous gray macadam. More than once she and Greg had been tempted to forget the time and their destination for a few minutes devoted to this view, but there was always a reason to keep on going. This afternoon, the shifting patterns created by the light wind blended, then distorted the mosaic. Like the thoughts she was collecting about strange disks, Dan Collins, and conversations in a tent; the leaves danced together, then apart, refusing to stay in place for very long. *Maybe that's best. Maybe, after this visit, I should let my thoughts sort themselves while I focus on work for the next several days.* When she reassembled them, they might come together as they never would have had she continued to prod and push them around. With a sigh, she finished the bagel, washed it down with the last sip of latte, and started the engine. *Now to find out where Dan gets his interns and pay a couple of them a visit.*

***

"Hello." Mat smiled at the student at the university career center. She started with the role she'd decided would elicit the most information. "I'm a reporter for a local newspaper. I'm doing a story on the experiences of interns at local businesses and wondered if you could help me. Any chance you could tell me who's working as an intern this semester?"

"Oh, I can't give out that information. Privacy and all that. But if you look at the job notices posted on the board behind you, maybe you can find out if they are filled. Then maybe you can find out who they hired." The student returned Mat's smile and turned back to the papers on her desk.

Mat looked over her shoulder at the board behind her. *There's got to be a better way.* She stepped over to a student who was also perusing the intern job notices.

"Excuse me, are you looking for an intern position?"

"What?" The young Asian girl glanced at Mat and continued her search of the board. "Oh. Yes. I hope there's one that's still available. They go so fast, especially the paying ones."

"Do you have any friends who have one of these positions?" Mat smiled in encouragement.

A few minutes later, she had the names and addresses of two students who had started working for the Collins firm about six months ago. The first was Kim, an Asian boy who was working on his master's degree in computer science. *Gotta find out if this Kim is still alive and well for a start.* The second was Rosa, a Venezuelan girl who was a senior in the Information Technology program.

***

Kim lived just off campus in a small bungalow that had been built thirty years ago. A waist-high chain-link fence ran from the front around to the back and down the side of a short driveway to the right of the house. The gate was long gone. Gutters pulled away from the eaves, and the downspout was missing from the right side of the house. Paint peeled away from the trim. Screens were patched and sagging. If the cars parked in front of the house belonged to the occupants, it implied very crowded living quarters.

Well, mused Mat, *in spite of the ramshackle appearance, the front step is swept clean, the grass mowed, and a small flower bed has been mulched. It seems the occupants are doing what they can to maintain the property.*

Mat pulled the screen door open and knocked twice. Immediately, she heard footsteps and a muffled "I've got it" before the door swung open. A young Asian girl looked her over, then glanced behind her as if looking for someone else. Dressed in loose black pants and mandarin collar

e-llegal code

top, she bowed slightly but didn't try to hide her disappointment. Then she brightened and asked, "Are you a friend of Kim's?"

"No," Mat began. "Is Kim not here? Have I got the wrong address?"

"Oh, no. He lives here," replied the girl. She hesitated before adding, "I thought you might be one of Kim's friends." She stopped as if hoping Mat would assure her she was indeed one of Kim's friends.

"No, I'm not one of his friends. But I would like to talk to him," Mat said, hoping to find this student alive and well. "May I see him?"

"He's not here," the girl replied, distress drawing soft lines between her eyes and around her mouth. "You don't know where he is?"

"No. I just wanted to ask him some questions about his job."

"I see," the young woman said, though Mat doubted she did. The lines between her dark eyes deepened as her distress increased. "Well, he's not here," she repeated, pushing her long black hair away from her face in a gesture of frustration and worry.

"Do you know when he'll be back?"

The young woman shook her head. "No. And none of his friends have seen him for a couple of days. He was supposed to be back yesterday afternoon so we could study. But he never came home." She was close to tears.

"Maybe he's still at work. I mean, they could have had an emergency. Maybe he spent the night with a coworker so he could go right back in the morning?" Mat asked, trying to provide a useful suggestion.

The young woman's eyes flashed in surprise. "Oh, no. He would never do that without calling me."

"Does he have family around here?" Mat tried again. "Maybe he went there."

"No. He is from Taiwan. His family is there and so is mine. They are depending on us to be successful and return to help them."

"Did you call where he works?"

"Yes. They don't know where he is either. I asked them if he'd seen Mr. Collins."

At the surprise on Mat's face, the young woman continued hastily as if afraid she'd said something wrong. "A couple of weeks ago he told me Mr. Collins had given him a special assignment. He said he'd be checking with him to find out when to execute the next phase."

"What was the next phase?"

"I don't know."

"When was Kim going to check with him?"

"Several days ago, I think. I'm worried. I talked to another intern who works there. She wouldn't tell me what he was doing. She did say she didn't like it. Thought Kim was crazy to get involved."

"Involved in what?"

"She wouldn't tell me. Do you think I should call Mr. Collins?"

Mat thought she knew what the young woman would hear from Dan Collins, and it might not bear any resemblance to the truth. *Still, it wouldn't hurt to see what Dan has to say.*

"It wouldn't hurt," Mat replied. Then asked, "If I give you my phone number would you call me when Kim comes home?" She pulled a bit of paper and a pen from her purse and wrote down her phone number.

"Sure." The young woman took the piece of paper and looked it over with interest. She looked up at Mat. "Do you think he'll come home soon?" The hope in the young woman's eyes tugged at Mat's heart. She was grasping at straws. Dan Collins would have no problem allaying her fears. For a while at least.

"I don't know," Mat replied, looking her in the eye. "But I hope so." She turned to go, then turned back to the girl. "I wonder, can you tell me the name of that other intern?"

"Sure. It's Rosa, Rosa Martinez." The girl tried to smile and failed, then closed the door as Mat turned away and let the screen door drift back into place.

What now? She considered the options and decided to search out student number two. She couldn't shake a growing sense of unease that seemed to increase whenever she got close to Dan Collins or anything related to him.

***

Rosa's apartment building was in a cluster of buildings south of the campus. It rose six stories and Rosa lived on the second. Mat entered the plain lobby, worn down with age. An Out of Order sign, hand-painted and taped to the doors of the single elevator in the lobby taunted her. To the left of the elevator, she found the stairs and pushed through the doors. Empty chip bags, gum wrappers, and greasy sandwich containers littered the steps. *It's broad daylight but this feels downright spooky,* Mat thought as she entered the dimly lit stairwell. *Still, it's just one flight up.* Mat paused, listened intently for the sounds of footsteps, and put a sneaker on the first step. The soft scurrying feet of tiny scavengers vanished before her into the dark corners of the stairwell.

On the second floor, Number 212 was at the far end of a narrow hall. At the door, Mat could hear the sound of drawers opening and closing and footsteps crossing the floor. She knocked and the sounds stopped at once. At the second knock, a floorboard creaked.

"Rosa?" Mat called. Perhaps it would help if Rosa knew a woman was on the other side of the door. "Rosa, I'm Mat Briscoe, a friend of Kim's." *Well, close enough.* Footsteps hurried to the door, bolts turned, and it opened on a chain. A young woman's dark, anxious eyes peered through. Rosa looked past Mat, searching for others.

"You're a friend of Kim's?" she asked. "Do you know where he is?"

"No," Mat said. "That's why I'm here. I'm trying to find him."

"I don't know where he is," Rosa said. She fixed dark, troubled eyes on Mat. "What do you want?"

"You work with him, don't you?"

"Yes." Rosa hesitated as if trying to decide whether to continue. "How did you know where to find me?"

e-llegal code

"A friend at the university," Mat replied, hoping this was the right answer. It seemed to satisfy the girl, who stepped back, eased the door shut, and slid the chain out of the lock. It opened once again as she stood aside to let Mat in.

"Sorry for the mess," Rosa said. Books were piled in boxes, and in others, small objects peeked from under their newspaper wrappings. Through another door, Mat could see clothes spilling from a suitcase on the unmade bed.

"Are you moving to another apartment?" asked Mat.

"Yes. No. That is, I'm going back to Venezuela," Rosa replied.

"Oh, you graduated! Congratulations," Mat said with enthusiasm.

"No," Rosa said, her eyes clouding with anxiety. "I have another year. Later, I'll return and finish." She took a deep breath and fixed her eyes on Mat. "Are you really a friend of Kim's?"

"Yes," Mat assured her, ignoring the outraged protest from her conscience. *Sometimes the ends do justify the means. Anyway, this information might help find Kim.*

"Will you do something for me when you find him?" Rosa pleaded. Her eyes, luminous in the soft light, filled with tears.

"Of course, if I can," promised Mat.

"Tell him to quit. They're onto him and he could get hurt."

"What do you mean, 'they're onto him'?" asked Mat. "Who's onto him?"

"He was working on a special project for Mr. Collins. It had something to do with the voting machines. I think he was doing something about the counting routines. It got him in trouble. I called his girlfriend, but she didn't want to talk to me."

"Is that why you're leaving the country?" Mat asked, and watched the tears glistening at the corners of her eyes. The frightened girl clasped her hands together, twisting them in endless loops. She nodded.

"I don't like Mr. Collins. I have this feeling. Kim likes him. He said even if Mr. Collins got into something that doesn't seem right to him or me, he's sure it's for a good reason and will turn out to be perfectly alright. I don't know—Kim trusts him, but I don't."

"Why not, I mean, why don't you trust him?"

"I, it's just, I mean .. " she trailed off. "I shouldn't have said anything."

"Look, I'm not a friend of Dan Collins if that's what you're afraid of."

Although she looked relieved, Rosa wouldn't say any more.

After a few more words, Mat wished her a safe journey and left the apartment feeling unnerved and more in the dark than ever. Rosa wouldn't tell her what she was afraid of, but whatever it was, it was enough to send her fleeing back to her family. Mat's heart went out to her. Rosa was intelligent, had achieved a lot, and her family had undoubtedly sacrificed a great deal so she could come to this country to study. Would she have the determination to come back and finish her degree? *This really is none of my business, but I can't just let it go.* She thought of Greg's response, *"Just remember, that's what got you in trouble before. You don't know when to quit even when the danger signs are everywhere."*

She was due at campaign headquarters by 3:00 p.m. to stuff envelopes. Dan said it was important that she get an idea of what it was like to be a regular volunteer even though he wanted her to work on the computer system. Mat didn't argue. She suspected he had other motivations for this arrangement, but it suited her needs as well. One often discovered a great deal by working in the trenches, and any information she could glean from Dan's admirers would be useful even if heavily biased. At 7:00 p.m. she was meeting Greg for pasta. She wondered what he would think of her plane trip and the day's activities both inside and outside of the campaign headquarters.

Chapter 8

Jim sat in the booth as far back as possible from the café entrance with his back to the wall. He surveyed the space around him and nodded. From earlier visits, he knew it would remain mostly empty at this hour of the night. One or two bleary-eyed students might wander in, ordering coffee in a desperate attempt to cram sufficiently for a passing grade, making up for prolonged bouts of inattention and partying during the semester. He dialed the familiar number and let it ring.

"Hello?"

"I figured you'd be up. You keep the same hours as these students."

"It's because I'm busy. What do you want?" The voice was sharp, tired.

"Reporting in as you wanted."

"So tell me already."

"You said you wanted to know if this guy was worth keeping on your radar, if he was worth the investment you'd made in his campaign."

"So?"

"He told me today to do whatever it took to win. Thought you'd find that interesting."

Silence. It lengthened while Jim sipped his coffee. His eyes darted around the room. He sat forward, then back, then forward again, arms on the table around his coffee cup, waiting.

Finally, he gripped the phone and said a little too loudly, "Are you still there? Did you hear me?"

"Yes, keep your voice down. I'm thinking."
"Well, do it faster."
"When do you meet up with Dan again?"
"Probably in a couple of days."
"Here's what you say to him."

Jim listened, nodding occasionally. When the voice finished, he asked, "Is that all?"

"It's enough for now. Let me know what he says."

Jim took a last sip of coffee, dropped a five-dollar bill on the table, and left the café.

***

"Mat, your imagination's really running wild this time," Greg said, frown lines appearing between his eyes. They sat outside a small café in Old Town Alexandria. The cool night air held the warmth of the summer-like day. The pasta was superb and the candlelight hypnotic.

"Yours and Rosa's," Greg continued. "Kids do crazy things. Kim will show up wondering what all the fuss is about. And that bit you heard on the other side of the tent partition. Are you sure you heard it right? Dan's got too much at stake. It doesn't make sense for him to jeopardize the election that way."

"But he is," insisted Mat. "He's doing, or going to do, something to make sure he wins."

"By doing something illegal? No, I don't buy it."

"Why not?" Mat felt the familiar nag of impatience coloring her voice. "It can't be coincidence that those students disappeared or are running away. And I know what I heard in that tent."

"Why can't it be coincidence, Mat?" Greg echoed. "You must have done unpredictable things when you were in school. I sure did, and we weren't the only ones. This time you just happened to run into two of them at the same time. Besides, I don't know what you think he's going to do to rig the election."

"I told you," Mat began, losing the battle to keep the impatience from her voice. "He's getting these students to change the software."

"And is somehow adding votes to his own? I repeat, I just don't buy it. Look, I know these kinds of things spin you up, but you need to keep your imagination under control. You could do a lot of damage with those kinds of allegations."

"Spin me up? And when did you become such a fan? I thought he was the 'fastest-rising son-of-a-bitch' you ever knew." Mat fought her knee-jerk tendency to take offense whenever she was challenged. *You know what happens when you let that take over.*

"I still think that, but I just don't see him as a killer. I just don't see these events as some nefarious scheme to swing an election."

"I'm not imagining this. I'm not," she insisted, the undercurrent of pleading in her voice begging him to understand.

"Look, Mat. I know you want me to believe what you believe. And I'm willing to, but not on imagination alone."

"Well, I guess I'll just have to prove it to you." She retreated behind a sullen poutiness that she couldn't help even though it appalled and disappointed her.

Greg studied her sour expression and suppressed a smile. "You can be such a child when things don't go your way," he chided.

"Yeah, whatever."

"Okay, come on. I think we're done." Greg motioned to the waiter to bring the check.

Mat bit her lip and sat back in her chair. The romantic mood was ruined and it was her fault. Until now she had felt safe sharing her wildest ideas with him. Now she felt chastened. The anger that welled up in response made her shoulders hurt. She took a deep breath in an effort to relax.

"Let's go back to my apartment. We can talk there." Greg's voice broke the spell. The desire to get past their disagreement rang loud and clear. She chose not to hear it. Abruptly she shoved herself back from the table and stalked off. Greg caught up with her at the curb, grabbing her arm as they crossed the street in the middle of the block.

"Look, Mat," he said. She heard the urgency in his voice and ignored it. "Mat, slow down, please. I just don't want you hurt." They had reached the median and stood facing each other as cars swept by on both sides.

"I don't believe you," Mat said. "The person you don't want hurt is Dan. You're siding with him. He's a snake and you can't see it." She regretted the words before they were out, but it was too late. Greg recoiled as if slapped, and his features retreated behind a cool mask.

"I'll take you home and we can discuss this another time," he said. He took her arm and guided her across the street. The ride home was dead quiet. Mat tried to think of a way to get back to the earlier mood of the evening, but it was gone. Their relationship, always bumpy, seemed to have entered a new realm. *Can we get past this? Do I care? God, yes.* Greg's studied indifference, heightened, she felt, by the distance between their bucket seats, seemed to grow more intense as the miles swept by. In the end, she put her head back and, with a sigh, closed her eyes until they arrived at the apartment building where she and Zorah were temporarily housed. Greg walked her to the front door, opened it, then dipped his head in a polite farewell. She had never felt so alone.

***

Am I asleep or not? Flowing gauze curtains that framed the open French doors blew gently over polished wood floors. The thin gray light edging the windowsill told Mat it was close to dawn. She rolled away from it and toward a growing sense of fear. In the dim light, two jewel-like eyes peered at her from the top of a bedpost. It couldn't talk, but she heard it say the trap had closed again. *"What trap?"* she asked. *"The one of your own devising,"* it said. With a rush of air and the sickening screech of claws against wood, it rose into the air and vanished.

But the screech went on and on. Mat blinked fully awake and sat up, heart pounding, looking wildly for the sound and its source. Again it came, from the far side of the room. She slipped out of bed and made her way in the pitch dark to the outline of the window. Behind the lace curtain, a glistening branch of the great oak rubbed the glass in response to the wild gusty winds of a late-night storm. All was dark, as if the world had been plunged into a lightless void. By her bed, the clock blinked furiously in the familiar frenzy of an electronic timepiece suddenly deprived of its life-giving juice. *What the hell? Ohmigosh, the electricity's out. What time is it?* She felt the dresser with her flattened palm until she found her watch, turning over its luminescent face to see 2:30 in brilliant green. *Damn. Just two hours of sleep but I'm wide awake. I won't be able to sleep for hours. I'll pay Zorah a visit at the studio.* Mat found a flashlight she'd squirreled away and checked the front rooms. They were empty of human occupants. She dressed in jeans and a black sweatshirt with "Save the Fledgling Artists" emblazoned in red across the back, and left the apartment.

At 2:45 a.m. the streets were immersed in a veil of quiet anticipation. It was Mat's perception that in the few hours before dawn the air seemed charged, as if preparing for the burst of energy the morning brings. Breathing in deep buckets of the cool night air, Mat drove through the deserted streets and was surprised at how her spirits lifted with each mile. At an all-night fast-food drive-through, she picked up a regular coffee and a tea for Zorah. Once again, she considered how nurtured she felt by the relationship. It was a feeling she couldn't explain. Zorah's work was the most creative her unschooled eyes had ever seen, yet the contradictions in her personality and her devotion to the mystical often left Mat speechless. Perhaps it appealed to her own impulsiveness that she rarely allowed freedom of expression. *Guess I do wish I could control everything. Make it all logical and predictable.* The absurdity of the idea almost made her laugh out loud. Another voice butted in: *That's why you find it so hard when someone disagrees with you. Someone you care about.* She drove on in silence, blindsided by her subconscious. *That can't be, can it?*

The dilapidated red-brick structure, once a warehouse in the thriving shipping port, appeared in the glow cast by the streetlights as Mat turned the corner a few blocks from the river. She pulled up behind Zorah's ancient, multicolored VW and turned off the engine. For several minutes she sat unmoving, held fast by a reluctance to emerge from the cocoon of her car. *C'mon Mat. If you don't get moving, Zorah will have cold tea. Not her favorite.*

The bulb high in the entrance foyer blinked intermittently as Mat found her way to the narrow staircase leading to the top floor. The steps creaked at each footstep announcing her ascent. At the threshold, she looked for Zorah's space. Grotesque shapes lunged at her peripheral vision as she made her way to the solitary light at the end of the room. Zorah turned to beam a welcoming smile at her approach, warming Mat's heart.

"What do I smell?" asked Zorah, rising from the stool in front of an immense canvas.

"Tea for you. I thought I'd bring some sustenance this time, for the spirit if not for the stomach."

"*Hmmm*, perfect," crooned Zorah, sipping from the Styrofoam cup. "I love it when you come bearing gifts."

"How's the work going?"

"Pretty good. I'm sketching out the mural on this canvas and then I'll transfer the outline to the wall I'm given. This way, I'll have all the perspectives and proportions worked out ahead of time and can concentrate on the details."

"How do you do that?"

"Use a grid. I'll draw a grid on the wall with chalk and dust off the lines after I'm done. This is the first time I've done it on something this big, but it'll work," Zorah said with satisfaction.

"Amazing," said Mat with feeling. As much as Zorah insisted on the supreme value of creativity and feeling in developing her paintings, Mat saw the precision of math and calculations in much of her technique.

Zorah smiled. "Thanks. I'm really pleased with the unicorns, goblins, and elves on the left. They'll be in all kinds of colors and patterns. That's to represent our individuality. How each of us is unique. Different. I've figured out the best way to draw the eye toward them even though they aren't in the center of the picture. You can't see it here, but it'll be great when the mural's done."

"Zorah, how do you know what works in a mural like that? I can't begin to imagine what it's going to look like once you're done." Mat eased herself down into the beanbag chair next to Zorah's easel.

The artist paused and sat back on her stool. She didn't answer at once, and Mat began to fear she was in for one of her infamous "thinking silences" whereby Zorah would withhold comment or conversation for minutes on end while working out an answer. How she'd triggered this one was a mystery.

"I have no idea," offered Zorah before Mat finished her thought. "I just seem to know. Ah, someone's coming." With that, the artist turned to face the back of the long, cavernous room, the dark black-on-black of the stairwell door at the end.

Mat followed her eyes but could see nothing. Then a faint tread on the steps and the accompanying creak of each board told her a visitor had reached the top of the stairs. In the dim light, Mat made out a large tent shape as it stepped through the door and headed their way.

"How do you do that?" demanded Mat, feeling the hair on her neck rise.

As the tent drew closer, its wild electric-blue color separated from the darkness. Minnie's face moved into the light, and she looked from Mat to Zorah and back.

"What are you doing here?" she asked in a voice flat and drained of emotion.

Mat bit back a retort. She was sure this immature girl-woman had information she needed. She'd do well not to piss her off.

"Keeping me company." Zorah jumped into the void, her voice bright with forced levity. "I get lonely down here sometimes and Mat brought me some hot tea." She held up the Styrofoam cup as proof.

"Oh." Minnie accepted the explanation, her sudden anger dissipated at once.

"Sit here," urged Zorah. She patted the crate next to her, its surface softened by an old quilt. The caftan moved toward the crate without reply. Zorah followed her movement, eyes filled with concern.

Mat felt only impatience and grew irritated with herself. *Get over it,* she admonished herself. *This is an opportunity, don't screw it up.* With a smile of sympathy, she turned toward the girl.

"What brings you here in the middle of the night?"

"I can't stop thinking about Lilah. Did the hospital ever say what happened? Why did she get so sick?"

Should I or shouldn't I? Mat thought Greene would say he'd told her about the doctor's concerns in confidence. Still, he hadn't *explicitly* told her not to say anything.

"Minnie, they're saying she had a miscarriage."

"Ohhh, no." Minnie's eyes darted from Mat to Zorah and back. Conflicting emotions flashed over her face: horror, guilt, and fear.

"What's wrong?" asked Zorah.

"Ohhh, no. A miscarriage?"

Mat nodded.

"Do they know what caused it?" She searched Mat's face desperately for an answer.

"I don't think they do, yet. They're doing tests to find out if she took something or if it was just, well, one of those things."

"She couldn't have, could she?" Minnie's eyes begged Zorah, then Mat for reassurance.

"Couldn't have what?" asked Zorah.

"Taken something? Could she?"

"We don't know. Why do you ask?"

"Well, it's just that we worked at that clinic and . . ."

"And what?" Mat pressed.

"Oh, Zorah, I didn't mean to. I never meant. Oh—" Minnie broke down into sobs that shook her whole body.

Slowly they coaxed it out of her. Minnie had an extensive herb garden populated with every variety of mint, her personal favorite.

"I make one of them, pennyroyal, into a tea to help with colds or headaches. It's an essential oil that can be used as an insecticide, believe it or not. An antiseptic too." Minnie's voice grew more strident as she continued, "But humans shouldn't mess with pennyroyal oil. It's very toxic." She started to cry. "I asked Steve about it." Minnie glanced up at Zorah whose brows knit together in perplexity.

"You mean my tall Amazon friend?" Zorah gestured with her hand raised above her head. "The one with short dark hair who has all these herbal remedies and works on them at Candlewick? She's into insecticides?"

"No! Well, maybe she is, but that's not important. I talked to her because she knows about all these herbs. I told her about what I was planting in my garden. She told me pennyroyal could cause miscarriages. I warned Lilah," Minnie insisted, sniffling and reaching for a nearby tissue. "I did warn her." She broke into a fresh bout of sobs.

"But she wouldn't take that stuff, would she?" Zorah asked. "I thought you said she was excited about the baby."

"She was. At least she told me she was."

"Well, there, you see. She wouldn't have taken anything to cause a miscarriage."

"I suppose. I know I told her about it. I'm sure I did," Minnie insisted again, misery and guilt filling her face.

"When you told Minnie about the pennyroyal, were you alone?" Mat interjected.

"Yes." Minnie tried to recall the moment. "Wait. No. Maybe. I can't remember. Dan might have been there." Her shoulders drooped as she struggled to recall. "He was interested in my herb garden, so I could have been showing it to him and Lilah. I don't remember for sure."

"Look"—Zorah regained control of the discussion—"the police or whoever investigates these things will find out what happened and they'll let us know. They will, won't they, Mat?"

Mat inclined her head in mute agreement.

"Minnie, you'll see it had nothing to do with your herb garden. You're just letting your imagination get out of control."

"Maybe you're right," Minnie continued. "Lilah worked at the women's clinic too. She would know about these things."

"How's that?" Mat asked.

"Well, the clinic provides information to women who are considering abortion. That way they can make good decisions," Minnie replied.

"How would something like pennyroyal come up? It's not one of the conventional options is it?"

"No, it's not. But women and girls come in with all sorts of old wives' tales about ways to prevent pregnancy and bring about miscarriages, or abortions, depending on your goal, I guess. The women who are trained in all this can tell them what methods are approved for all that and which are not. They also tell them about ones that might be on the market soon or might be available in another country."

"What methods?" Mat couldn't restrain her curiosity.

"Well, there's something called dilatation and evacuation. That may not be exactly right. Anyway, you have to go to a hospital for that. It's the typical method when you're in the second trimester. Then there's a new pill that's approved in France, but not here yet. They called it RU486, I think. I can't pronounce the real name of it," Minnie continued. "Hector explained a lot of that to me when I first started working there. I was trying to figure out what I could do to be a more useful person. Guess I still am." She seemed to retreat into her memories.

"Hector?" Mat said, surprised.

"Yes." Minnie sat looking at her hands, smoothing then twisting a Kleenex tissue in a nervous gesture. Her tear-stained face was mottled from crying. "She was filling in for the regular doctor at the clinic."

"Hector? You really said Hector?" Mat tried to grasp what she had heard.

Minnie looked up, her face twisted with impatience. "Yes, that's what I said. Hector. She's a doctor. I asked her to fill in."

"But how do you know Hector?"

"She's my mother." Minnie looked at her hands and the shredded piece of Kleenex again, unaware of Mat's astonishment. "I know it's a funny name, but that's what I've always called her. I don't like calling her Mom."

"Hector's your mother?" Mat repeated. *Boy, anyone listening to me would think I was demented.* She looked at Zorah and found her suspicions confirmed.

"She didn't come around too often, but she came through when we needed her," Minnie added.

"Did she supply you with RU486?"

"No! It's illegal here. I told you."

"Right, you did. Still, if it's legal somewhere else, a determined person could find a way to get it or bring it here."

"Are you suggesting . . .?" Minnie looked at Mat, her eyes wide and round with sudden understanding. "Hector would never do something like that!"

Mat returned Minnie's incredulity with raised eyebrows. "So, other than that or this hospital procedure you mentioned, there's really nothing else?"

"Mostly."

"Mostly?"

"Well, that pennyroyal oil I mentioned is supposed to be effective, especially early. They told us stories about it at the clinic, but I never knew anyone who tried it."

Maybe you do now. "How do you get that? The oil I mean."

"Oh, well, I guess you could get it out of the plant yourself if you know how. I don't think it's complicated."

"Do you know anyone who would know how to do that?"

"Other than Steve? No."

Zorah turned from the outline for the mural when she heard her name. "What's that about Steve?"

"You know, your friend with the glittery eyes."

"Mat, she's off that stuff. I told you."

"Oh, right."

"*Really*," Zorah emphasized the word and dared Mat to argue.

"Okay, okay. It's just my skepticism coming out."

"It's just that it puts a bad karma around her and that affects people who are close to her, like me." Zorah paused to drive home her point, then turned back to the mural.

"Sorry. I didn't realize." Mat tried to feel serious about what Zorah was saying but found it hard to believe the statuesque nutritionist had really turned her back on whatever drug she'd been using when Mat last saw her.

"Look, guys. I'm sorry to be a wet blanket here"—Zorah turned back around to face them—"but I really need to work on this mural if I'm going to get it into that show. It's only a couple of weeks away. If I don't win, I don't know how I'll eat, and you're distracting me with all this talk about bad herbs and killing babies."

"Zorah, that's not fair. Look, you've upset Minnie again." Mat put an arm around Minnie who had started to cry in earnest.

"Sorry, sorreee. I just need some peace and quiet," Zorah mumbled as she turned back to the mural.

Mat helped Minnie get up from the crate, handed her a tissue, and guided her toward the door to the studio. It was clear she wasn't going to get anything else out of either one of them for the rest of the night.

Chapter 9

The next morning, Mat sat at her computer staring at the disk. *What are you hiding? You have to be what Dan wants so badly, but why?* She inserted the disk into her machine and watched the system display the icon in the directory. She had contacted a hacker who worked for the FBI. It hadn't taken him long to break the access code for the disk. She clicked on it and entered the ID and password.

The shrill from her phone made her jump, nearly toppling her coffee mug. She grabbed at it and the phone, then dropped the phone. She retrieved it from the floor, pushing the small desk in the process and adding a screech from its short journey across the floor. Taking a deep breath and willing the adrenaline away, Mat finally answered the phone.

"Hello?"

There was silence on the other end, then a tentative, "Matilda Briscoe?"

"Yes. This is her, rather that's me, or I'm Matilda Briscoe," she stammered. She took a deep breath. "Who is this?"

"I remember you as more articulate than that. What in the world just happened?"

"Lynn Peterson?" Mat recognized the familiar voice. "Professor Peterson? You were the graduate assistant in my Political Science class when I was a freshman at the university."

"The very same," replied the voice. "You were one of the sharpest students there, but you loved those machines more than politics. As I recall, you said something about gray areas and having to compromise your ethics to get anything done."

"Well, I'm a little more realistic now. But you, a professor! I didn't realize you wanted to be an academic."

The voice chuckled. "I didn't either. I always enjoyed the subject but didn't think much beyond the fun of classes. But what do you do with a Political Science degree? I should have thought about that before I graduated." She laughed ruefully. "So I decided the only thing to do was stay in school. One thing led to another, as they say. Anyway, I'm working on tenure here and started advising the Collins campaign as part of my research."

"The Collins campaign?!" Mat's astonishment underscored her words. "Then you're just the person I want to talk to. Do you have time to catch up over a coffee?"

"Sure. I just finished classes for the day. A coffee break sounds like just the thing. Tell me where."

***

The local coffee house was crowded, but Mat and Lynn found a table and two chairs in a remote corner of the shop. Mat took a sip and put her cup next to a small notebook she'd brought for notes.

"First you have to tell me how you found me."

"You're not going to believe this," Lynn began, "but you made quite the impression on a couple of the guys at Collins's campaign headquarters. I overheard them talking about a new computer expert Dan hired. Said you were a hot number. A strawberry blond instead of the usual platinum blonds Dan gathers around him. They figured you were Dan's latest conquest, and maybe you are." Lynn smiled at Mat and twisted her coffee cup between her fingers. "They were putting a flyer together to let people know who to contact to help on the campaign. It had pictures showing a group of staffers and there you were. I asked who you were but didn't recognize the name. Still, I knew it was you."

Mat scrunched her nose in protest. "They didn't ask me before they did that."

"I found your phone number and thought it was worth a call to see if it was really you. Why the different name? Are you married? Are you using a middle name for your first name?"

Mat held her hand up to stop the barrage of questions.

"No, still not married. I'm doing a little investigating for someone and need to use a different name. I didn't think anyone would see a picture and recognize me."

"I'm probably the only one who would. I don't think many other people are doing research on voting trends and knew you way back when. Interesting, though, that we should connect this way. So, what are you investigating, if I may ask?"

"To be honest, Lynn, there's one direction this could go that would make it wise not to know too much. I'd prefer to keep you at arm's length until I know it's not going there."

"You really know how to be mysterious, even a little frightening, Mat. Are you sure you're not getting in over your head?"

Mat brushed off Lynn's concern, "I'm being careful. I'm working with a cop on this, but no one is supposed to know that, understand?" She looked at Lynn, who nodded her head in agreement.

"I just want to know what you think of Dan Collins. You know, what sort of person he is."

"Okay, if you think that's useful. I'm only telling you some of this because I've always felt I could trust Matilda Briscoe with my deepest, darkest secrets and I'm assuming that's still true." Lynn looked pointedly at Mat, who nodded in agreement. "Good. Looks like we're still on the same wavelength as far as that goes."

Lynn settled back in her chair and took another sip of coffee. "I first got interested in Dan Collins's campaign when he ran for office the first time. He seemed like a rising star, and I wanted to follow someone who had the possibility to go state-wide or even national. My research is on the loyalty of voters through a series of campaigns. I really needed to find someone who had a good chance of winning and moving up. This research is so important to my career. I'm going up for tenure next year. If I don't make it, I'll have to start over at another university."

Professor Peterson looked down at her coffee cup, twirling it around again in a nervous gesture. "I have too much invested in this research to start over. This just has to go the right way for me."

She looked up at Mat, a mixture of desperation and determination filling her eyes. She sat back, seeming to will herself to relax. "Anyway, I know many voters stay with a candidate throughout their careers, but I want to know the details of how stable that base is when scandals and bad press affect their candidate. I'm studying an angle others have ignored in the past, and that's all I'm going to say about that." Lynn smiled conspiratorially. "I have cards I play close to my chest too."

"Understand. You don't want anyone stealing your research ideas." Mat smiled back. "Is there anything about Dan that makes you think he will be in for a scandal or two?"

"That's really the risk in my research, that he's squeaky clean and I'll have nothing interesting to study. But I doubt that, and the more I hang around him and his cohorts, the more I'm convinced that won't be the case."

"Why?"

"I'm not naïve, and I know politicians spout half-truths and sometimes outright lie. It's all part of the game. But Dan seems especially coldhearted about relationships and seems to delight in delivering bad news."

"Can you give me an example?"

"Let me think. Ah, here's one. I was at his campaign headquarters when he called over one of his staffers and upbraided him for missing an entire street when canvassing a neighborhood. He went on and on about the number of votes that could cost him. Dan chewed him out in front of the entire office and seemed to enjoy doing it. It was embarrassing for all of us." Lynn looked down at her coffee. "I guess he didn't care that he lost that person's vote. I think Dan figures volunteers are nobodies who couldn't possibly have an impact on the outcome. There are enough waiting in line to take his place. I've seen candidates get angry with staffers before, but Dan is a superstar in that regard. There's a viciousness in his personality that's frightening, to be honest."

"Why would anyone work for him after that?"

"Most are young, or enthralled, and don't think it will ever happen to them. They justify Dan's outburst by thinking the staffer had it coming. I also don't think most want to think ill of Dan. They are mesmerized by him and don't see what's underneath. I expect you haven't either, have you?"

"You're right. I've noticed how mesmerizing he can be, but only because someone pointed it out to me. I was flattered, if I'm honest, when he hired me with no questions asked. I can see how people fall under his spell and don't look any deeper or question his ethics. I'm sure they dismiss anything amiss as an anomaly and unimportant." Mat thought about what she had just said. "You're right. It is frightening."

"On the one hand, this is just the personality that's needed to tough out the bad times and come out ahead. On the other hand, he could make a big mistake that could end his career. That would mean I'd have to start over. There's not enough time to do that before the tenure committee meets."

"Sounds like his success means a lot to your career."

"Well, I don't want to make too much of that. There's a long way to go and my instincts are that his campaign will work out. I've learned to trust them. If I come to any other conclusions, I'd guess you want to hear about them?"

"You bet," Mat assured her.

"That said, I'm reminded of something a couple of my students said about him," Lynn continued. "They said he's ruthless. He reminded them of kids who tear wings off insects and watch them struggle to fly. Some people never outgrow that impulse, they just hide it but it's always there." Lynn looked up at Mat. "There's another thing I'm pretty sure about. I think he would do anything to make sure he wins this time. *Anything.*"

***

After saying goodbye to Lynn, Mat arrived at Dan's campaign headquarters to continue her volunteer work stuffing envelopes. She was picking up the last stack of unfilled envelopes when she heard the sound of Minnie's voice, angry and strident. Looking up, she saw the familiar voluminous caftan, this time a tie-dyed profusion of color that was in stark contrast to the muted colors and conservative attire of everyone else in the room.

"Where is he?" Minnie demanded of no one in particular. Everyone in the work area stopped and stared.

"I know he's here! His office said he'd be here all day," Minnie insisted. "I need to talk to him. Now!" She looked around in a vain search for her target.

"Perhaps I can help." An older staff member approached her, attempting to calm her with his voice. "Who are you looking for?"

"Dan. Dan Collins. Who do you think?"

"He's busy at the moment. Perhaps I can help?" he repeated.

"No. This is between him and me. Where is he?" Minnie demanded, her voice rising in pitch with her words.

"I told you he's busy. Maybe I can get you some time with him later. I'll be glad to make an appointment for you—"

"No! I want to see him now. I don't care if he's busy!" she shouted. "This is important." Minnie stopped abruptly as her eye caught movement in the back of the room.

"What's going on?" asked Dan, emerging from the short hall leading to the rooms in back of the office. "I heard someone shouting."

Minnie brushed past the aide, caftan billowing out behind her. She strode up to Dan, her face contorted with anger, fists clenched. "You bet I'm shouting. You killed her! I know you did!"

"Hold on, Miss. I don't know what you're talking about."

"Yes you do! You gave that drug to her. You killed her!"

Dan raised both hands in an attempt to halt her tirade. "I don't know what this is about, but I'm sure we can sort it out if you'll calm down."

He stepped to the side to put a hand on Minnie's elbow. Urging her forward, he said, "Let's go to my office and sort this out. I'm sure it's not as bad as all that."

Minnie shook his hand off angrily but started walking toward the back of the office. She continued her tirade as they walked, "Oh, it's bad." Dan raised a hand and waggled it in a "no" gesture at his aide's pantomimed query to call the cops, then disappeared with Minnie into his office.

"Okay, everyone," the aide announced to the room, "back to work. Just someone upset about a friend's political views I expect. Dan will take care of it." He chuckled to lighten the mood.

Mat stacked the envelopes she'd completed and pushed the empty ones behind some flyers on her desk. She got up and headed toward the back.

"Out of envelopes," she murmured to the aide as she passed him. He nodded and returned to his task of analyzing poll results.

Mat listened for raised voices to decide which of several offices opened onto the short hall behind the main work area. Immediately, she heard Dan behind the last door on the left. She approached quietly, turning around as she reached the closed door to see if anyone else had come back to this part of the suite. She heard his tense voice attempting to soothe Minnie.

"Look, I'm as upset about what happened to Lilah as you are. I don't know why you're so mad at me."

"You gave it to her, that's why!"

"What? I gave her what?"

"Pennyroyal from my herb garden, that's what."

"You're crazy. I don't know what that is and why would I do that anyway?"

"You do know. I remembered you were with Lilah that day when I showed her my herb garden. I showed her the pennyroyal plant. It's what they told us about at the clinic. I wanted her to know what it looked like for real. You were there. You used it to make her have an abortion!" The sound grew louder as hysteria crept into her voice.

"Even if I was there, I don't remember anything about this pennyroyal plant!"

Mat could hear the undercurrent of impatience and anger in his clipped words as he struggled to keep his own voice even.

"Yes, you do!" Minnie's voice rose stridently with the need to convince Dan. "Lilah told me you asked her how long it took to work. Why would you ask her that if you didn't plan to use it?"

"You're not making any sense, Minnie."

"I am too! You didn't want the baby!"

"Maybe it seemed that way at first. I mean it was such a surprise." Dan took a deep breath. "Look, Minnie, I loved Lilah and having a baby with her was wonderful news. The voters would have accepted it."

"That's what Lilah told me you'd say, that at first you were worried about how it would look. Then she said you told her you got over that. *Humph!*" Mat could imagine Minnie crossing her arms, stubbornness and cynicism taking over her self-control. Her voice stayed loud as she continued, "Well, know what I think? I think you didn't get over it. I think you were so worried about how voters would see it that you needed to get rid of it."

"You're crazy." Dan's voice had a new menacing quality that Mat could hear through the door. "This has gone on long enough. Now you need to leave so I can get some work done."

"You think you can just turn your back on this and tell me to get out?"

"That's exactly what I think, and if you don't leave, I'll call the cops."

The silence that met this last exchange was unnerving. Mat heard heavy footsteps crossing the room. A second later, lighter footsteps seemed to be coming her way. She stepped over to a box of envelopes as the door jerked open.

"Oh, I'll leave alright," Mat heard Minnie say as she stopped on the threshold, her back to the hallway, her attention on Dan. "I'll leave, but you haven't heard the end of this. There are all sorts of ways to keep this issue in front of the voters. You'll see."

Minnie swept past Mat, who knelt, pretending to search for envelopes in the boxes of office supplies. She heard Dan step to the threshold and then the sounds of a cell phone call. The door slammed shut as she heard Dan say, "Jim? Get in here now!"

Mat grabbed some envelopes, returned to her workspace, and gathered her keys and jacket.

"Got an errand to run," she told the nearest campaign worker and hurried out the door. She had an overwhelming need to find Minnie, fast. Miss Meek and Mild sure had another side, one that reminded her of a mother bear protecting her cub. She didn't know what Dan might do, but she couldn't ignore the hairs prickling her neck at his last words.

Chapter 10

"Thank you so much for meeting me for dinner tonight." Mat sat across from Lynn Peterson at the bar where she and Greg often met. "I know we just talked, but something happened at the campaign headquarters that is really bothering me."

"I'm all ears." Lynn spun some spaghetti on her fork, glancing up to encourage Mat to continue.

"First, I need to update you on another aspect of Dan's world. Perhaps you knew he had a steady girlfriend he kept in an apartment in town."

"Yes, I knew about her. There aren't many politicians I can think of who don't have something like that going on."

"Had you heard she was pregnant?"

Lynn sat up, leaning toward Mat across the table. "No, I hadn't heard that. How is Dan reacting to that?"

"Depends on who you ask. Let me explain. Lilah, that's her name, has a friend named Minnie who claims the two were happy as pigs in sunshine. They didn't plan to marry. Apparently, Lilah thought it a repressive institution. Anyway, last week Lilah was rushed to the hospital suffering from what appeared to be a miscarriage. Unfortunately, she died. The doctors are trying to determine if she took some kind of drug to induce a miscarriage and it went wrong."

"Wow! That's quite an 'aspect of Dan's world.' I'm sure he doesn't want that to make it into the tabloids."

"I'm sure of it. To round out this tale, her best friend, Minnie, stormed into Dan's office today, threatening to let everyone know about Lilah's baby and accusing him of giving her something called pennyroyal to get her to miscarry. Minnie is convinced he gave her too much and that's why she died. You can imagine Dan was not happy. He denied it all. Right after he hustled her out of his office, he called his campaign manager and told him to get over there, *now*."

"And you know about this, how?"

"I found a way to listen in."

"I won't ask. So Dan was unhappy and called his campaign manager?"

"Yeah. Thing is, I can't shake a bad feeling about this. So I decided to try to find her to make sure she's alright."

"You always were a sucker for the underdog."

Mat smiled ruefully. "I know, but this time I really think she could be in danger." Mat gave Lynn a rundown of all the places she'd looked for Minnie.

Lynn sat back and took a drink of her wine. She sighed. "I wish I could say Dan is more bluster than bite, but I'm not sure that's true with him. Still, if you're thinking of super bad stuff, like murder, that's quite a leap."

"I hope so," Mat replied. "I just can't shake a bad feeling about this." She smiled again, amused by the familiar term. She twirled the stem of her wine glass, watching the ruby-red liquid slosh gently from side to side. It held its color to the top of the pour, signaling a strong, mature blend several years old. She leaned back against the booth and stared at the liquid as if she could divine Minnie's whereabouts in its depths.

"So," Lynn summarized, "you've asked Hector. You asked her friends, visited the art studio where Zorah works ..." She paused. "Candlewick is it? Anyway, it seems you followed up every lead they gave you." She sighed. "I don't really want to encourage this, but it's barely been twenty-four hours. Isn't it possible you just haven't asked the right person the right question?"

"I suppose, although I don't know who else to ask. I just feel like I'm spinning my wheels, asking the same questions and getting nowhere. I can't help thinking she's out there somewhere, afraid and probably close to panic by now."

"On the other hand, there's always the possibility she's gone to ground where you'll never find her. She could be safe and sheltered with friends who are reluctant to tell anyone where she is."

"But if she doesn't know someone is after her, she might not know to go to this shelter you're referring to."

"Mat, you're thinking about her as a helpless victim. Maybe she isn't as helpless as you think. Maybe she's hiding and doing a very good job of it. After all, you said she wasn't afraid of taking Dan on face-to-face."

e-llegal code

"Or . . ." Mat's face filled with distress at another thought. "Dan or Jim or one of his hirelings has found her already."

"That's thinking positively." Lynn made a wry face. "Aren't you being a little overdramatic?" She looked up and locked eyes with Mat.

"I know you think I'm making a mountain out of that molehill. But I just can't help thinking . . ."

"Thinking . . . what?"

"That this is not going to end well."

"Well, whatever happens, you can only do so much. And it could be for someone who may not need your help." Lynn drained her glass and reached for her jacket. "I enjoyed this, but I've got papers to grade and an early class." She slid out of the booth and stood to put on her jacket.

"Thanks, Lynn. Truly. I needed someone to shine the light of day on this." Mat looked up but didn't move. "One more day, then I'll go back to fighting Greene's decrepit machines." She slid her glass, still half-full, to the center of the table and got up. "Just one more day." She followed Lynn out of the bar. On the one hand, she was relieved to have shared her fears with someone who might be less biased than she was. Sure, Lynn had her opinion of Dan, and it wasn't flattering, but she was a relative outsider to the other events swirling around Mat. That helped balance her panic-prone feelings of the moment. Still, try as she might, she couldn't escape the sense that her fears for Minnie were more than justified.

***

Two days later, Minnie's body was found in a ditch in a remote section of the county. A state mower clearing brush that obscured the view of approaching cars saw a piece of colorful fabric waving in the breeze and went to investigate.

"Was just inside the county line on our side," Greene explained. "So we got the body. Just came in. You been tellin' me you're worried about your friend's friend. Said she wore this kind of thing. So c'mon, tell me if you recognize her."

Mat felt sick. She'd returned to work that morning and was working on backups for one of Greene's older machines. Punching the keys for the shutdown routine, she grabbed her jacket and fell into step behind Greene. She thought desperately about how she might have done a better job trying to find Minnie in the last forty-eight hours. *I stayed away from my job as long as I could, but when someone wants to disappear, it's like looking for the proverbial needle and this area is a big haystack.* They opened the door to the morgue and knocked on Hector's door. It drifted open and they looked around an empty room.

"She must be here, she'd never leave her office open like this," Greene announced. Raised voices reached them from the lab and they looked through the large glass window that let Hector keep an eye on the activities in the main lab. Hector was draped over one of the gurneys, her back heaving in cries of anguish just barely audible through the glass. Greene slapped his badge against the window and tapped loudly. One of the attendants who had been standing to the side hurried over and opened the door to the lab.

"What is going on?" demanded Greene, covering the distance to the gurney in two strides.

Hector's head came up as she recognized Greene's voice. She turned to face them, tears streaming down her face, grief distorting her features almost beyond recognition.

"She's dead! My baby's dead!"

***

"That's when it hit me," Mat had found Zorah twirling around in Mat's office chair that she'd brought over from the house.

"What hit you?" Zorah asked, slowing the chair until she was turned to face Mat.

"What are you doing?"

"Oh, when I hit a brick wall in my art, I like to do something physical to shake up my mental processes, you know, kind of give my creative side a nudge. If I get going around fast enough and stop suddenly, sometimes I get a whole new perspective on things."

I wonder how long it takes your brain cells to realign. Maybe that's the point, you don't want them to.

"What hit you?" Zorah repeated her question.

"I remembered Minnie was her daughter."

"Whose daughter?"

"I just told you." Mat tried to contain her frustration. "Hector's. She's Hector's daughter and she's dead."

"Who's dead"

"Minnie! Haven't you paid any attention to what I've been saying?"

"Omigod, you mean Minnie, Hector's daughter, *our* Minnie is dead?" Zorah visibly paled, her childish delight at spinning around in Mat's chair fading fast. "Oh, Mat."

"I'd forgotten. Remember, Minnie told us that when she was talking about her work at the women's clinic." She saw tears beginning to stream down Zorah's face.

"Oh, Zorah, I'm so sorry! I didn't mean to just blurt it out like that, but I was so shocked." She went over to the sofa across from Zorah. "I've been trying to find her for the past two days. Remember, I asked you if you had any ideas about where she could be."

"I know," Zorah sputtered, "and I told you not to worry, she was probably just off with friends somewhere burying her grief in some weed or other. Some friend I am." Zorah snatched a tissue from the box next to her. "I feel awful. I don't know how I can work tonight. The aura from this is going to stay with me for days, I just know it." Zorah blew her nose loudly and tossed the used tissue in the trashcan next to the sofa. "Do you know how it happened?"

"Someone strangled her, used a thin wire like that poor student. I just can't get past the idea that the two are connected but, for the life of me, I can't figure out how."

"Wait, what's connected?" Zorah asked, her brow furrowed in confusion.

"Minnie and that student. You know, Kim with the disk in his pocket."

"Oh. Well, I just can't believe it," Zorah lamented, skipping over the reference to Kim.

e-llegal code

"First Lilah, now Minnie." She looked at Mat, eyes narrowing with suspicion. "So you suppose someone has a vendetta against us? You know, people who don't conform. We suffer so much for our art and individuality, it just isn't fair!"

"Zorah, I appreciate that the lifestyle of you and your friends can seem strange to the rest of us, but I really don't think there's a vendetta out there aimed at you."

"You don't? Well, I'm not so sure." Zorah sat up suddenly, eyes focused on Mat. "Do you really think the same thing happened to that student and Minnie? How could that be? They weren't anything alike. They didn't even know each other, did they?"

"No, I'm not saying they knew each other. I just think there's a connection."

"Why?"

"Well, the strangulation with the wire and finding the bodies out by the side of the road. No other injuries, at least from what I know." Mat sat silently musing over the different but similar events.

"Isn't there some sciencey thing they can do to find out what's the same about both of them?"

"You mean a forensic analysis? I expect they are doing what they always do. The question is whether they are comparing those two bodies in particular."

"Can't you get Greene to suggest that?"

"I can try. He gets testy if he thinks I'm interfering too much." Mat sighed. "Well, we're not going to solve it tonight and you need to get to work."

"Oh, Mat. I don't think I'll be able to work tonight. Could you if you thought your best friend was out smoking dope and she was really getting strangled somewhere? This will affect my work for days," Zorah moaned.

Hmm. This is the first time you've described Minnie as your best friend, but what do I know? Maybe she was. Best friend means different things to different people.

"Look, I know you like ice cream. I haven't had dinner. Let's go get a sundae and see if we can get you back in the mood to go to your studio tonight."

Zorah rewarded her with a broad smile, lifting her spirits too.

Chapter 11

"It's about time! What took you so long?" Mat's frustration boiled over.

"Hey, I'm doing you a favor, remember? I don't need to tell you any of this," Greene snapped back.

"Sorry, really. It's just been such a landslide of awful things, I'm not . . . I'm sorry."

Greene had called Mat into his office and was sitting behind his beat-up desk, twirling a pen in his right hand. He glared at Mat for another moment, then continued, "The kid's name is Kim something or other. I got it written down."

"Kim?"

"Yeah, why?" He shoved a piece of paper toward Mat. "Foreign exchange student. Some kind of computer whiz. Been here about eighteen months."

"Kim was the name of one of the interns Dan Collins hired."

"Must be this kid. According to this report, he got an intern position with Dan Collins two months ago. I'm gonna go talk to Dan about him tomorrow. You might be there stuffing envelopes or whatever you do there. Thought you should know."

"You *have* to believe me now," Mat argued. "I just know Dan is involved and this proves it."

"I don't know that it proves anything," Greene retorted, the florid hue of his face increasing with his irritation.

Mat was trying to think of something smart to say when her cell phone rang. She looked around, trying to identify the sound.

"It's that phone thing you got in your pocket. Go find someplace else to talk on it. I can't stand these one-sided conversations that are starting to pop up all over. It's like announcing your life to the whole world. And shut the door behind you!"

Mat left the office and pulled the cell phone out of her pocket, aware of eyes on her as it continued to ring.

"Mat Briscoe. Can I help you?" She squelched the impulse to demand "what?" at the top of her lungs.

"Yes you can, please don't hang up."

"Why would I . . . Greg?"

"The one and only. I've missed you. Can we call a truce and talk?"

"Oh, Greg. Yes, let's do that. I'm so glad you called, really I am."

"Are you? That makes two of us. I don't know where you are. Can I pick you up?"

"No, I'm at work. Why don't I meet you at that little bar around the corner from the house?"

"Perfect, in about thirty minutes?"

"Perfect." Mat hung up, returned to the office, and finished the backup routines. She gathered her laptop and jacket and headed out the door with her mind humming. *What should I tell him? How much should I tell him?*

***

"I've been asking myself how much to tell you." Mat ran her fingers up and down the stem of the wine glass. She sat across from Greg, who held a tall beer stein by the handle. He took a big swallow.

"Why not tell me everything?" He paused, then continued, "Because you don't know if you can trust me. It's written all over your face." Greg set the stein down between them. "After all we've been through together, I really hoped you'd know you could by now."

"I guess it's not so much trusting you . . ." Mat struggled to sort out her feelings. "It's . . . Oh, I don't know, maybe it's that I'm not sure you'll take me seriously."

"Okay. I know I've been a little quick to dismiss some of your ideas, but I promise I'll suspend disbelief as much as I can. I'll let you know when I think things are getting out of hand without flying off the handle. At least I'll try. That's all I can promise."

Mat sat staring at the wineglass, then at Greg for a few moments. She took a deep breath. "I don't know why this is so hard, but I suppose we won't get very far if I go on keeping you at arm's length."

"Whew." Greg smiled. "I wasn't sure where that was going to end up."

"Neither was I, at first. Just don't make me regret it." Mat tried to smile back.

"I'll do my best.

"Okay, here goes. You remember that kid who was strangled?"

"How could I forget it?"

"Then that medical examiner was attacked, and Zorah and I moved into Lilah's apartment after she died. Lilah, not Zorah." Mat managed a weak smile to go with her attempt at humor.

"Right, and the doctors found some drug in Lilah's system. They don't know if it was suicide or a homicide. Then you started working for Dan at his campaign headquarters." Greg smiled in return.

"Right. That's where I found out about the interns. I got the name of one of them, Kim, and talked to a friend of his, Rosa, who worked for Dan. Rosa told me he was involved in something that frightened her, frightened her enough that she's leaving town."

"But she didn't say what that was?"

"No. But she did say they hadn't seen Kim in almost a week and she was afraid something had happened to him."

"And you thought Dan was what happened to him. I thought it was farfetched and we parted ways for a bit." Greg sat back. "I gather that's not the end of the story."

"Far from it." Mat tapped her fingers on the checkered tablecloth and went on. "Well, Minnie showed up at Zorah's studio and told us about her herb garden. She was proud of it and had shown it to Lilah."

"That doesn't sound so ominous."

"Not on the surface, it doesn't. Thing is, she grows pennyroyal in that herb garden."

"What?"

"Pennyroyal. It's a plant that helps with pest control and some other things, but the key is that it can cause miscarriages if a woman takes it early in a pregnancy. She made sure Lilah knew not to touch it. She swears Dan was with her to hear that too."

"And you think Dan was and gave some of it to her." Greg's skepticism was increasingly apparent.

"I know, I know. But then, out of the blue, someone I knew at university, Prof. Lynn Peterson, called. We met for coffee, and I got an earful of what she thinks of Dan Collins. It wasn't pretty."

"Hmm. Okay."

"Then a couple of days ago, I was in the front room when Minnie stormed in. She insisted on seeing Dan. At the top of her voice, I might add. She didn't see me, but Dan took her to a back room near the supply shelves and I was back there getting envelopes. She accused him of giving Lilah pennyroyal."

"Did she tell you that?"

"Tell me what?"

"That Dan was there when she and Lilah talked about the penny whatever in her plant garden."

"Pennyroyal in her herb garden."

"Whatever. How do you know about that?"

"I listened in."

"Of course you did."

"Convenient."

"Yes, very. Anyway, when Dan threw Minnie out of his office, he called someone named Jim and told him to get there right away. He sounded angry and desperate."

"Probably was."

"That was three days ago. Yesterday they found Minnie's body on the side of the road."

"You've got my attention now." Greg sat up and leaned his arms on the table. "What happened? Was she hit by a car?"

"She was strangled with a garrote."

Greg whistled, all humor disappearing from his face.

"I was in Greene's office when you called." Mat looked down at her drink. "He wanted me to identify Minnie." Mat swallowed several times at the memory. "Hector was nearly hysterical." She took a deep breath. "That's not all."

"There's more?" Greg's eyes widened and the lines between his brows deepened with concern.

"Yeah. Greene told me they'd identified that kid's body and it was Kim, one of Dan's interns. Remember Dan said one of his interns was missing and had something of his? Remember he was killed with a garrote and left by the side of the road? Remember what I just told you, that I talked to a friend of Kim's who's leaving the country because she's scared?" Mat sat back and watched Greg's reaction.

Chapter 12

"Neat setup you got here." Greene sat back in the chair opposite Dan, his eyes roaming around the room. It was lined with posters from Dan's campaigns, taglines emphasizing his virtues and skills over other candidates.

"I figure it doesn't hurt to remind people that I'm a veteran at this. Not some wet-behind-the-ears newbie." Dan smiled in an attempt to take the arrogance out of the statement. "So, what can I help you with?"

"We got another body you might be interested in."

Dan visibly stiffened, the smile wiped from his face. "What do you mean 'another' body? Why would I be interested in it?"

"This one was that girl's friend, your girlfriend."

"I know about Lilah." Dan frowned. "She broke my heart when she killed herself. Don't know why she did that."

"Oh come now. She was gonna have your child. You tellin' me you didn't know that?"

"*My* child? That's not true. She would have told me. Anyway, you can't prove it."

"Actually we can, and it's a pretty good motive given your current ambitions. But I'm here about something else."

Any color in Dan's face fled, replaced by an ashen hue.

"You okay?" asked Greene, pleased with the reaction his words had produced.

"I'm fine!" retorted Dan. "What about a second body? It couldn't possibly have anything to do with me. You're wasting my time." He blustered and moved some papers around on his desk. "I'm a busy man in case you hadn't noticed."

"That second body was Lilah's girlfriend."

"So what?"

"She came in here last week. I understand she was pretty upset. Can you tell me what she wanted?"

"People come in here all the time. How am I supposed to remember her?" Dan's voice was petulant.

"Because she was Lilah's friend. You know, the one with the herb garden, the one growing pennyroyal." Greene had hoped for a reaction, but he got more than he'd bargained for. Dan was on his feet in an instant.

"How dare you come in here and accuse me of causing Lilah's miscarriage! Whatever anyone says, we both wanted that child!"

"Thought it wasn't yours."

Dan blinked and swallowed. "Well, she may have said something, now that I think of it."

"But you didn't want her to tell anyone about it."

"That was to protect her. People can be incredibly mean to women having children out of wedlock." Dan was getting even more agitated, something Greene would not have thought possible.

"So you didn't plan to marry her?"

"I would have if she wanted that. *She's* the one who didn't want to get married."

"We'll never know, will we? Shall we get back to Minnie?"

"Who? What about Minnie?" Dan's confusion was genuine. It suited Greene perfectly. The more rattled suspects got, the more they tended to contradict themselves.

"She's dead."

"I . . . I didn't know that." Dan looked at Greene, then away. He picked up some papers from the desk and put them back down. "I don't know why you're here asking about her."

"Because she was here last week and was upset when she arrived. You do remember that? I want to know why she was upset."

"I don't remember."

"Maybe some of your colleagues can tell me. From what I understand, it had something to do with you giving Lilah pennyroyal."

"That's crazy. I didn't even know she was growing pennyroyal, or whatever, in her garden."

"I didn't say she was."

Dan paled even more. "That was just an assumption. She talked about her herb garden all the time. I just assumed that was something she'd grow in it."

"So you say." Greene got to his feet. "You don't need to see me out." He started toward the door, then turned back to Dan. "Make sure you don't leave town without telling me."

"But I have campaign stops to make. They're all over this district."

"Just be sure to tell me." Greene left the room and Dan slammed the door after him. He picked up the phone and dialed a familiar number. "Jim, I need you in here, *now*."

***

Hmmm. Early the next morning Mat was seated at her computer on the small desk in Lilah's living room. *Now to figure out what's on it and what it's there for. It was in Kim's pocket, but was it his? If not, who gave it to him? And why?* The algorithms displayed on her screen were written in machine code. *Thank heavens, I took that operating system course. I sure learned what I didn't want to do with my life, but it's coming in handy now. First, it's checking for a date range. Then it's reading input of some kind until it encounters a certain value. Then it drops through to a counting procedure and maintains a 51 percent value for a specific parameter.* The routine looped until it encountered the code for "end of input" and exited. Mat sat back in her chair and stared at the screen. *What is this? Or rather, what would you use this for?* She thought about Kim working for Dan and an unpleasant thought occurred to her. *I need to talk to someone who counts votes.* She glanced at her watch. *Too late to go back to bed and I'm too wired anyway. And it's also too early to find anyone in the office.*

In the midst of her musings, Mat heard the faint click of a key turning, a latch releasing, and a door opening behind her. She whirled in her chair in time to see Zorah semi-crouched in the door frame, her arms and hands full of painting

e-llegal code

materials, a canvas bag over her shoulder, and keys hanging from her mouth.

"Zorah! Is it really that time?"

"*Mmoof, hmmoof,*" Zorah responded as she kicked the door closed and dropped her bundles on the floor.

"Hit a wall," she said, spitting the keys out of her mouth. They joined the pile of bundles on the floor. "Walked around for an hour and decided a change of scene, maybe a hot bath and herbal tea, might get the creative juices flowing. They should jell by tonight. Didn't want to wake you, but I can see that wasn't an issue."

"Maybe you need another challenge circle," Mat teased her.

"Didn't work. Worth a try, though. Want some herbal tea?"

"Great idea. Your timing is perfect."

"It is? Really?"

"I've figured out what's on this disk."

"This what?"

"Disk. You write on it what you want a computer to do."

"Why would you want to write on it? Never mind. I couldn't handle any more of those long words you string together. Although, maybe I could work some of that into my art. *Hmmm.*"

"I just thought you might want to hear about it, but if it's too boring, we can skip that."

"Oh, it's not *that* boring. I'd really like to hear about it. Just keep it simple and don't mind me if I seem to tune out. I'm probably just seeing something on canvas." Zorah perked up at the thought of something new to come. "You always have the most interesting stuff to talk about. And you don't mind when I tell you I've had enough. Anyway, you never know, I might get inspired by something you say. Remember those paintings I did showing the planets in the universe that got smaller and smaller until they resembled those itty-bitty things you said we are all made of? Aha! Maybe that could be part of my mural for Lilah." She disappeared into the kitchen.

Mat shut down the computer, stepped around the pile of Zorah's painting materials, and headed for the kitchen.

A little while later, they were comfortably seated at Lilah's kitchen table on the second pot of tea. The sun was enveloping their feet in its warmth and creeping slowly up the table legs.

"But that's not right, isn't it illegal or something?" Zorah had become increasingly concerned as Mat explained what she had discovered.

"Of course it is."

"I mean, it sounds like someone is trying to do something with the votes, make them come out a certain way. Isn't there a fancy word for that?

"You mean fraud?"

"Yeah, something like that."

"Isn't that illegal?"

"Of course it is."

"But that's not right."

"Of course it isn't. Yes, it's illegal. Yes, it's fraud. No, it's not right."

"But who would do that?"

"There's a piece of this I haven't told you."

"What? Why wouldn't you tell me?"

"Because I want to be sure. Anyway, I've probably told you too much already. You'll be safer if you don't know any more."

"Safer? OMG! You don't think they'll kidnap me again?" Zorah's eyes filled with tears and she stood abruptly, rattling the mugs on the table. "I couldn't go through that again. Really I couldn't!" She turned and left the room, the intimate mood created by sharing the secret of the disk destroyed.

"Zorah, wait!" Mat jumped up and ran after her, narrowly missing the pile of paints and boxes on the floor. She followed Zorah into the bedroom.

"Zorah, wait. No one is going to kidnap you again." She recalled with dismay her last adventure when some thugs had kidnapped Zorah. They'd hoped to scare Mat away from her investigations at her former employer, Kinross Associates. She went on to solve that case with Detective Greene. Zorah claimed she was no worse for the wear from the adventure. Maybe that was only a brave, but fragile, front. *I sure hope not, although I'm afraid this relationship will never survive a repeat performance like that.* "No matter who is behind this, they have no idea I'm involved. And they'd need to know that before connecting me to you. They don't know we're here. Besides we're having that new security system put in at the house, remember? No one can get in there when it's set, and we'll set it every night."

Zorah was sitting on the side of the bed, sniffling loudly and clutching a box of tissues.

"Do you really think so? Oh, promise me that won't happen again."

"Zorah, what happened that time was so unlikely to work. Those men had no idea whether I'd care what happened to you. They were fools. It was a stupid thing to do no matter what was at stake. I think these guys are smarter than that. Anyway, I'll do everything I can to make sure it doesn't happen again. I promise." *Why do I keep on making promises I'm not sure I can keep?*

"Mat, I know I said it wasn't so bad, but when they dragged me out of the kitchen I was so scared."

"I know. You really handled it well and helped solve the case."

"Did I, really?"

"Absolutely. It made what I was saying more credible to Greene." Mat wasn't sure about that, but it made sense, and if it helped Zorah come to terms with what had happened, what did it matter?

"Well, I'm willing to do my part to help," the artist sat up straighter on the bed. "As long as I don't get kidnapped again!" She added a shaky smile to punctuate her words.

Chapter 13

The next morning, Mat called Professor Peterson, who was grading papers for an extra credit project.

"Mat! How are you? Thanks for giving me a break from these papers. I know I'm not an English teacher, but I have to confess, I resent having to correct grammar along with logical non sequiturs! I don't remember being this inarticulate as an undergraduate. You certainly weren't. What can I do for you?"

"Not that you were really asking, but I think formal grammar was more important when I went to school, not to mention when you did."

"Are you calling me old?" Mat could hear the smile in Lynn's voice.

"No, of course not." Mat smiled back. "As to what you can do for me, do you remember what we discussed about Dan Collins the other night?"

"Of course. What's he done now?"

"Nothing yet, that I can prove anyway."

"Too bad."

"It's early days, things are still evolving. Anyway, I need to find out how voting machines work. Do you know anyone I could talk to?"

"Funny you should ask. I do have a colleague who specializes in automated voting methods. His name is Professor Quick. Give him a call."

"Thanks so much. I really appreciate it."

"No problem. I guess I need to get back to these papers. I dream about students coming after me with pitchforks if I don't get them back as promised. Come to think of it, I dream about the ones who don't get an A coming after me when I'm done."

"Sounds like you need a good pair of running shoes."

"Very funny. Promise you'll tell me how it goes with Professor Quick."

"Will do, thanks."

***

Mat walked through the double glass doors of the Political Science Department, which opened onto a spacious lobby. She stopped and looked around, trying to decide which way to go to find the office. To her left she saw an older man coming toward her from the corridor. He stopped and blinked at her from behind coke-bottle glasses. Pure-white hair, a mass of corkscrew projections, surrounded his head and merged into a full beard and mustache. He stared silently, then peered on either side of her as if looking to see if she was alone.

"You look lost. Can I help you?"

"I hope so. I was looking for Professor Quick in the Political Science Department. I have a couple of questions about voting machinery."

At the mention of voting machinery, his eyes widened and a wide grin lit up the parts of his face visible amid the mass of white curls.

"Well, in that case, I'm, uh, probably your guy, uh, person." He spoke quickly with a surprisingly thin, high voice, punctuated by quick breaths as if he were perpetually short of air.

"Super. That would be great. Oh, by the way, I'm Mat Briscoe. I work at a local technology company." She held out her hand.

"Professor Quick." He laughed as if at a private joke. "But you know that." He grinned broadly. "You just caught me. I was heading out to my hot yoga class. It's the latest thing, you know."

"Hot yoga?"

"Yes, it keeps me limber, and at my age, everything helps."

"Well, it's my lucky day then." Mat smiled back.

"It surely is. Follow me." With that, Professor Quick turned abruptly and went back the way he had come; Mat increased her stride to keep up with him. He passed several doors, each one not more than ten feet from the one beside it. At the third one he stopped, produced a key, and swung it open. It settled against a wall of bookshelves that stretched along the ten-foot length of the room to a small window at the end of the room.

Professor Quick turned to the bookshelves and ran his fingers along the shelf, his index finger beating a silent rhythm along the spines. He paused, pulled out two, and turned back to Mat.

"Voting machines, eh?" His quizzical expression begged for an explanation. He settled himself in one of two chairs in the office and pointed to the other one. "Have a seat."

Mat sat down. *What to say?* Her idea sounded so preposterous when put into words. On the other hand, it explained a lot.

"Well, it's complicated." She paused to gather her thoughts. Professor Quick waited patiently, rocking back in his chair, just missing the wall behind him. "What if I wanted to make sure someone running for office got enough votes to win?" Mat noted Professor Quick's raised eyebrows. "I know, I know, who would do that? Let me explain."

"Oh, I don't doubt it's done, perhaps more than we know." Professor Quick put his feet up on his desk, a wry grin on his face. "What's your interest in such nefarious deeds? Please start with the facts, just the facts, ma'am." He chuckled at the reference to the old Dragnet TV show. "Inside joke," he added, looking at Mat's blank face.

"As I said, I'm a computer consultant and I've been hired to audit a candidate's computers to see if anyone has hacked into them." Mat gestured at his desktop. "Maybe to find out his strategy, stuff like that."

"I see."

"I started thinking what if someone wanted to get into the voting machines themselves and not into a rival's computers? They could affect the outcome without even knowing what the strategy of their opponent was."

"That's some out-of-the-box thinking for sure."

"All I want to know is if it's possible. Is there some way the results could be manipulated to give one candidate more votes than he or she actually got?"

Professor Quick sat back in his chair and stared past Mat at the whiteboard on the wall behind her. After a minute, he turned back to Mat.

"Can you tell me which precinct you want to know about? Even which state? The machinery isn't uniform across all the states. I don't know if you realize that."

"No, I didn't. I'm interested in the race Dan Collins is in locally."

"Ah, indeed. Interesting history on that one. A story for another time perhaps."

Professor Quick stood and stepped over to the large whiteboard.

"First some basics." He drew a couple of boxes and lines connecting them on the board.

"The precinct that race is in uses Votomatic machines."

"Votomatic? You're kidding. I've never heard of a Votomatic machine."

"Then either you've never voted, and I hope that's not the case"—Professor Quick winked at her—"or the precinct where you came from used another method. Anyway, as I said, the precinct Dan Collins is running in uses Votomatic machines. They use Hollerith cards. Ever heard of Hollerith cards?"

"Of course. That's how computers were programmed in the early days. Those went the way of the dinosaur for the most part a long time ago."

"Not so much for some voting machines, although they are on the way out there as well. For now, the Votomatic machine collects votes punched into a ballot card, a version of the Hollerith card."

"How do the votes get punched into the cards?" Mat interrupted.

"Okay. Let's start from the beginning. When an election is scheduled, a given number of blank cards are delivered to the voting places. The number is based on estimates from past voting events at the location."

"And where is this Votomatic machine?"

"Votomatic machines are what voters use at the polling site. Here's how it works." Professor Quick returned to his chair and settled in.

"A couple of facts to start with: candidate names are not printed on the cards but rather on the pages of a ballot label which is arranged as a booklet. It also holds the card. This is part of the Votomatic setup. The voter gets a ballot card and slips it into the ballot holder. The voter then turns the pages of the ballot to expose candidate names lined up with a column of numbered positions on the underlying card." Professor Quick looked up at the ceiling as if mentally reviewing what he'd just said.

"Right. Then voters use a stylus to punch through the card at the numbered position of the candidate they want. After voting, the ballot card is removed from the ballot holder and collected for counting."

"So there's no way to tell who used which ballot card?"

"No, no way at all. Even the precinct number is initially not on the ballot. Anyway, to continue, ballots are collected and put into a box with the precinct's label. They are taken to a central location and tabulated using card readers and attached computers. The reader senses which position on the ballot card has a hole and the software summarizes the number of votes for each candidate. Also, since the computers need to be dedicated to this task when votes are counted, no other processes can be running on them at the same time." The professor paused to catch his breath. "This is a security feature that ensures no outside processes can affect the count. They do an audit of the software right before it's isolated to be sure nothing has been added since the last authorized update to the code."

"Sounds like they thought of everything."

"It's actually a pretty good system. A number of major voting precincts, particularly big city environments use them. The machines are lightweight, inexpensive, and uncomplicated." Professor Quick glanced at his watch and sat up in his chair.

"So sorry, I was going to be early but now I'm going to be late to my yoga class. Need to run." He grabbed his briefcase and hurried to the office door, turning to make sure Mat was close behind him. She grabbed her jacket and hurried after him.

"Thank you for giving me so much time, this has been very helpful," Mat called to him as she closed the door behind her. She raised her voice as he trotted down the hall ahead of her, "Is it alright if I check back with any questions?"

"Of course. Glad to help, yes indeed, glad to help." He disappeared around the corner and Mat listened to his receding footsteps as she slowed to a leisurely pace. *Interesting fellow. Good resource for sure. Now to figure out how this information fits into what I found on the disk and how it involves Dan Collins's campaign, if at all.*

Chapter 14

Mat returned to Lilah's apartment and caught Zorah before she headed out to Candlewick. As she neared the door, the whirling dervish music she had heard from the lobby grew louder. When she eased the door open, the sound engulfed her as did the sight of her roommate. A portable cassette player, the source of the music, was on the floor and Zorah was twirling around, keeping time with her feet. She was lost in a blaze of bright red and orange that swirled around her. Mat stared, mesmerized. The music picked up speed and Zorah kept up, her feet nimbly dancing around and around in circles. Mat rescued a small statue from the coffee table just before the caftan swept across the surface. All at once, the music hit a pinnacle in volume and stopped abruptly. Zorah collapsed into a colorful heap of red and orange on the floor. The artist lay there panting with a broad grin on her face.

"Well, it's not Bolero, but close enough," commented Mat. "What was that all about?"

"Oh Mat, I'm so glad you're home," Zorah began when she caught her breath. "The most exciting thing happened today. I just had to release some of this energy or it would ruin my painting tonight. I've tried a lot of things, like running up and down stairs several times or doing jumping jacks or putting on a belly dancing tape. Have you ever seen me belly dance?" She grinned at Mat. "I'll show you sometime, but then I thought the people downstairs might not like it, well maybe they wouldn't have minded the belly dancing, but I can't find that tape, so I put on this from a mix of whirling dervish music I got a while back. It's a lot more fun than running up and down stairs." She paused to catch her breath. "Whew, I think it's done the trick!"

"I'm sure the neighbors hope so."

"Oh gosh, do you think the music was too loud?"

"Well, I could hear it from the front door several floors below us."

"Someone should have knocked on the door."

"They might have, but you probably wouldn't have heard them with the music so loud."

"Oh, Mat. I'm sorry. I get caught up in things sometimes. I'll go around and apologize before I go to the studio tonight. At least to the people who are home. Do you think they'll be mad?"

"Probably not if it didn't go on too long. So what was the exciting thing that happened today?"

"Oh yes!" Zorah brightened immediately, her whole face suffused in a delighted smile. "Someone saw my sketches of the mural I'm doing for Lilah. You remember?!"

"Yes, I remember. Something about lots of red."

"Exactly. Well, it's not just red. Lilah was so spiritual. I added lots of dream-quality images. That brought in some blues and purple. I'm using some swirling and spiral ideas to show Lilah's spontaneity, and how she touched so many aspects of people's lives. Anyway, this man saw my sketches and wants me to create a mural for

e-llegal code

his new art building. Isn't that the best news? It'll get lots of attention. I sure hope it brings me lots of work."

"Where is this mural going to be?"

"I'm not sure exactly. I think he said something about an abandoned railroad yard and the art projects he is sponsoring."

"Zorah, if it's an abandoned railroad yard, who's going to see it?"

"Maybe not many people at first, but the area is going through something he called 'gentrification.' That means lots of people with money will soon be seeing it."

"Okay. So, how much is he paying you for this mural?"

"Honestly, not all that much. But it'll pay for a few months' rent at the house and at the studio. And, like he said, the point is to get my work out there for people to see. Don't you think it's exciting?"

Mat went over to Zorah and gave her a big hug. "Absolutely, I think it's exciting. So many journeys to success start with small steps. I think you're on the way!"

"Thanks. I know it's not the big time, but you gotta start somewhere, and I'm really not in a position to be choosy."

"Not yet, anyway." Mat gave her friend another hug and went into the kitchen to make some tea.

Zorah followed her. "I'm sorry I was so excited I forgot to ask how your investigation is going.

"Good question. I think the first thing is to figure out how to explain to Greene what's going on."

"You can't just tell him like you told me?"

"Problem is"—Mat pursed her lips as she considered how to answer Zorah—"I have to show him the code in a way he'll understand. He won't just take my word for it."

"How are you going to do that?"

"Read the code in detail and create a flowchart."

Zorah considered this bit of information.

"Sounds, no offense, super dull to me."

Mat laughed. "And very interesting to me."

"Different strokes, I guess." Zorah turned to leave the kitchen, all interest fading away. "I'll have some tea later. I'm late and I still have some of that energy to get rid of. I think it's the right amount to keep me going all night! See you in the morning."

Mat smiled to herself, picked up her mug of tea, and wandered over to the table she'd set up as a workspace. *Is a flowchart the way to go? I already know what it's doing. Still, maybe that would be a good idea if only to help Greene and others understand what's going on.* She settled in front of the computer, pulled out a notepad, and started to draw. An hour later she sat back and reviewed her work. Satisfied, she picked up the phone and dialed a number.

"Yeah?" barked Greene. "It's late. What do you want?"

Mat held the phone away from her ear. She'd completely forgotten the time.

"Sorry. It's Mat. Got a minute?"

"What for?"

"I figured out what's on the disk. I think you'll be interested in what it's doing."

"Good. Are you going to tell me or keep it to yourself?"

"I'll tell you, but it's best done in person."

"Why's that?"

"It's a bit complicated but I have a couple of pictures that show what's going on."

"I'm not two years old, you know."

"That's not what I mean. It's complicated and even techies use these pictures to help keep themselves straight when they are programming."

"Okay, okay. When do you want to meet?"

"How about first thing in the morning?"

"Done." Greene slammed down the phone.

***

The next morning Mat spread the flowcharts on the small table in Greene's office.

"These the pictures you were talking about?"

"Yes. They describe, visually, the process a designer wants the computer to follow. The programmer writes code to make the computer do this."

"This is what the disk is doing?"

"Yes. Do you know what a Votomatic machine is?"

"A what?"

"A Votomatic machine. They are used in the precinct where Dan Collins is running for office."

"If you say so. What does this Votomatic machine have to do with this disk thing and the code you say is on it?"

"I'll explain the Votomatic machine first, then explain how the code on the disk fits into the picture. A Votomatic machine is what voters use to cast their votes. A voter uses a punch card . . ."

"A what?"

"A punch card, Hollerith card, one of those cards programmers used to use to write code. A programmer would end up with a deck of cards that got fed into the machine to tell the machine what to do."

"Okay."

"Nowadays, programmers key code directly into a computer." Mat noticed Greene's eyes starting to glaze over. She moved on. "It's not important. The point is a Votomatic machine uses those same cards to record a voter's candidate choice. The card is collected after someone votes, then is bundled up and taken to a central counting facility. There, it's read into another computer that reads each card and tallies up the votes for the different candidates. Are you with me so far?"

"Yeah. Mostly. So what does this have to do with that thing we found on the kid's body?"

"The code on the disk replaces the code in the computer that receives the count from the card reader. It reads the ballot card and compares the vote to a running total for all the candidates for a given position. Here's where it gets interesting." Mat pointed out an area on the charts. "The instructions on the disk are to maintain a percentage, say fifty-one percent, for one of the candidates as it counts the cards. That's assuming there are two candidates for a position. The percentage could be different depending on how many candidates there are."

Greene was silent for a moment. "So you're saying someone is messing with the totals in the election."

"That's what it looks like to me."

Greene gave a long, low whistle. "So what was this kid doing with this disk thing?"

"I don't know. Maybe he developed the code, but if so, who was he going to give it to? Why was he killed before he could hand it off? Was that the intention?"

"So the kid knew what was on it?"

"If he programmed it, he certainly knew what was on it. If he didn't, why did he have it?"

"Maybe he got cold feet and someone wanted him dead before he ratted on them."

"There's another angle that I just thought of."

"Oh?"

"They do a security check of the vote counting computer before it is used to count votes."

"Why?"

"To make sure no one has messed with the code. I'm sure they make note of any changes to the code that were made since the last audit and determine if each change was authorized with an ECP."

"A what?"

"Engineering change proposal. Doesn't matter. The point is they want to make sure there are good reasons for any changes made to the code since the last election."

"So, if they do that, wouldn't they see that this other code was put in before the election?"

"They would, assuming the audit came after the code was put in."

"When do they do the audit?"

"Right before they isolate the machine to process votes."

"What do you mean 'isolate' the machine?"

"According to Professor Quick, no other processes can be run on the computer at the same time as the votes are counted, so they isolate it."

"Professor Quick?"

"Sorry." Mat checked her notes. "He's a professor in the Political Science Department at the university. He studies voting patterns at the precinct level. He teaches classes in the Political Science and Computing and Informatics departments. I talked to him about the Votomatic machines."

"*Humph,*" grunted Greene. "I still think you made up that name."

"I didn't, cross my heart." Mat crossed her heart and held up her hand. "I promise."

"So where are we?"

"From my perch, we've got voting fraud." Mat noted Greene's look of skepticism and amended her comment, "*Potentially.* Also, we've got a disk with code on it that *appears* to alter voting counts and I'm betting someone, *possibly* Dan Collins, is going to use it to stack the deck in his favor in the upcoming election."

"How do you figure that?"

"The disk was found in the pocket of a student who worked for Dan who is a candidate in the next election."

"That's a lot of *potentially, appears,* and *possibly*. Still, maybe you got something there. Got any *potentially*s or *possibly*s about that second death? Who *might* have murdered her, and the student, for that matter."

"And how and when is the code on the disk put into the vote counting machine? We haven't even talked about how the code is removed." Mat sat in a chair beside Greene's desk. "If it's still in the machine by the next time an audit is done, it'll be found and the vote will be thrown out. If they are smart, they'll do another audit right after the election results are certified."

"Add *might*s and *if*s to the list and all we have is speculation and circumstantial evidence. And even the circumstantial evidence is . . . choose a word . . . *iffy* does it for me."

"I wonder if Lilah's death is connected in some way," Mat mused, already pursuing another angle.

"As if we didn't have enough *possibles* here."

"There are still a number of questions to find answers to," Mat went on, excitement putting her on the edge of her seat. "How does the code get into the machine and how does it get removed, assuming it does? That's a mighty big risk they're taking if they just plan to leave it in. Also, there's a date range for this code to execute and a section of comments. I haven't looked at those too closely yet. Usually, it's just information about the code and what it does generally like 'tallies or counts.' There might be more information there that will help."

"Look, before your imagination runs away with you any faster, we're assuming this disk is even intended to be used in this election." Greene sat back in his chair, pencil twirling in his right hand. "One thing's for sure. All of this is meaningless if we can't get any proof."

"What if we take this disk to Dan and see what his reaction is?" Mat leaned forward in her chair, as if pinning him down with her body. "I can tell him what I found on it and that one of his employees had it on him when his body was found. It's logical. It's what we should do anyway, right?"

"You got a point there." Greene sat up, putting his elbows on his desk and clasping his hands in front of his face. He stroked his chin with one thumb. "We need to find out what he knows about that thing. I'll tell Dan to make time tomorrow afternoon. It's too late today. Meet you there tomorrow." With that, Greene shoved his chair back from his desk, grabbed his jacket, and left the room without a backward glance.

***

That evening, Mat and Greg sat in the kitchen of Lilah's apartment with a bottle of wine and the remains of sushi take-out on the kitchen table. Mat lifted her glass and saluted Greg.

"Congratulations on winning your latest case. I knew you were going to pull that one off."

e-llegal code

"You're the only one who did. As much as I prepare and think I've covered every base going in, there can always be something to surprise me and change the outcome. Especially when a jury's involved."

"Well, whatever you say, I had a feeling you were going to win."

"Now you're beginning to sound like Zorah!"

"I heard that!" Zorah crossed the small living room and came into the kitchen, her arms loaded with papers and bits of brightly colored fabric.

"What sounds like me?"

"Just me telling Greg I had a feeling he was going to win his case."

"Oh Greg, intuition is nothing to laugh at! If you can just learn to trust them and give them space to intensify, you'd be surprised how they'll lead the way. I'm sure Steve has something to help nurture that. And we have exercises that help you bring those feelings out." Zorah's enthusiasm for all things spiritual was infectious.

"Anything like challenge circles?" Mat couldn't resist a reference to Zorah's attempt at dispelling artists' block.

"Actually, it's sort of like that," Zorah answered in all seriousness. "It's called Intuition Intensification. You take this supplement that Steve has, but instead of sitting in a circle with other people, you sit by yourself. You surround yourself with objects you want to get sensations about, like a picture or piece of clothing from someone, or a map if you want to improve your sense of direction, or a piece of your artwork if you want to get inspiration. Then you focus on the sensations that emerge as you focus on the thing. You choose a meditation method or chant and do that at the same time. You'd be surprised at how it works and what it does."

"I'm sure," Mat commented, trying not to let her cynical reactions to Zorah's obsession with the occult and spiritual auras get the better of her.

"Seriously," Zorah continued enthusiastically, "if you're consistent about doing this, you'll be amazed. And Steve's supplements just about ensure success."

"Success at what?" They all turned to see Steve, an herbal nutritionist and artist, on the other side of the kitchen threshold.

"Steve!" Zorah gushed. "You're here. See"—she turned to Mat and Greg—"it's true. I was focused on the work Steve is doing and here she is. I just know it's because I was concentrating on her and her work."

"What about the objects and chant and her potion?" asked Mat.

"Potion?" asked Steve.

"Or supplement. Whatever you call it to help with this focus thing."

"Zorah, I told you your friend wouldn't understand. Here's proof. She's making fun of you and me."

"Steve, I'm sorry. I wasn't making fun. I just don't understand." Mat tried to deflect the conversation away from the focus topic. "How did you get in here anyway? I'm sure I locked the door."

"Lilah gave me a key so I could drop some supplements by anytime she wanted them."

e-llegal code

"What supplements?" asked Mat.

Steve didn't answer but looked at Mat and Greg. "What the hell are you two doing here?" she demanded. "This is Lilah's apartment. Or was. Anyway, it's not yours. Zorah said she was staying here, but you two don't belong here." She tilted her head and, squinting one eye, looked from one to the other. In a malevolent tone, she stated, "You're trespassing. I should call the police."

"Steve," Zorah interrupted, "Mat's staying here with me, and Greg's her boyfriend. What did you come here for anyway." She steered her friend into the living room. Steve turned her focus to Zorah.

"I gave Lilah some herbal anti-nausea supplements and other stuff. I wanted them back. You knew she was pregnant didn't you?"

"I do now. When did she tell you?" Zorah's voice betrayed a tinge of jealousy that she'd not been among the first to know.

"Right after she found out, I think. A couple of months ago."

"What other stuff did you give her?"

"Just stuff."

"C'mon, Steve, what stuff are you talking about?"

"I don't know if she would want me to tell you."

"Can it matter now? Maybe it'll help us understand why she died."

"Do you think she was allergic to something in the supplements? I told her what was in them, and she said she wasn't allergic to anything."

"What did you give her?" Zorah continued to pressure the nutritionist.

"I told you, just something to help with nausea and nerves."

"Why did she need something for nerves?"

"I think she wasn't sure about her boyfriend's reaction."

"Do you know who that was?"

"No, do you?"

"Steve." Zorah took a deep breath. "Did you give her something to end the pregnancy if she wanted to?"

"I don't know what you're talking about."

"Well, what *stuff* then?"

"Stuff to help her nausea and for nerves, like I told you."

"Yeah, I know. What other stuff?"

"That's all. Look, if you're going to give me the third degree, I'm leaving." Steve turned and left, slamming the door behind her.

Mat heard the door slam and came into the living room.

"I couldn't help but hear. What do you think that other 'stuff' was?"

"Huh?" Zorah transferred her eyes from the apartment door to Mat.

"I said, what do you think that other 'stuff' was?"

"Oh. I don't know . . ." Zorah gathered up her design papers. "Look, I'm really late. I need to get to the studio." She headed for the door. Greg came from the kitchen to stand beside Mat. They watched Zorah's caftan slip through the closing door as it trailed behind the artist.

"You two really need to change that lock. I thought Greene had done that."

"I did too. If Steve had a key, I bet Dan has a key..."

"Maybe I should stay the night." Greg turned Mat around to face him.

"*Hmm.*" Mat rested her forehead against his chest. "Did I ever tell you how glad I am that Zorah works at night?"

"No, why don't we finish the sushi and you can tell me all about that."

Chapter 15

In the morning, the sun shone brightly into the small kitchen that was such a contrast to the vibrant red of Lilah's bedroom. Its art deco–style black-and-white-checked floor tiles and white walls complemented the small black table and chairs.

"More coffee?" asked Mat.

"Thanks, but I'm done for now, at least with the coffee," Greg replied. "We never got around to bringing me up-to-date with your volunteer work on the Collins campaign. Got anything else on that?"

"A few things. I'd really like to hear what you think."

"I'm all ears, as they say."

"I'm pretty sure the only thing you don't know about is Professor Quick and the Votomatic machines."

"The what?"

"I'd have thought you would have heard of them since you're so tight with Dan Collins."

"Hardly. What are Votomatic machines?"

"They are used to record votes in the precinct where Dan Collins is running for office."

"Okay. I'll bite. Why is that important?"

"Well, it works like this. The voter gets a ballot card and slips it into the ballot holder. Then voters use a stylus to punch through the card at the numbered position of the candidate they want. After voting, the ballot card is collected for counting. The software summarizes the number of votes for each candidate."

"Sounds aboveboard so far."

"But," Mat continued, "if the algorithm on the disk alters the way the votes are counted, it could mean one person would win no matter how many votes he or she got."

"So now you're adding *possible* election fraud to the list of things that are *possibly* going on here."

"You sound like Greene." Mat drained the last of her coffee and went to the counter for a refill. "I know it sounds farfetched, but I'm sure all of this, the three murders as well as the disk fit into the picture somehow."

"Have you been trying Zorah's Intuition Intensification exercises? That might have unintended collateral consequences."

"What?"

"Just playing with words. Seriously, you do have a habit of letting your imagination run away with you."

"As I recall, the last time you accused me of that, I turned out to be on the right track."

"Once doesn't make it a rule."

"Oh, Greg. Can't you give me a little credit? There are just too many coincidences, and I don't like coincidences. Not when they pile up like this."

"Okay. You're right, that disk is something to check out. The other stuff is possible, maybe. But you need to leave this to Greene. If you dig deeper, you might find yourself in over your head."

"It's going to be hard to leave me out entirely. I'm Greene's reason for going after Collins at this point. We're going to meet with him later today."

"You mean you're going to take these suspicions to him directly? Mat, you're playing with fire."

"Possibly." Mat couldn't resist a smile to accompany her comment. "We're going to see what a few questions gets us."

"I wish Greene would leave you out of this."

"He may be able to soon. But right now he has no solid evidence, and I'm the only one who can talk about that disk and what's on it. I think he'd get lost in the explanation if he goes it alone at this point."

"Well, I don't like it, but at least you're going together."

"I appreciate your concern, really I do." She pulled his head down for a kiss. "But I need to see this through, at least until there's enough evidence for Greene to move forward officially. After all, as you said, right now all we have is speculation."

They both turned as Zorah came barreling into the apartment, sketches and loose bits of colorful fabric flying out of her arms.

"Oh, you two. I'm so glad you're still here!" She continued to talk as she dumped the armload of papers and detritus of her artistic endeavors on the sofa, "I had the most amazing conversation with Steve around two thirty this morning. It was so inspirational but also so amazing. Well, I said that, but it's true. She was talking about her herbs and told me, I promise you want to hear this, she talked about getting the oil, or extracting it out of pennyroyal. The extraction thing is what was amazing to me, but you'll be interested in the other thing, the oil thing." Zorah paused to catch her breath.

"Take it slow, Zorah. Let's all sit down and hear what you have to say." Mat and Greg sat next to the pile of papers on the sofa and Zorah moved over to the single chair opposite them.

"Oh, Mat, it's so exciting, this extraction thing. It means you're getting something out of a bigger thing, the essence of it. It's inspirational! I'm going to use it as an image for Lilah's mural."

"Extraction?"

"Yes! I'm going to 'extract' Lilah's essence from her earthly existence and paint it in the mural. It's absolutely the answer." Zorah's excitement was palpable and infectious.

"Zorah, I'm really happy for you," Mat said to the artist's beaming face. "What about the oil thing."

"That is what you'll really find interesting."

"I'm all ears."

"Steve does these lectures sometimes on her herbs and nutritional supplements, you know, as a way to bring in some extra cash. You'd be surprised at how popular they are."

"That's good I guess."

"Oh, it is. It helps her buy new herbs and things she needs to create her supplements. It's also a way to let people know about her and what she does."

"The oil?"

"Oh. Yes. Well about a month ago she gave a presentation on the mint family and talked about the different kinds like pennyroyal. She sends these flyers around neighborhoods and gives them to her friends, so they get a wide distribution. She puts them under windshield wipers and in mailboxes, in church lobbies, places like that."

"I see. The oil, Zorah."

"I'm getting to it. I just wanted you to understand how this could have happened."

"What could have happened?"

"Mat, don't be so impatient. I'm getting to it."

Mat clenched her teeth and gave Zorah what she hoped was an encouraging smile.

"Sorry, please go on."

"Well, at that presentation, guess who was there?"

"I have no idea, please tell us."

"Dan Collins." Zorah sat back with a satisfied grin on her face.

"No!"

"Yes!"

"Dan went to this presentation on pennyroyal?"

"Yes, and Steve explained all about how toxic the oil was and gave a brief explanation of how the oil is extracted. She's really very good at explaining stuff like that."

"That is interesting. Greene told me Dan denied knowing anything about pennyroyal. Zorah, you're sure about this?"

"Of course I am. Steve went on and on about how he really stood out, dressed in that suit with his big "I AM A CANDIDATE" button in his lapel. He's not a short person anyway, and everyone else was in jeans, clogs, caftans, and such. Steve said he stayed after to ask her a couple of questions about how the extraction process worked. Real curious, he was."

Mat turned to Greg, who had been sitting back listening to Zorah. He raised his eyebrows and gave her a little shake of his head. Mat took one of his hands in hers.

"I know what you're thinking, but I can't keep this from Greene. And it'll be more convincing if Dan hears it from me. It's already second- or thirdhand. If Greene says he heard it from a friend of a friend of a friend, etc., it just makes it less meaningful. You must see that Greene needs me right now."

Greg sat up facing Mat and took both of her hands in his.

"I can see it looks that way to you. I still think if you tell Greene this, he is more than capable of making it as meaningful as it can be. All you're doing is telling Collins that you know all about it and that puts you in danger. That's assuming he has anything to do with this at all. Any involvement he has in Lilah's death is still just speculation."

"There's another piece I haven't told you about." They both turned to look at Zorah who was still sitting across from them amid the pieces of fabric she'd brought home.

"What's that?" they said in unison.

"About a week before Lilah died, Dan came by the studio and bought some pennyroyal plants from Steve."

Chapter 16

"Thank you for giving us some time this afternoon." Greene and Mat were sitting in front of the desk in Dan's office in the rear of his campaign headquarters. Posters, banners, and flyers from his current campaign had been added to the ones papering the walls around the desk. Dan was seated behind it, arms crossed. He leaned back, a welcoming smile on his face.

"What can I do for you? Mat, have you come up with something in my computer systems that requires the police?" He sat up, smile fading, uncrossed his arms and put them on his desk. He looked Mat in the eye. "I'm sorry you didn't feel you could come to me first so we could discuss whatever it is you found. It might not have been necessary to involve the police. After all, we know Detective Greene has a lot on his plate. There might be a perfectly good explanation for whatever you found, one that I can provide."

"Actually," Greene spoke up before Mat could answer, "I have some questions about what we found on the dead student."

"So you *did* find something on that body. You told me you didn't after I said he had something of mine." Dan leaned forward, his focus shifting to Greene. "You lied to me!"

"I didn't. It didn't have your name on it. How was I to know it was yours?"

Dan retreated into silence, glaring at Greene.

"Back to the dead kid. You remember, the one you said worked for you. The one we found strangled to death and dumped in a ditch across town."

Dan acknowledged his admission grudgingly, "Yes, I remember. Such a tragedy. I've spoken to the family. They are devastated. The young man had some employment benefits coming that will help defray the costs of burial. I told them I would make sure that got to them as quickly as possible."

"That's all well and good," Greene said, "but my questions have to do with what is on that thing, that . . ." He turned to Mat for help.

"Computer disk."

"Right. Mat's here because I asked her to figure out what it was. Looked like something from a computer and she knew right off what it was."

"Is that right?"

"She said it was some kind of program that would tell a computer how to count votes in an election. Seeing how it was found on someone who worked for you, and you insist he had something of yours, and you are running in the current campaign, I wondered what you could tell us about that."

Dan's pallor had gone increasingly white, and the smile fled from his face. He adjusted his position in the chair and sat back, the fingers of his right hand beginning a slow drumming on the armrest of the chair.

"I'm not sure why you're telling me this. Just because that—disk, did you say?—was found on that kid doesn't mean it has anything to do with me." Dan regained some equilibrium with these words and the drumming stopped.

"Well, someone who knew the dead kid said that he was doing something special for you, something exciting but not exactly on the up and up."

"I have no idea what that might be. I certainly don't condone any behavior that is not exactly on the 'up and up' as you call it."

"So the kid's friend was lying?"

"Of course. Kids these days, they'll say anything for a laugh. You should know that."

"What was it you wanted from the kid?"

"What do you mean what did I want?"

"You called me after I found the body wanting me to find something he had on him. Was it the disk?" Greene leaned forward. "Just so you know, there was someone else in the room. I have a witness."

"Uh, that was a while back. I don't remember exactly what I wanted. Whatever it was, I must have gotten it back from someone else. I don't think I'm missing anything at the moment." Dan readjusted his position in the chair.

"So you don't have any thoughts about what that disk might have to do with vote counts?"

"No, none at all."

"Let me tell you how it looks to me." Greene settled further back in his chair, his beefy hands clasped over his stomach. "I find it more than a little coincidental that an employee of yours, a dead employee, has this disk with a vote counting procedure on him, that you wanted something he had on him, and that you are running for office, which could be affected by this vote counting procedure. I think you had this kid create this procedure, and he told his friend, who told us about it. Then, for whatever reason, you had him killed but didn't get this thing back before the body got dumped. How am I doing?"

"This is crazy! I had nothing to do with that kid's death and I don't know anything about a disk."

"What I can't figure out is why you felt it necessary to kill that kid. So they wouldn't tell anyone? Seems an extreme measure."

"I'm telling you I didn't kill anyone!"

"Possibly not, but I think it is in the realm of possibility that you had someone do it."

Dan stood up and pointed to the door. "Get out, now!"

Greene leaned forward, arms on his knees.

"We can go now, but I'll be back because I have something else I want to ask you about."

"What's that?" Dan remained standing but dropped his arm.

"I understand you have an interest in pennyroyal oil."

Dan, caught off guard, looked past Greene, his eyes darting around the room before answering the detective.

"That plant? Why do you think I would be interested in that?"

"So you do know what it is?"

Dan blinked, caught off guard for a second time.

"So what? I must have heard Lilah or her friend talk about it."

"Or maybe you talked to her friend Steve. You know the herbal nutritionist." Greene glanced at Mat to be sure he had the right term. At her nod, he continued, "Apparently, you wanted to know all about how to get oil from it."

"Did I? Maybe I was just curious." Dan set his jaw and glared at Greene.

"Seems a strange thing to be curious about. Also a funny thing to be spending time on in the middle of a political campaign."

"So now I murdered Lilah too!"

"How did you know Lilah was murdered?"

"I didn't, don't." Dan's face had grown increasingly red and he was close to shouting. "You're trying to confuse me so you can pin something on me."

Greene stood up and Mat followed suit.

"I can tell you two things. It's only a matter of time before we find something to link you to Lilah's death and to a case of planned voter fraud. And that won't be a matter of trying to pin something on you, it'll be fact."

Suddenly Dan sat back down in his chair. A smile slowly spread over his face. He threw his hands up in the air and shrugged his shoulders, admitting defeat.

"I give up. Oh, it's not what you think," he responded to the confused looks on Greene's and Mat's faces. "If it'll get you off my back, I'm going to tell you something that isn't any of your business and will probably get me in trouble with the Feds."

Greene sat back uncertainly. "The Feds?"

"I know there's something funny going on with the Votomatic machines."

The perplexed expressions on Greene's and Mat's faces were identical. Greene asked, "So what do you think is going on?"

"A while back, I was contacted by someone in the federal government, a Gilbert something." Dan paused at the sidelong look Mat gave Greene. "What's up?" he asked.

"Nothing," Mat answered. "Go on."

"He wanted me to help them find a group that is trying to rig voting machines so the candidate they want to win actually does, no matter what. I said I'd do what I could. I can't tell you any more than that. I expect I'm already in hot water for telling you this much."

Mat and Greene sat in silence, trying to absorb this turn of events. Dan relaxed in his chair, a hint of a smirk at the edges of his mouth. He stood again, defiant and back in charge.

"Now, I'm going to ask you both to leave my office. And you, Ms. Briscoe, are fired. Don't come back to either my campaign headquarters or my company or I'll have you arrested on the spot."

Greene rose from his chair and headed for the door with Mat close behind him. He paused at the door and glared at Dan.

"I'll be taking another look at this whole mess." Jabbing a finger at Dan, he added, "Your story doesn't check out, I'll be back." He slammed the door behind them.

Dan picked up the phone and punched in a number.

"Jim? Get in here now!"

***

Outside, Greene headed for the squad car they had come in and slammed the door as Mat got in.

"What the hell?" Greene asked. "What is this Gilbert guy doing messed up in this anyway? Last time he came around it was all about drugs. I thought you said he was DEA."

"How should I know what he's doing mixed up in this?"

"Well, you should know. He's your friend."

"He's not my friend. He just turned up last time. I don't keep up with his schedule or his assignments," Mat snapped at Greene. She thought briefly of the burly, dreadlocked, British-accented agent. He was Jamaica born and bred, educated at Dartmouth, and worked for the DEA—a perfect undercover agent who had helped her solve the case at Kinross Associates.

He looked at her sideways. "You don't have to blame me, I didn't fire you."

"I'm not blaming you," Mat snapped again.

"Have it your way. Answer me this. How does Dan know about this Gilbert person if he's not into drugs? Do we have to make this about drugs too?"

"I told you, I don't know. I think Dan is just throwing up a smokescreen. Why didn't he tell us about Gilbert earlier?"

"Maybe it was what he said, the Feds don't want him telling anyone about their little project. I've had those guys on my ass before and it's not a good feeling. Nothing my boss likes less than riling up the Fed folks. It always comes rolling right downhill to my desk."

"Well, I don't buy it. I think all he's done is buy himself some time to clean up his mess and you're falling for it, hook, line, and sinker! He's conning you, and you're going for it." Mat was confused, confounded, and certain that Dan was not helping the Feds. *He can't be, can he?*

"I'll tell you who's been conning me." Greene turned in his seat to glare at Mat. "I've let you drag me into this kind of situation before—"

"And I've been right!" Mat interrupted.

"Once doesn't make it a slam dunk. This one is just too iffy, too coincidental, and too much about *your* suspicions. I'm not moving another step on *your* suspicions."

"But I just *know* he's behind Kim's murder and is trying to manipulate the Votomatic. I *know* it!" Mat was close to tears from frustration.

"You don't *know* anything," Greene said, his florid complexion growing redder as his tone of voice rose in exasperation. "And until you do *know* something, I'm not listening to you another second. We have no proof and now we've just interfered with a voter fraud investigation."

"You don't *know* that!"

"I *know* it as much as you know what you've been going on about. I should never have let you convince me to come over here and start on him. My head's going to be on a plate for sure." Greene turned away, his shoulders hunched in disgust.

"Look, I'll find Gilbert." Mat sought to reassure the distraught detective. "I'll see if what Dan is telling us is true."

"Be my guest, but you're on your own. You are off this case as far as I'm concerned. I don't want to see or hear from you unless you have the kind of news I want to hear."

"What about your computers?"

"Don't push me."

They drove in silence back to Greene's office and parted company, heading for opposite corners of the virtual boxing ring that seemed, too often, to define their relationship.

Once back in her own car, Mat sat in silence for a time, lost in her dark thoughts. Finally, she started the car and drove aimlessly around, trying to get her head around this new situation. *Where did I go wrong? I just know I'm right. All I wanted to do was to rattle Dan into making a slip. Now what am I going to do?* She continued to drive in a directionless manner, not really seeing the streets and buildings she passed. She was vaguely aware of crossing the 14th Street bridge and heading north through the District of Columbia and the suburbs of Maryland. At the beltway, she turned right without thinking and continued around the northeast suburbs of DC without emerging from the mental fog created by the tumultuous interview with Dan and its aftermath.

Is Dan really in league with Gilbert? What does Gilbert have to do with voter fraud anyway? I have to give Dan a lot of credit if he came up with that story on the fly. One thing's for sure, I'd better not underestimate that guy.

The evening rush hour was in full swing by now and it took her another hour to get back across the Wilson Bridge and onto the street where Lilah's apartment building was nestled among others just like it. As she pulled into a parking space, she noticed a nondescript gray sedan drive past in her rearview mirror. As she turned in her seat to watch it, it sped up and exited the parking lot, turning right and disappearing from view. *I feel like I've seen that car before.* She got out of the car fighting an increasing sense of unease. *Maybe it just looks like so many others around here. Now you're really getting paranoid. Get a hold of yourself!* She shook herself, gathered her purse and jacket, and went inside, determined to shake off the negative feelings from the day. *What I need is a good book, a glass of wine, and some soothing music.*

She had just settled down on the sofa and poured a second glass when the phone rang. She stared at it and considered whether to disturb the growing buzz in her head from the wine. Curiosity won. She picked it up and heard a familiar voice.

"Greg! I'm so glad to hear your voice."

"I'm glad you're glad. Glad enough to share a bottle of a really good red and some sushi this evening?"

"Sounds fabulous. You have some catching up to do on the wine, but food sounds perfect and I'm famished."

"Be there in thirty minutes."

***

e-llegal code

When Greg walked through the door, Mat put her arms around his neck and gave him a big kiss. Sushi in one hand, a bottle of wine in the other, Greg was reduced to a semi-hug with his arms while returning the kiss with as much fervor as he could muster under the circumstances.

"Whoa," he said when Mat finally released him. "That's quite a greeting. Tell me what I did to deserve it. I want to do it again."

"It's more what I did." Mat stepped back a little sheepishly. "I'm just so glad to see someone who doesn't hate me, at least I hope you don't."

"That's a guarantee." Greg set the sushi and bottle down on the coffee table and noticed her glass and the already-opened bottle next to it. "Looks like I'm late to the party."

"You might enjoy it if you like pity parties," Mat said ruefully, sitting down, tears threatening to overwhelm her.

"Pity party? Whose?" Greg sat down beside her.

"Mine. I've been fired. Twice."

Greg chuckled lightly. "You're kidding."

"No, and I'd appreciate it if you didn't laugh."

"Wouldn't dream of it. Truly." He wiped the smile off his face, taking her hand. "So what happened?"

"Well, you know I was volunteering for Dan Collins."

"I remember, according to me, the 'fastest-rising son-of-a-bitch I've ever met.'"

"He fired me today."

"What? Why?"

Mat filled him in briefly on the visit she and Greene had made to Dan Collins at his headquarters. She presented her suspicions and all the evidence, admitting it was all circumstantial, and said Greene agreed with her initially.

"Then Dan comes up with this unbelievable story about being on assignment with Gilbert. Remember him?"

"Vaguely."

"Gilbert with the DEA."

"Oh, yeah. Dreadlocks and a British accent. Hard to forget."

"Dan *claims* he's helping Gilbert with an investigation into voter fraud and we've just barged in and screwed it up. He fired me from my volunteer position on his campaign and from the audit of his company's computers."

"What did Greene say?"

"After we left, Greene started in. Said he'd let me convince him to go after Dan based on hearsay. If Dan went to the Feds, his head would be on a plate, Greene's that is. He told me not to interfere in his work again. More or less fired me too. He did say I could continue to do maintenance on his computers. I guess that's something."

Greg sat back, looking at her. "*Humph.*"

"Is that all you have to say?"

"One thing I'd say is you really know how to stick your nose in where it isn't welcome."

"Thanks, that's really helpful."

"What do you want me to say? This is as big as last time when you were only dealing with the Mafia. This time it's possibly them *and* the Feds."

"But I know I'm right," Mat insisted, her face tense with certainty. "I just know Dan's behind all this. I think he murdered Lilah too. Can't you see that?"

"What I see is that you got lucky last time. This time, *if* you're right, you just poked the hornet's nest and who knows what will come swarming out. I think you should wait until there's more proof before confronting someone as powerful as Dan Collins. Remember what I said about him, the 'son-of-a-bitch' part?"

"Yes, but—"

"No 'buts' involved. He has that reputation because he can be dangerously ruthless when need be. I only know about his business practices which don't, as far as I know, include murder. However, backstabbing, reputation-ruining insinuations and innuendos, which he exploits to the fullest extent possible, are all part of his repertoire. He could make sure you never work in big business around here again."

"You can't be serious?" Mat felt the first stab of fear push her anger aside.

"I wish I were. Look, I'm not suggesting you apologize, but just lay low for a while and see if he forgets all about it. On second thought, maybe an apology would be a good idea."

"No way am I apologizing to that son-of-a-bitch." Mat could feel her eyes fill with unshed tears. "What would you suggest I do? Let two murders fade away without finding the killers and let fraud take over the next election? We won't know if Dan Collins won on his own merit or on the merits of a stacked vote counting algorithm."

"You're assuming Dan is going to win."

"I'd just about bet my life on it." Mat's anger at the injustice of her treatment reasserted itself. "He'll win and be on top of the world and no one will be able to prove anything different."

"So you think you're the only one with the skill and ability to ferret out the bad guy, assuming there is one in this case? You're the only one who can come riding in on a white horse and save the day, the election. You're the only one who can identify the murderers of Lilah, Kim, and Minnie? Do you really think the police are so incompetent that they won't be able to figure this out?" Greg sat forward and sighed as frustration, concern, and impatience flitted across his face. "Mat, honey, I care about you more than anyone, but you have to see reason on this."

"And reason means giving up, letting things play out so Dan wins and no one's the wiser."

"No. Yes. I mean let the police handle this. They have all the experts and resources to figure this out. Why does it have to be you?"

"Because I'm afraid they'll be too intimidated to pursue it and those three deaths will be viewed the same way. As soon as they get close to anyone powerful like Dan, there will be threats, bribes, and intimidation. Any investigation will get dropped." Mat couldn't hide her bitterness.

"Look, we've seen what he's capable of, assuming you're right about all of this. Do you really want to get involved in that world? And where did this lack of faith in our legal system come from anyway? I grant you it really looks like a dangerous situation, but maybe you're watching too much TV." Greg's attempt at lightening the mood fell flat.

"Hardly. The real world is more sordid and uncaring than those stories on TV. I think serial killers die in their beds just like Dan Collins will if no one stops him."

"And you don't think the police will?"

"I just said I don't."

"Do you still have that disk?"

"Yes."

"I suggest you return it to Greene as soon as you can. He can keep it in a safer place than you can and keeping it will only put you in more danger."

They sat in silence for several minutes before Greg rose and gathered up the empty sushi boxes.

"I wish I could convince you the police aren't as incompetent as you think they are. They just need the room to do their job on this. Why don't I call you tomorrow and we'll go out for a nice dinner. In the meantime, lay low, do your job, and don't attract attention. Hopefully, Dan will forget your meeting with Greene today. Maybe Greene will too."

"I guess there's nothing else to do." Mat felt childish and sullen but couldn't shake herself out of feeling lectured by everyone.

"That's my girl." Greg pulled her up and gave her a big hug, which she returned unenthusiastically. He stepped back and looked at her, his hands on her arms.

"Try to relax, get some sleep and think about where you'd like to eat tomorrow."

Mat nodded silently, too overwhelmed by her sense of abandonment to speak and unable to share her feelings, even with this man that she realized she, too, cared more about than anyone else. She watched as he picked up his jacket and headed to the door, turning to give her a smile and a thumbs up as he walked out and closed it gently behind him.

A couple of hours later, Mat stopped flipping aimlessly through TV channels, watching images and hearing nothing while her mind swirled around the events of the day. She turned off the TV and wandered into the bedroom, marveling again at its relentless crimson shades. She crawled under the covers determined to meditate her way to a deep and dreamless sleep.

Chapter 17

The crimson colors of the bedroom were repeated in ever-deepening shades on the canvas before her.

"Zorah," she asked, "why is it only shades of red?"

"Because that's what she was," replied the artist.

"I don't understand."

"She was vibrantly red, alive with it, embraced it wholeheartedly, didn't you see it?"

"No. I mean, clearly she liked it, but there were other colors too."

"You're wrong. Those other colors were only shades of red too."

"That's not true, there was green, yellow, and white. Don't you remember?"

"That's only in your imagination, Mat. Come see the mural when it's finished, you'll see."

Mat turned and caught a glimpse of Dan staring at the mural. He was dressed in a red shirt and matching tie.

"Hello Mat," he said. "Lovely day for an unveiling, don't you think? Aren't you going to congratulate me on my win? Nip and tuck there for a while, but the final count said it all."

"Congratulations!" Mat turned to see Greene. He was raising a glass of champagne.

"Congratulations!" Zorah stood beside her mural with a glass of champagne.

"Congratulations!" Greg was behind her, raising a glass of champagne.

They all turned toward a giant hearth of red brick. Glasses of champagne were being hurled against it in a grand finale of toasting to the mural and election. Mat turned in the direction of the glasses and saw Lilah, Minnie, and Kim laughing as they tossed glass after glass at the fireplace and joined in the chorus.

Mat woke with a start, bathed in sweat. She sat up, heart pounding. *I can't let that happen!* She slid off the bed, searched for her shoes. There was enough light from the moon to see her way to the bathroom, so she made her way in the dark. Some cold water would clear the fog and ease the approaching panic brought on by the dream. Better yet, a midnight drive with windows open should really clear out the cobwebs. The nightlight in the bathroom had been sufficient for a quick splash of water and she returned to the bedroom in the dark, focused on her plan for a midnight drive. She dressed quickly in jeans and a sweatshirt against the cool night air and headed out. As she approached her car, she saw Zorah's psychedelic VW come into the lot. It pulled into the parking place next to hers.

"Zorah," she exclaimed, trying to keep her voice low to keep from waking sleeping residents.

"Why are you whispering?" the artist emerged from the VW, laden with fabric and art supplies.

"Guess I think I'll wake someone. Silly. Why are you home so early?"

"Why are you up so late?"

"You first."

"I got stuck again. Just couldn't get past the outline in one section. I thought some meditation and tea might get some ideas going. I'll jot them down for tomorrow. Tired too. I tried dancing around the studio to dispel some of this nervous energy from staring at red all night long. Didn't work." She shifted the load of fabrics, then dumped them back in the car. "Don't know why I brought these back. I'll just take them back to the studio tomorrow. What about you?"

"What about me?"

"Why are you up at midnight?"

"Oh. I couldn't sleep. I thought I'd drive around a little and see if that helped."

"To each his own. Me, I'm done driving around at night."

"I'll be back soon. I'll try not to wake you."

"Ok, thanks." The artist grabbed her other supplies and headed for the apartment while Mat drove out into the silent streets.

***

In the apartment, Zorah quickly made some tea and went into the bedroom. She settled down on the braided rug on the far side of the bed near a window. Her back was to the corner with the dim light of a streetlamp coming in over her shoulder. After a few sips of the fragrant, warm tea, she closed her eyes and began to murmur a familiar chant. She began with her hands, willing them to relax, then her forearms, elbows, and upper arms. As she progressed through her limbs, up to her neck and head, and then down her torso, the repetition, combined with the soothing aroma of the herbal tea, deepened her sense of weightlessness. She seemed to float above her body, drifting into an increased state of relaxation that surrounded everything around her.

Abruptly her eyes popped open, her ears alert to a noise in the living room. She turned her attention to the darkened room opposite the bed.

"Mat?" she called. "Is that you? Are you home already? It's okay to turn on the light, I'm awake." The silence continued except for a single creak of a floorboard.

"Mat? Did you hear me?" Her sixth sense kicked in, making her hyperaware. She stood and took a tentative step toward the living room and the floor creaked under her. *Shit!* Was it her own footstep she had heard or . . .? She moved slowly into the living room, partially convinced her imagination was getting out of control.

"Mat? This isn't funny." *Where is that light switch?*

As she turned toward the front door, she almost put her nose into a black nylon jacket and stopped short, panic running wild through her veins. Before she could react or cry out, an arm spun her around and encircled her neck, putting pressure on her carotid arteries. The pressure increased and she found herself losing consciousness and sinking onto the floor. She struggled to get a hand under the arm or behind her to grab her assailant but found herself grabbing air or muscles of steel. She couldn't catch a breath deep enough to satisfy her starved lungs; her panic was reaching a fever pitch. She couldn't breathe; she had to get air. She gasped and felt walls closing in around her, drowning her.

She was vaguely aware of skin against her ear and a menacing voice.

"Tell that roomie of yours to back away from Dan Collins or next time she'll end up on one of Hector's morgue slabs." The pressure increased until blackness enveloped her. She sank to the floor.

***

"Zorah, Zorah!"

Mat could see Zorah struggling to regain consciousness. Zorah fought, flailing her arms and blinking her eyes rapidly.

"Zorah!"

Zorah pushed Mat away and sat up, looking around, terror etched on her face. Suddenly she looked into Mat's face and broke into tears.

"Oh Mat, I was so scared."

"Oh, thank heaven. I was just about to call an ambulance. Maybe I should anyway, you look like you've seen a ghost."

"No, don't do that. I don't want to ride in that thing."

"Okay, we'll leave that for now. Just tell me what happened."

"I'm not sure. I was in the bedroom meditating when I heard a noise. I called your name, but you didn't answer. I came in here and a man grabbed me around the neck. Then you were shaking me." Zorah dissolved into tears. "It was so awful!"

"A man? What man? Are you sure?" Mat was kneeling beside her friend, her eyes filled with worry. She put her hand on Zorah's arm. "When

I came home and saw you on the floor I thought maybe you'd gotten a notion to sleep out here. You were lying there so peaceful. But it was cold on the floor. I tried to wake you, but you didn't move, so I started to shake you. That's when you woke up."

Zorah looked at Mat and blinked. "I wouldn't sleep on the floor! That's stupid. It's cold. I know you think I'm weird, but I'm not *that* weird." She broke into fresh tears.

"I'm sorry. I'm just trying to understand."

"Well don't start by thinking I want to sleep on the floor. How could you think that?" she repeated, hysteria edging her voice.

"Zorah, what happened after he grabbed you around the neck?"

"I don't know. I must have lost consciousness."

"Okay." Mat tried to get a picture of what had happened. "Tell me again about a man coming in here."

"Mat, I need a minute to think." Slowly Zorah sat up, pulled her legs up, and rolled onto her knees. She put both hands on the floor in front of her. She raised her rear into the air until she was on her hands and toes. Then she stood from a cat stretch position.

"Wow," Mat's voice held both relief at her recovery and awe at her acrobatics. "That's really neat. You need to show me how to do that."

"Sure, anytime." She looked around the couch. Muttering, "I need my robe, I'm cold," she got up and retreated into the bedroom. A minute later she emerged wrapped in an enormous fake-fur poncho that reached almost to the ground. She walked over to the couch and sat down, trying to wrap her bare feet under the folds of the poncho.

"Let me get you some tea, hot with plenty of sugar. It helps with shock." Mat went into the kitchen where soon Zorah heard the sound of crockery and water being poured into a kettle.

"Are you sure you don't want an ambulance or to go to one of those new urgent care places? You don't look good," Mat called anxiously from the kitchen.

"No, no, I don't need to do that," Zorah replied absentmindedly. "Mat," she said as her friend returned a few minutes later carrying a tray with cups of tea, sugar, a pitcher of milk, and some fruit cookies that claimed to be nutritional as well as satisfying to one's sweet tooth.

Mat busied herself setting a cup and a small plate of cookies in front of Zorah. "What?"

"I'm remembering something. Or maybe I dreamed it."

"What is it?"

"A message for you." The artist stared at her friend, locking eyes with an intensity that was unnerving.

"What message?"

"Tell that roomie of yours to stay away from Dan Collins or next time she'll end up on one of Hector's morgue slabs." Zorah swallowed and began crying again. "It was so awful. He was so mean, and ugly." She sniffled at the memory, reaching for a tissue. "I thought I was going to die."

"What do you mean, ugly? Did you get a look at his face?"

"No! He just sounded mean and ugly and mean, and ... and ..." She folded into herself, arms wrapped around the poncho, hugging its warmth.

Mat sat back thinking through all the events of the past few days. "Zorah, I'm so sorry this happened to you. But what I don't understand is how he knew we were here. We came here to hide. How did he know where I was?"

"Know what? Who's 'he'?"

"The man who attacked you. How did he know we were here? Zorah, they've found us."

"What do you mean, 'they've found us'?" Mat heard hysteria creeping back into her friend's voice.

"You said someone broke in and attacked you, right?"

"Yes." Zorah began to tear up as she dabbed at her eyes and fought to keep control.

"Well, I don't think you're in real danger."

"How can you say that? I told you what just happened."

Mat hastened to calm her. "Look, they clearly knew you weren't me. But they wanted to leave a message for me. They just chose a scary way to do that."

"They sure did." Zorah's voice trembled at the memory.

"I think he, whoever he is, expected to find me alone. When it was you, he switched gears and told you to warn me. They probably didn't even know about you until now."

"Really, you're serious? You think they didn't know I'm here?"

"I think it's a good bet. Why would it occur to them that I have a roommate who works at night? If they were bold enough to break in last night, I'll bet they were sure I'd be here all alone. They aren't after you."

"But I always get in the way," the artist complained, her voice rising with the thought. "That's my karma with you. One day they'll kill me, I just know it!"

"Zorah, give me one good reason they would kill you instead of me. What could they hope to gain?" Mat tried reason to calm her friend. "Giving me a message is one thing, killing the messenger is another. That's what happened before too."

Zorah sat back, looking at her friend. "I never thought about that." She took a deep breath. "What if they make a mistake and kill me anyway?"

"I think it's about as likely as getting killed in a car accident, probably less. Besides, how would they get the message to me if that happened?" Mat was close to convincing herself.

"But what about you? What do they want? Do you think they'll come back? Shouldn't we call the police?"

"I wish I thought that would help. But you're not visibly injured; the door is not damaged. They might just think you had a bad dream."

"Yeah." Zorah took a deep breath and sighed. "Even I'm starting to wonder if maybe that's all it was."

"A bad dream? Do you sleepwalk too?"

"Well, no."

"I don't doubt someone came in and grabbed you. It sounds to me like he used some kind of choke hold that made you lose consciousness. Once they realized you weren't me, they changed plans. Or just decided to give you the message instead of me." Mat sat up and clasped her hands between her knees. "What I want to know is how they knew we were here. Someone must have followed me when I left Dan's office." Suddenly she saw the image of a gray car slowing, then speeding up after she pulled into the apartment parking lot. "And I think I know when that happened."

"Oh Mat, you can't go back there then."

"That's taken care of already." Mat filled Zorah in on her last conversation with Greene and Dan, when both men fired her.

"What I want to know," she continued, "is how Dan knew about Gilbert. He's your friend, isn't he? Last time I saw him he said he was undercover, DEA I think, hanging out at your studio. Have you seen him lately?"

"No, I haven't seen him for weeks. His area looks abandoned. I thought maybe he was gone for good." She thought about that for a minute. "I'd sure like his space if he's gone."

"Don't be too hasty. Apparently, he's not gone, at least not from this area. Of course, that depends on how much you believe Dan. As far as his studio space goes, I have no idea if he's walked away from that."

"How can we find out?"

"Does he pay rent for his space? Is there anyone who works out the space assignments there who would know if he still plans to use it?"

"I can ask Miranda. She's the one I went to when I wanted a space in there. She does fabric art, gorgeous stuff. Trees, landscapes, portraits, beautiful things, and you just can't imagine how she does it. I'm sure if she's not doing the rents anymore, she'll know who does."

"That would be terrific, thanks."

"Mat."

"What?" She watched her friend who was close to dissolving in tears again.

"I'm not sure I can stay here all alone today. What if they came back and you weren't here? They might come after me again just because I'm here." Mat could hear Zorah's anxiety increasing with every word.

"I think you have a good point," she replied, attempting to reassure her friend. "Although I think they got what they came for."

"What was that?"

"To scare me and get the disk. I see that it's gone." She gestured to the desk in the corner.

"Oh. Right. That must mean it's important, huh?" Zorah pulled her feet up beside her, adjusting the fur poncho around them again. "Well, I still don't want to stay here today. The effect on this place is already getting to me. Mat, you know he left emanations from his aura here."

"His what?"

"Emanations. From his aura. Everyone has one, an aura I mean. It's the energy around you. It comes from who you are, your essence, the result of your life with all the ups and downs." Zorah paused, her brow crinkled in an effort to explain.

"I'm not using the right words, Salee could explain it better. She can actually *see* them, the auras. She says mine has a lot of violet in it. She says it 'indicates my extraordinary creativity, clairvoyance, intuition, vision, and even magic.' Isn't that exciting? The thing is, our auras affect those around us and remnants of it stay in an area when we leave. It doesn't stay forever, but for a while. Anyway, I'm sure his has a lot of red in it. I can feel it. There's a lot of negativity. It's dark, threatening, full of violence."

"His emanations?"

"That does it. I'm not staying here today."

"Zorah, it's probably alright for you to go back home. The alarm people were supposed to finish yesterday. I'll call them and get them to meet us at the house. They can explain how the system works." Mat stood up, stretching her legs from the cramped position on the floor. She looked around the room. "As for whoever broke in here, they've sent their message, and they took the disk. I expect they are happy for now."

"They took the disk?"

Mat pointed to the blank space on the desk next to her computer. "Frankly, I'd be surprised if they hadn't."

"Okay. Maybe you're right and they're happy now," Zorah conceded doubtfully.

Mat attempted to reassure her and provide an acceptable alternative, "If you don't want to go home, maybe you could go stay with a friend, maybe Salee."

"Oh, she wouldn't want me around today, not with all those bad vibes from the man who attacked me. If my aura is affected by them, yours is too. They cling, you know, and take a while to disappear."

"I didn't know."

"Well, they do. We are seriously going to have to do an exorcism here. I wouldn't want to leave this place with such bad vibes for the next occupant. I'll talk to Salee. Mat, you should leave, too, and find someplace else to spend the day. Maybe you should go home too?"

"I guess that's best. We'll take our things home, then talk to the security folks. After that, I've got to work on some things for Greene's computers. You can call me when you've had a chance to talk to Miranda."

"Okay. I'm going to pack up what I need for now and leave. The negativity is really getting to me."

With that, Zorah picked up the sheets of paper, artist supplies, and satchel she brought with her and disappeared into the bedroom, where Mat heard her pulling open drawers and rifling through her clothes in the closet. She got up and went into the bedroom to join her.

"Here," she said, "I'll help you and pack up my stuff at the same time."

They worked in companionable silence for a while until everything was stuffed into a suitcase or plastic bag and parked by the front door.

"Let's do one more sweep," Mat suggested, "then I want to take another look at what's on that disk before packing up my computer."

"How are you going to do that? Didn't they take it?"

"Yes, but I made a copy." Mat winked at her friend. "A cardinal computer rule that many people don't follow: always make a backup of your work."

Zorah stared at her friend as if she were speaking Greek. "Oh. Okay."

Mat laughed. "Let's finish up. You start in the kitchen. I'll start in the bedroom." Mat heard cabinet doors opening and closing and larger items being moved across the linoleum floor as Zorah checked out the kitchen. She started with the chest of drawers next to the door and continued around the room to the closet. As she took the last clothes out of the closet and slid their hangers to one side, she noticed a darker shape on the floor in the far corner. Curious, she bent down and pulled the object across the floor. It was a small cardboard box with no identifying marks. She picked it up and sat down on the bed, running her hands over the lid.

"Zorah!"

The artist came running in from the kitchen with a dish rag in her hand.

"What's wrong? I was just wiping up some dirt from behind the coffee maker. I'll come help in here as soon as I'm through."

"Look at this." Mat pointed to the box. "I found this in the far corner of Lilah's closet. I think we should take a look at what's in it."

"You do?" Zorah sat down next to Mat, her eyes on the cardboard box. "What do you think is in it?"

"We won't know by staring at it." With that, Mat raised the lid to reveal its contents.

"Letters! I wonder if they're Dan's love letters!?" Zorah's eyes lit up in anticipation of a titillating romantic read.

"Maybe, but these first ones aren't." Mat picked up one of the letters. "It's to her mother, they're just letters to her mother."

"Oh." Mat heard the disappointment in Zorah's voice and realized she shared it. She rifled through the stack.

"I wonder why they were never posted?"

"You mean they haven't been mailed?"

"Right. These aren't *from* her mother, these are *to* her mother, but they don't have a postmark on them. Why would she keep letters she wrote to her mother and never mail them?"

"Zorah, was her mother dead? Maybe these were just her attempt to communicate with her mother in some way."

"I think you're onto something! We had a session with Salee about staying in touch with a loved one after they passed. She talked about how spirits can read letters you write them, but it can take them a while to find them, so you should save them and hope the spirit you wrote them for finds them."

"Really?" Mat commented skeptically. "What do you say we make sure that's what's going on here." She pulled open the flap of the letter she held and took out the paper. The page was from a small pad of ordinary lined yellow paper. It had a date at the top left. After scanning the first lines, she looked up at her friend.

"What?"

"It's a diary, not a letter to her mother."

"What do you mean, a diary?"

"I mean these look like letters to her mother on the outside, but these are pages from a diary. Look here, it talks about working in her herb garden and visiting the women's clinic. It's written like you would write in a diary, I did this, then this, then this. I felt this, dreamed about this, and so on. She's not really writing to her mother, but keeping a diary. I wonder why she did it this way?"

"I think I know. I suggested she do some journaling once to help sort out her feelings for Dan and she said she couldn't do that. She said she tried when she was young but a girl she didn't like broke into it and read what Lilah thought of her. She'd never been able to keep a diary since. Maybe this was her way of getting around that experience and keeping one anyway."

"You could be right. In any case, I think we should take it with us and see if there's anything in it that might explain what happened to her."

Mat helped Zorah finish packing. After loading their cars, they drove out in the brightening dawn.

Chapter 18

Mat considered the events of the new day. She and Zorah had survived the ups and downs of her adventures so far. Now she wondered if, once she'd had a chance to absorb what had happened, Zorah would find a way to tell Mat she'd had enough, that she needed to find another roommate, one not so prone to life-threatening investigations.

Once back in the old Victorian, Mat sat down at her computer. She opened the backup copy of the file to refresh her memory and review a section of unexecuted code that she had seen. Usually, such code was identified as a comment and may have been part of an original design that turned out not to be needed. It was ignored or overwritten if space got tight. She navigated to that section and was surprised to see it was not a section of programming code, but an actual comment in English.

"Well, I'll be," she murmured aloud. She read it over, then reread it and whistled out loud. *Well, if this isn't the proverbial smoking gun! Greene may not want me involved, but he can't ignore this.* She thought about how to present it to Greene and decided that more work was needed. She spent the next half hour carefully reviewing and documenting the code so it would be understandable to Greene. She called Greene and was told he was out on a case and would not be back until the next day.

What to do until then? Do I confront Dan with this? What do I still not know? Mat fixed a fresh cup of tea and pondered the document in front of her. *Maybe Greg can help me sort through this.* She picked up the phone and dialed his number.

"Good morning, beautiful." His cheery voice reminded her that the day had just started for most. "What did I do to deserve a call from you so early in the day?"

"You only have yourself to blame, you keep coming back. Seriously, it's been an interesting night and I need some advice."

"Can it wait until later? I have some appointments that I really can't reschedule aside from life-or-death situations."

"I think that already occurred last night. But yes, it can wait until later, preferably later today."

"Wow, so enticing. You know how to tease me on a number of levels. Let me get through these meetings and my evening is all yours. And then some." She could see his smile at the other end of the line.

Two hours later she was completing the upgrades to several programs on Greene's office machines. They were overdue and she was still responsible for that work as far as she knew. After an hour, she saw him enter the room and make his way to his desk in the back. He didn't greet her or acknowledge her presence in any way. *Well, be that way, but I bet you'll be glad to hear this bit of information.* She got up, passed by the intervening desks, and stopped in front of Greene. He looked up, a sour expression replacing the half smile on his face.

"What?" He glared at her across the desk. "I told you you're off the case. I don't see how your work on those computers out there gives you an excuse to bother me."

"Do you want to know what else is on that disk?"

"You finally figured it out? I'd have thought a smart lady like you would have done that long ago. Just write it down and put it on my desk. No need to interrupt what I'm doing." Greene turned back to the reports he was reading, dismissing Mat with a wave of his hand.

"Okay." Mat took the papers with the flowchart and code and tossed them on the desk in front of Greene. "Here it is, written down, on your desk. Good luck." She turned around and headed back to pick up her briefcase and backpack. *Jerk! If that's your game, I can be hard to get too.* She ran through the shutdown routines and turned off the monitor and computer in record time, grabbed her things and walked out, determined to focus on dinner and civil conversation with Greg later on.

On the drive home, the morose mood returned in force. *Why do I even try? Maybe Greg's right. It is none of my business and I should keep my nose out of it. Three people dead, Zorah's been assaulted, and I've been threatened. What do I care who wins that election? Let the police deal with the rest of it.*

By the time she reached home, she was thoroughly wrapped up in self-pity and anger. *I don't owe Greene a damn thing. I just wanted to help, and he threw me out, won't even look at that flowchart I spent so much time putting together.* Fuming, she parked the car and stalked into the house.

***

At 5:00 p.m. Mat got in the car and drove out to the house Kim had shared with his girlfriend, kicking herself all the way for choosing rush hour to make the trip. *Won't I ever learn?* She figured she was in luck when there were cars parked in front of the house. Indeed, the same young Asian girl opened the door at her knock.

"Oh, I remember you," she said behind the screen door, her voice filled with anxiety. "Have you found Kim yet? I haven't heard from him, and he hasn't been home since I saw you."

OMG. I never thought she wouldn't have been told.

"I do have some news. May I come in?"

The girl's face brightened, and she eagerly opened the door and gestured to Mat to come in. She stepped into the small entryway and turned to face the young girl.

"I don't know how to say this . . . I'm sorry, I don't know your name."

"Mei," the girl said, the initial hope fading from her face.

"I'm afraid it's not good news. He's been killed."

"What?!" Mei's dark eyes filled with tears and she gasped. "How is that possible? Who would do that? Kim wouldn't hurt anyone!" She turned and made her way into the living room and sank into one of the overstuffed chairs around a small table. She turned tear-filled eyes to Mat.

"His parents will be . . ." She couldn't seem to find the words. "Who will tell them? Do they know? I know I wasn't anyone special but . . ." She clasped her hands together and looked down at them, then started to rock silently front to back on the seat, moaning into her hands.

"I'm so sorry." Mat stood opposite her, awash in anguish of her own. "I'm sure they are the first people the police and the school will be contacting."

She stood there a little while longer, aware that Mei seemed to have shut out everything but her own sorrow. Tentatively, she asked, "Does anyone else live here? Can I call someone to come over and sit with you?"

"What? No, I mean yes, there are two others who live here, Cheng and Hua. They'll be home soon. They are the only ones I'm close to besides Kim." Mei sank further down into her chair, silent sobs racking her body.

"What if I sit here with you until they come home? Can I fix you some tea or something to drink?"

Mei didn't answer and Mat wasn't sure she'd been heard.

"Can I fix you something to drink?" she repeated a little louder.

"Oh, sorry, no, thank you," Mei whispered.

"Mei." Mat sat down in a chair opposite her. "I don't want to intrude, but do you mind if I ask you a question?"

Mei seemed to shake herself, and she sniffed in an attempt to pull herself together.

"I guess not." She sighed and said, "Kim was so kind and sweet. I met him when he helped me with a programming problem last semester. When one of the students living here graduated we asked him to move in. He didn't like where he was anyway."

"Do you know how long he worked for Dan Collins?"

"Oh, he didn't work directly for Mr. Collins."

"He didn't? But I thought you said he was working on a task for him?"

"He was. I talked to Rosa yesterday before she left. She said Kim was working for the company that did the programming for the machine that took input from a Votomatic machine, that's a machine that people use to vote." She looked at Mat to see if she understood.

"I know about Votomatics." Mat nodded her head encouragingly.

"Well, Rosa said Mr. Collins was friends with the head of programming for this company and told him he would arrange for someone to try to break into the vote counting code to see if it was secure. He got Kim, who was volunteering on his campaign, to do this. He promised Kim it was okay. Kim thought it would be fun, but Rosa didn't like it. If I had known, I'd have tried to talk him out of it but . . ."

"Did Kim ever tell Rosa exactly what he planned to do?"

"No, but he told Rosa he put a safeguard in the code. I don't know what he meant by that or what it was."

"That's alright. I think I know what it was."

The door to the house swung open and another young Asian boy charged in through the entryway.

"Mei, I just heard that something's happened to Kim!" He took in the scene in the living room. "Who's this?"

"A friend," Mei answered, tears filling her eyes. "She just told me about Kim. How did you find out?"

"It's going around campus. The police have been in the computer science lab asking questions. They aren't saying much." He turned to Mat.

"How did you know about it?"

"I'm also volunteering on the Collins campaign and just heard about it. Now that you're here, I think I'll go."

"Yeah, okay," Cheng said with uncertainty. He turned back to Mei. "I don't know how they do things here, but they'll probably want to talk to us soon. Are you going to be alright?"

Mat left them to face the chaos and sadness Kim's death had brought to their world. She remembered how fresh and new everything had seemed in college. Anything was possible, nothing hideous like murder could possibly happen. How wrong she had been about so many things.

Chapter 19

"When we talked I'm not sure I thought a pub would be the place for a 'nice' dinner, but I'm willing to give it a try." Greg slid into the booth opposite Mat.

"Sorry about that. I'm afraid I'm not in the mood for a nice dinner. Can we do that another time?"

"Sure. Why don't we order drinks and see if we can work on improving that mood."

"I'd love a drink but improving my mood could be a real challenge tonight."

"Now I'm really intrigued. So, let's hear it, mystery lady. You've already been fired twice. What could be worse?"

"I think what happened last night, or rather early this morning would fall into the 'worse' category."

"Okay, okay, I'll bite. What happened last night?"

"Someone broke into the apartment, attacked Zorah, and threatened me."

"What?" Greg sat up, his hand reaching for Mat's across the table. "You're right, that is worse. Are you alright? How did he threaten you? Have you called the police?"

"I'm fine. He told me to stay away from Dan Collins and stole the disk. No, I haven't called the police."

"My God, Mat. Why not?"

"Neither of us was hurt. They'll think we made it up."

"Why do you think that? What happened?"

"I couldn't sleep and decided to take a drive to clear my head. Zorah was just coming home early from her night's work. She was meditating in the bedroom and heard a noise. When she stepped into the living room, a man grabbed her. She says he twisted her around so she couldn't see his face. I think he put her in a choke hold. He told her to tell me to stay away from Dan. Then she lost consciousness. He must have found the disk on my desk and took it with him when he left."

Greg sat back and stared at her for a few moments. "And you haven't called the police? Or gone to the doctor, I'm willing to bet."

"Zorah didn't want to go to a doctor. And I told you, he didn't leave any marks or tear the place up. He didn't break the lock or smash a window . . ."

"On the third floor?"

"Whatever. Anyway, I really don't want to share this with anyone else. Well, except you."

Greg squinted his eyes in consternation. "Why not? Mat, this is getting beyond dangerous. At least come home with me tonight. They won't know where you are."

"I don't think they'll be back tonight. They've delivered their message, and anyway, I won't be at Lilah's. We're back home. Plus, Zorah won't go back to Lilah's until Salee does an exorcism."

"You're kidding?!"

"No, I'm not. She kept talking about how his aura had infected the place and you know that stuff lingers."

"I did not know that. Are you joking with me? Because I don't think this is funny."

"Neither do I, nor does Zorah. She's perfectly serious."

"Knowing Zorah, I bet she is."

"There's more."

"I should have known."

"I found an area in the program where comments had been stored. Comments having to do with the code. I also diagrammed the logic of the code so I could explain it to Greene."

"Back up a minute. What were those comments about? You said they are about the code, but what about it?"

"It said that he wrote the code as part of an exercise to show the voting officials how vulnerable their computer system was to being hacked. If anyone had questions and he wasn't available, they should ask Dan Collins, who gave him the assignment."

"Sounds innocuous on the surface."

"It does until you know what the code is doing."

"So enlighten me. What is the code doing?"

"It is guaranteeing that one person wins the election for a position no matter what the voters say."

"Say that again."

"This code changes the vote tallying algorithm to stack the deck in favor of one person, who is guaranteed to win."

Greg took a deep breath and let it out slowly.

"When are you going to tell Greene?"

"I left the chart and code with Greene today. He was still pissed at me, so we didn't talk. I also left him the information about Lilah's diary. The ball's in his court now."

Greg perked up. "Whose diary?"

"Oh. Thought I told you. Lilah left a box of letters to her mother that she never mailed. After looking through them, Zorah and I figured out it was really a diary. Proves that Dan gave her pennyroyal."

"Talk about a smoking gun! Who else knows about this?"

"No one other than you, me, Zorah, and Greene if he looks at the material I left on his desk. Of course, Dan knows about the code along with anyone else he's told."

"And Dan doesn't know you know?"

"Depends on whether he thinks I've figured it out. Even if he thinks I have, he may be hoping I haven't documented it. Even if I have, he could still make it my word against his. Without the disk, who would you believe?"

"I see what you mean."

"Do you think he knows about the comment piece?"

"Doubt it."

"What do you want to do?"

"I don't know. I could just wait for Greene to look at the copy I made of what was on the disk."

Greg smiled slowly. "You made a copy. Of course you did. Smart lady, but then I knew that."

"It's one rule I take very seriously. So many people still don't think to back up their work or make a copy of it. Too often they lose everything if the computer crashes or a file is corrupted. I learned that lesson the hard way early on and I've never forgotten it."

"Sounds like you've got this all worked out. What do you need my advice for?"

"It's more of a favor."

"Just ask."

"I'd like to give another copy of that disk to you for safekeeping."

"Of course. Just hand it over."

"I also want to run that diagram by you to see if it's understandable to someone like Greene. I did it in a hurry, but I also want someone else to know what it says."

"I always liked puzzles. Let's take a look." Greg's wry grin held warmth and an acknowledgment of the serious nature of this game.

Mat showed him the flowchart and where the count for a given candidate was artificially held at a certain percentage. She pointed out the date range in the code and showed him the section where Kim had named Dan Collins as the person who gave him the assignment.

"One other thing that may not be important, but I thought was interesting. Kim wasn't working directly for Dan in his company."

"Really? Then how did he get involved in this?"

Mat repeated what Mei had told her about Kim's job with the programming company for the Votomatic computers.

"That's why he left that comment in the code, the one that says who hired him. Either he was a super cautious young man, or he had doubts in spite of Dan's assurances. He was a smart kid in more ways than one."

"All that promise gone in one evil act." Greg looked at Mat. "You don't suppose it's the same person who attacked Zorah?"

"I hadn't thought of that."

"If it is, he sounds like a trained commando type with a garrote and choke holds. Are you sure you don't want the police to know about this?"

"What is it you said about Collins? You are 'persona non grata'? Well, I think if I stepped into Greene's domain for anything other than computer maintenance, he'd throw me out without hearing a single word."

"I could talk to him, make him see reason."

"I don't think it would make a difference. But if it makes you feel any better, I expect he'll be contacting me shortly to make sense of the flowchart and code I left with him."

"I don't feel like leaving this to the chance he'll want to talk to you about that code."

"Okay. If I don't hear from him by tomorrow evening, I'll give him a call and see if I can get him to listen to me."

"What if I stay with you tonight in case this bad guy takes another shot at you?" Greg asked, adding a smile as he continued. "After all, it wouldn't hurt to make sure your house, in particular your bedroom, is safe from intruders."

Mat smiled back. "It should be with the new alarm system. Anyway, he thinks I'm still at Lilah's. I expect he'll want to see if this warning stops me in my tracks. That should leave us plenty of time to make sure my bedroom is safe from intruders."

Chapter 20

The next day, Mat drove over to Candlewick Studios to find Miranda in hopes that she could help get a message to Gilbert. She found the artist near the back of the studio, not far from Zorah's space. Trees with autumn leaves, frosty branches of a winter tree, and whimsical puffed faces of elves and forest sprites hung on the wall beside her. Miranda was standing in front of a large canvas with lines that could be an outline or just the beginning of a piece on railroad tracks. Her buzz cut framed an angular face that was just short of beautiful with eyes, nose, and lips that were well positioned in relation to each other. She had unexpectedly dainty eyebrows. Large dangle earrings stood out against the spare features of her face and sparse haircut. As Mat's footsteps paused behind her, she spoke without turning around.

"Do you like fabric art? This is a new piece, actually just the outline. I'll add possibilities for fabrics and colors before starting the actual piece."

Mat was mesmerized. "I didn't know you could do art like this with fabric, your things are gorgeous. So creative."

Miranda turned around to get a good look at Mat. "You're not an artist, are you? I've seen you hanging around Zorah. How do you know her if you're not an artist?"

"She's my roommate. I love her stuff, yours, too, but I'm not blessed with any artistic talent."

"You'd be surprised. Could be you've just repressed it all your life." She studied Mat for a moment then continued, "Zorah's not here, she works nights, but I expect you know that."

"Yes, I do know that. Actually, it's you I wanted to talk to."

"Really? About what?"

"Zorah said you manage the rental space in the studio."

"Yes, boring bean counting, but someone has to do it. Can't recall how I got roped into it, but there you are. What about it?"

"Zorah said Gilbert Cullings has a space here. I'm trying to find him, and I thought if he has space here maybe he comes on a regular basis and I could manage to catch up with him."

"Ah. Gilbert. Even by our standards, he's different."

"How so?"

"Well, he's not an especially gifted artist and he's only here once in a while. I don't think he's taking it seriously."

"What do you mean?"

"His art. It's not for me to say, but I don't think he's going to get any better unless he devotes more time to it. His space stays empty a lot of the time and there's a waiting list of artists who want space here. It's selfish to my mind." She turned her back and began to rummage through a stack of fabric squares. "What did you want to know?"

"Um, I was going to ask if you knew when he comes in."

"Not regularly, that's for sure. He did tell me he was going to be gone for a while. That was a couple of weeks ago. Not that I'd notice."

"Any chance there's a way to get in touch with him if you needed to? Like if he owed rent or something like that?"

Miranda paused and thought about the question for a moment. "I guess he might have put something down on his rental application. I never looked. If you can wait a minute, I'll go check."

"Sure, that'd be great," Mat agreed. "Where's his space? Maybe I'll see what he was into."

"Over by Zorah's. They seemed to get along, by the way. You'll be able to pick it out." Miranda turned back to her work in dismissal.

Mat wandered over to the area where Zorah's space was evident from the large colorful paintings and what looked like the start of a design for a mural taped to the wall. A little ways down from her space was a break in the energy and creative vitality so evident in the other spaces. Mat paused in front of it. There was an artist's easel with a blank canvas, a small desk with brushes and other tools of a painter's trade arranged neatly next to a small pad of paper. On a shelf behind the desk, several bottles and cans of paint-related solutions were lined up. She could see no personal objects, finished works, or even the start of a new one. It looked unoccupied, even abandoned. *This looks as if he might never come back.*

"Here," Miranda's voice startled her out of her musing. She thrust a piece of paper at Mat. "This is all I have on Gilbert. Leave it on my easel when you're done if I'm not around." She turned and strode back the way she'd come.

So much for client confidentiality. Mat scanned the document for relevant information and turned the piece of paper over in her hands to see if there was anything on the back. It was blank. There wasn't much on the front other than the preprinted information and spaces for a renter to fill in. Gilbert had provided a phone number and address. *I expect they are bogus, but it's a place to start.* She left the paper on the easel as instructed and headed back down the stairs to her car.

As she turned the last corner to home, her phone rang on the seat beside her. She jumped and grabbed it, trying to maintain control of the steering wheel at the same time. *Damn! When am I going to get used to this thing?!* She answered and coasted into a parking place next to the house and turned off the engine.

"I need you to get over here now and explain this!"

"Detective Greene?"

"Who else did you think it was?"

"Good point. What can I do for you, sir?"

"You left some papers on my desk, said they had something to do with that voting computer."

"The Votomatic?"

"Yeah, that one. How do you expect me to understand what you left here? You need to get over here and explain it."

"Right away, sir."

"And don't 'sir' me!"

e-llegal code

"No sir, uh, no. I'll be there right away." With a sigh, Mat restarted the engine and headed over to Greene's office. At his office door, she knocked lightly. At his bellowed "come in!" she opened the door and poked her head in.

"I'm here."

"*Humph,*" Greene grunted. "Well, don't just stand there. C'mon in and tell me about this." Greene pointed to the diagram on the paper in front of him.

"It's a flowchart," Mat replied, pulling a chair up and leaning over to point out a section of the diagram. "It starts here. As you can see the basic idea is that it counts input, in this case, information from a voting card. Normally, it would send a total for each candidate to the computer for formatting, reporting, and storage. However, in this case, as you can see here"—she pointed to another section of the diagram—"the code takes a detour. If it is counting votes for a certain office or position, it first checks to see what the totals are for each candidate for that position. If the vote would put another candidate ahead of the preferred candidate, the code gives the vote to the preferred candidate instead."

"What exactly are you saying?"

"The code makes sure a preferred candidate always has a winning percentage."

"You're kidding!"

"I'm not. It's right there in black and white."

"How do I know you're not putting me on?"

Mat worked to keep her tone civil. "Detective Greene, if you really believe that, now is the time to fire me again because if you think I'm putting you on, you shouldn't allow me to get anywhere near your computers."

"Okay, okay don't get your hackles up, I was just asking."

"If you want proof, get another programmer to look at this and tell you if I'm putting you on."

"I said okay. That won't be necessary. We don't need to bring anyone else into this."

"So what makes you think Dan is behind this?"

Mat sighed in exasperation. "Because Kim says so!" She pulled a section of the code from the pile of papers on his desk and pointed. "Here, he specifically says Dan Collins gave him this assignment. Who else could it be?"

"We still can't assume he was going to use this and that it was anything more than you said it was, just an exercise to show them it could be done. Not that it was done or would be done."

Mat sat back in her chair, stunned by his stubbornness.

"How can you say that? He's a political candidate running for office and he asks a kid to create this code. A kid who works for the organization that runs the vote counting software. This isn't just a software exercise, it's a plan to make sure he wins!"

"I'm just saying how the defense will work this. It's still just circumstantial." Greene sat back in his chair, bristling belligerence. "I won't let you talk me into another meeting with Collins that gets me into trouble."

Mat stared at him in disbelief. Greene leaned forward and continued his rant, "And another thing. I told you once before, don't go talking to Collins and interfering in that investigation. We're done here. Take all this paper with you." He shoved the offending documents toward Mat, turned to his computer, and began typing as fast as his hunt-and-peck ability would allow.

Mat sat in silence for another moment, then gathered up the documents, stuffed them in her backpack, and left. In the car she phoned Greg. After unloading her thoughts about slow-witted detectives and the exasperation of circumstantial evidence, they agreed to meet at the same bar as the day before.

***

"This still doesn't feel like it's special enough for a 'nice' dinner," teased Greg.

"This isn't about a 'nice' dinner." Mat fingered her glass of wine morosely. "I can't believe Greene could look at that flowchart and not see what is going on."

"He may not understand what you are trying to tell him," Greg commented.

"But I went over it again and again. He kept saying it's all circumstantial and I'm still forbidden to talk to Collins again."

"*Hmmm.* To be honest, I have to admit I agree. Strong as it is, as damning as it all is taken together, it's still circumstantial. And given the political forces at work, I guess I can understand his hesitation." Greg mused thoughtfully for a minute, "He must really be spooked. What he needs, in my opinion, is irrefutable, concrete, slam-dunk evidence and this isn't it."

"It's so frustrating," Mat whined again. "I mean, someone killed that student and threatened me. I just can't see how that doesn't all fall at the feet of Dan Collins." She sighed and sat back. "But more than that, why do I care? I've been asking myself that since Greene and I met. Why can't I just walk away and let the chips fall where they may? They meant to frighten me, and they sure did in the moment." Mat sighed again in frustration. "Now I'm just mad. I'm also convinced he's involved in the deaths of Lilah and Minnie, but that evidence is even more 'circumstantial.'"

"Maybe"—Greg leaned forward and took her hand in both of his—"it would be better to hope that Dan just forgets all about you. Let's have something to eat and talk about something else." He jiggled her hand and smiled. "It's worth a try isn't it?"

"You're right. Maybe I need to put it aside for a while. I'm not getting anywhere going over and over what's happened. I mean maybe Dan is legit. Maybe he's not conning us. I just can't help feeling he is." Mat smiled back, masking her uncertainty and anxiety.

***

The next morning, after Greg left for work, Mat pulled his shirt around her and wandered into the bathroom. She turned on the shower and looked around at the razor, comb, and toothbrush left scattered on the sink. She'd forgotten what it was like to share this space with someone special. She gulped in a ragged breath and sat down on the edge of the antique footed tub next to the shower. *What is wrong with me? I can't seem to move forward and there's no turning back for sure. What does this man mean to me? Am I going head over heels just to have my heart stomped on again? How do you know? On top of that, I've been fired, twice this time, and everyone thinks I'm chasing ghosts. Problem is, I don't think I am.* Quickly, she showered and dressed, vowing to go back over the chain of events and find something, anything, that would convince Greene she was right.

Chapter 21

Mat opened the door to the old Victorian house she shared with Zorah and immediately felt a change in the atmosphere. Something was wrong.

"Zorah?" she called. Silence. She walked into the living room, the hairs on the back of her neck rising.

"Zorah!" Her voice echoed through the empty room. Hesitating, she took a tentative step toward the kitchen.

A male voice came from somewhere near her, "Keep your voice down. You'll wake her."

Mat looked around and saw a dreadlocked Rastafarian sitting at the kitchen table, a cup of coffee nearby. His knit cap of black, red, green, and gold stripes lay on the table beside him. She gazed at him, momentarily speechless, once again finding his ebony skin mesmerizing in its beauty. One day, she'd have to tell him that.

"Want some coffee?" he asked, standing up. "I made a fresh pot."

"Oh! Yes." She strode quickly over and put her arms around him, hugging tightly. "Gilbert! You almost gave me a heart attack! How did you get in?"

"I got here at the same time Zorah did. She's gone upstairs to get some sleep but invited me to make a pot of coffee and wait for you to get back. We assumed you'd want a change of clothes on the off chance last night was more spontaneous than planned." He grinned broadly. "Did you have a good time?"

Mat smiled sheepishly. "As a matter of fact, I did, but that's another story. How are you? I've been wanting to talk to you. How did you know?"

"Miranda told me. I gave her an extra tip if she'd call a special number should anyone come around asking for me. We go a long way back, I knew I could trust her. She described you pretty well. That artist's eye for detail, you know. What's up?"

"*Hmm*. Where to start?" Mat poured herself a cup of coffee and sat down opposite him at the table. She sat staring at it, eyes glazing as the moments passed and the steam rose..

"It seemed so important yesterday. Now I wonder if I'm just letting my imagination run amok. That's what everyone else thinks. I don't know what's true and what isn't, and I don't know where to start."

"The beginning seems as good a place as any." Gilbert got up, poured himself a fresh cup, and sat back down.

"Okay. Remember Detective Greene?" At Gilbert's nod, Mat continued, "After I left that job at Kinross, I decided to start my own consulting business. He gave me my first contract to do maintenance on the computers in his office, installing software, new versions of applications, backups, that stuff."

"Got it. Go on."

"A couple of weeks ago, maybe three, I was working on one of the computers and Greene told me to come down to the morgue with him. He introduced me to the medical examiner,

Hector something or other. I never got the rest of her name. Odd little gnome of a person."

Gilbert raised one eyebrow in response. "This is getting interesting already and you've just started."

"They had found the body of a student in a ditch. He'd been strangled. They also found one of my business cards in one of his pockets, a computer disk in another, as well as part of a letterhead from the Dan Collins campaign. Greene wanted me to figure out what was on the disk. He also wanted to know if I knew who the kid was."

At the mention of Dan Collins, Gilbert sat up straighter in his chair. "Now this is really getting interesting. Dan Collins, you said."

"Yes. I decided it might be a good idea to see what Dan Collins knew about this kid. Greene had asked him, but he was evasive. I thought there was more to it, so I volunteered to help out on his campaign."

"Of course you did." Gilbert's wry smile brought back memories of the last time they'd met. She'd been convinced her company, Kinross, was involved in e-commerce involving illegal goods. She'd been right but had nearly paid for it with her life.

"I started asking questions, then Greene and I confronted him. He denied it all. He said he was working with you. Is he?"

"Is that all?" Gilbert asked, ignoring her question.

"No. Greene told me to stay away from Collins or he would get into trouble. Then someone broke into the place where I was staying and threatened me, telling me to stay away from Dan. Is he working with you?"

"Short answer, no."

"I didn't think so. Aren't you DEA? What would you have to do with political campaigns?"

"That was the short answer. The long answer is a bit more complicated."

"Okay. Your turn." Mat leaned back in her chair and settled in.

"This all really started back when Dan was in college. Believe it or not, he started out in pre-med but switched to political science after a year or two."

"That's quite a switch."

"An interesting factoid is that the medical examiner, the one you called Hector, was in pre-med at the same time. Her name kept coming up as a frequent acquaintance of Dan's during that time. There were also rumors that she got pregnant and had a baby sometime around then."

"She did, and I met her daughter, Minnie, through Zorah. Unfortunately, Minnie was murdered sometime after Kim, that student. It's complicated, but I think Dan is involved in that death too."

"Why do you say that?"

"It's complicated as I said, but basically, Minnie was friends with Lilah who was Dan's girlfriend. Lilah got pregnant and died after taking an abortion med. Minnie thought Dan killed her and accused him of it. I think he murdered her to shut her up. By the way, I think he killed Lilah too."

"You're kidding."

"Not in the slightest."

"Well, I hate to tell you, but that particular situation is not in my job jar. Surely Greene is looking into that?"

"Yes, he says he is but I'm not sure he's giving it one hundred percent. Doesn't seem to want to push Dan too much."

Gilbert shrugged. "The truth is, Dan is an important political figure and he's got powerful backers. At Greene's age, I'm sure he's looking at a nice retirement in a few years and doesn't want to mess that up."

Mat bowed her head and squeezed her hands together. "I just don't want to think it's going to end up a cold case."

"Let's focus on this money laundering. You never know what washes up when everyone is hung out to dry."

Mat had to laugh. "Gilbert, I think the world of you, but that is the best example of a mixed metaphor I've ever heard. My ears hurt."

Gilbert smiled in response. "Sorry, couldn't stop myself." He took a sip of coffee. "Shall I continue?"

"Sure."

"Apparently, Dan was always interested in politics and volunteered for several campaigns in his freshman and sophomore years. Then he switched his major entirely. I think he decided waiting ten or fifteen years to start making money didn't make sense. If he could get into politics that would be a faster route to a secure future, at least that's how we think he saw it. My involvement in all this came via surveillance on a specific drug lord who started funneling funds to Dan's campaign. Apparently, he and Dan have an agreement for Dan to start backing policies favorable to this drug lord's business interests if the drug lord helped get Dan elected. But there's only so much money can do. To ensure Dan gets elected, it seems they're working on something to do with the Votomatic machines."

"I knew it!" Mat exclaimed, sitting up in excitement. "I know what it is! That disk I mentioned? I decoded the information on it and the code is making sure one item in a list gets more than the rest. I just knew it had something to do with an election."

"You're saying that disk you found on the dead student's body had code on it that makes sure a candidate gets the majority of votes?"

"Essentially, yes."

"Some things are starting to fall into place," Gilbert mused. "Dan knows about me because I approached him to help us trap this drug lord. At the time, I didn't realize he was in on the scheme to launder drug money through donations to his campaign."

"What did he say?"

"He said he'd think about it. I've got to contact him to follow up. In the meantime, I put a mole on his campaign team to keep an eye on what he's doing."

"Who's that?"

"Better you don't know." Gilbert leaned forward. "If you figure it out, let me know.

Someone else may have too. We may need to get them out in a hurry."

They drank coffee in silence for a few minutes. Gilbert spoke first, "Mat."

"Yes."

"Greene may not want you involved, but I do. I think you could help us get Dan on this voter fraud thing."

"How could I? Dan doesn't want me around. Greg thinks we should hope he just forgets about me. I'm beginning to agree. Showing up again in any way might not be good for my health."

"Hear me out. If you don't want any part of this, just say so. No hard feelings either way."

"*Hmmph*. Go ahead."

"We need to rattle Dan's cage. If we do what I have in mind and he's innocent, he'll go to the police. If not, we'll know he's in this up to his neck."

"What do you have in mind?"

An hour later, Gilbert left to put the first phase of their plan in motion. Mat was to continue with her maintenance tasks for Greene and wait for the phone call to start her part of the plan.

***

Jim picked up his coffee from the clerk and returned to his place in the back of the café. As he slid into the booth, his cell phone rang.

"It's about time. I left you a message two hours ago."

e-llegal code

"Can't be helped," the voice rebuked him. "Classes just let out. What's your problem?"

"This is getting complicated. Keeping my stories straight between you and Dan is getting harder."

"Dan is the only one you need to worry about. If he catches on, this whole thing could go sideways. Don't forget what I promised you. There'll be none of that if you slip up."

"If any of us get caught, there'll be none of that anyway."

"So don't get caught! Just keep an eye on Dan. It'll all work out."

Jim hung up without a reply. This whole thing was close to getting out of hand.

Chapter 22

Dan's campaign headquarters was in the middle of a block of brick buildings in midtown. It was nearing the end of the workday when Gilbert arrived. He stood under an awning at the corner across the street, watching the front door as most of the staff and volunteers left to go home. Jim, Dan's chief of staff, left shortly after 5:00 p.m. carrying a briefcase and posters under his arm. The bulk of his biceps and torso was apparent under the summer-weight suit. Gilbert knew that Jim was a combined bodyguard, enforcer, and campaign manager. They had met when both joined the Marines but went separate ways after basic training. Gilbert always thought he was the perfect material for a SEAL Team with an unwavering focus on a goal, grit to see it through, and an attack-dog approach to obstacles in his way. His loyalty to Dan was likely unquestioning and he was immune to pity or empathy. He was a formidable opponent, physically as well as intellectually. He was also into more than politics and someone Gilbert had been tracking for over a year.

After twenty minutes, when the building had emptied itself of most workers and rush hour was in full swing, Gilbert crossed the street and went in the front door. He found Dan alone in his office at the back of the suite. He entered silently and closed the door forcefully.

Dan looked up. "Wha—!" He stood as Gilbert approached his desk. "I didn't hear you come in."

"That was the plan." Gilbert smiled as he sat down in one of the chairs in front of Dan's desk. "You can sit back down, this is a friendly conversation."

"It had better be short too," growled Dan, sitting. "I'm busy."

"Just got back and wanted to see if you've thought about my proposal."

"The one where I help you trap these drug lords you say are laundering money through my campaign?"

"You've got a good memory." Gilbert smiled. "That's the one."

Dan sat back in his chair and relaxed. "I've thought about it and I'm willing to help under two conditions."

"What are they?"

"It won't interfere with my campaign obligations or make me a target."

"On the first, it won't, and on the second, we'll make sure there's someone close by at all times in case things get out of hand."

"Can I know who that is?"

"No. It's better if you are completely unaware of that person. That way you can act naturally and not give the person's identity away."

"What if I need help but don't know who to go to?"

"Don't worry about that—"

A soft knock preceded the slow opening of the office door. A young girl stuck her head in, accompanied by a middle-aged woman with a bunch of posters in her hand.

"Sara," Dan greeted the young girl, "and Sheila. You're both still here. What can I do for you?"

"Sorry to interrupt," Sheila said, "but Sara wanted to know if she should put these posters on the schedule for distribution tomorrow. She didn't want to interrupt you, so I volunteered to knock. I hope that was alright." She smiled broadly and enthusiastically at Dan.

"That's fine. Good catch, Sara. You can interrupt me any time for that."

Sara beamed self-consciously and both women withdrew, closing the door softly behind them.

"What was that smirk for?" he demanded, catching Gilbert's ghost of a smile out of the corner of his eye.

"Oh, just admiring how devoted your volunteers appear to be." Gilbert's smile broadened. "They are on top of every detail."

Dan leaned back in his chair, self-satisfaction on his face. "They know being part of my campaign is a unique experience. I'm alone in proposing truly transformational policies that will affect thousands for the better. Others have tried some of them, but I know how to implement them and make them work." He paused. "Sorry, I'll get off my soapbox. That's not what you came for."

"No, it's not. I'll leave you to it. I've got a phone call to make, and you must be busy with your policies." Gilbert stood, shook Dan's hand, and left as quietly as he had arrived.

***

That evening after dinner, Mat was sitting on the back porch of the old Victorian when her cell phone rang.

"Hello, Gilbert?—So he's willing to help you trap the drug lords?—Right, I heard you, be careful because he may be conning us both. Something else?—He did what?—Your mole said he's put a contract out on you? Sounds like I'm not the only one who needs to be careful—Okay, phase two. I'll start that tomorrow." She hung up and thought about what tomorrow would bring.

"Oh, I'm so glad you're here." Zorah flew through the screen door to the back porch, the folds of her caftan adding to the breeze coming through the trees in the yard. She sat next to Mat, bangle bracelets jangling and the beads of her necklace adding to the tinkling sound.

"Guess what?"

"What?"

"Someone saw that mural I painted on the abandoned building, remember? And he wants me to paint some murals on the new addition to the downtown mall. Isn't that fabulous? I'm so excited!"

"Zorah, that is wonderful, truly! I'm so happy for you." Mat smiled at her friend. "When do you start? Are they paying you what you're worth? Do you have time to celebrate before going to the studio?"

"Not sure. *Hmmm*. I'm thinking my name on that mural will be worth more than any payment at this point. Yes, let's have a glass of wine! Oh, did you see Gilbert when you got back? I wasn't sure when you'd get in and I didn't know how long he could wait. I told him to fix himself some coffee. I hope you saw him."

"He was here when I got home this morning. Miranda came through."

They returned to the kitchen and Mat opened a bottle of cabernet. She poured two glasses, handed one to Zorah, and sat down opposite her friend at the kitchen table. Zorah took a sip and looked at Mat, her eyes brimming with curiosity.

"So tell me! What did he say?"

Mat smiled at her friend's enthusiasm. "I guess the last time we talked about any of this was when we found Lilah's letters to her mother."

"Did you tell him about those?"

"No, we didn't get into that. He's only interested in the voter fraud."

"Okay. So did he tell you why he's involved? You said he was only involved in the drug stuff."

"Yes. Apparently, some drug lords he was watching want Dan to win this election so he can push a platform that favors their agendas. They're donating to his campaign as a way of laundering the drug money."

"Wow."

"Yeah. He wants me to help him trap Dan." Mat sat back and sighed. "I told him I was not wanted on Greene's turf or on Dan's. He still thinks there's a way I can help."

"Oh, Mat. You didn't agree, did you? They've already come after you once. If they find out you're working with Gilbert . . ." Her horror at the thought of anyone coming back to find Mat, and maybe her, too, was written on her face. She blanched, and her brows rose over wide eyes as she covered her gaping mouth with her hand.

"Don't worry," Mat hastened to reassure her. "We have that alarm system on the house now, remember? Anyway, I don't think they'll do something as stupid as kidnapping you. How are they going to know you're anything more than a roommate to me?"

"Those other people didn't know that either, but it didn't stop them."

"These people aren't that stupid. If they come after anyone, it'll be me. And Gilbert will be close by."

"I still don't like it." Zorah frowned in disagreement, worry furrowing her brow and adding a tremor to her voice.

"I know, but I can't let go of this. I thought I could, then Gilbert shows up and has this plan—"

"What plan?" Zorah interrupted, fear and anxiety raising the tone of her voice. "Did you let him talk you into something? I like Gilbert, but he can be rash. Anyway, he's not a very good artist so I bet he's not very good at this stuff either."

Mat smiled at Zorah's twisted comparison of Gilbert's artistic talents and his job skills. "I don't think I'll be in any danger, and if this works, it'll nail Dan and his cronies." *Where did I learn to lie so easily?*

"Well, I don't like it." Zorah took another gulp of her wine. "Mat, promise me you'll be careful. If something happens to you, the bad karma of it will be so intense Salee won't be able to do enough exorcisms to get it out of here and I . . . I . . ." Zorah struggled to express her worry and affection. "I don't want to move," she finished weakly, her eyes begging Mat to understand.

Mat got up from her chair and went over to Zorah. "Hugs?"

Zorah nodded and they put their arms around each other and held tight. Mat stood back with her arms on Zorah's.

"I promise, you won't have to move," she said, smiling at her friend. Zorah smiled weakly in return. "Try to forget we discussed this. It'll all be over soon without you even knowing anything is going on. Just remember to set the alarm like I showed you if you leave when I'm not here."

"Okay, will do. And I'll try to put what you told me in my 'tomorrow' jar. That's from *Gone with the Wind*. Scarlett was always saying she'd worry about something tomorrow. It works, and after all, I have this new commission." She brightened at the thought. "I have to make notes on some ideas I have already. It's going to be magnificent!" She gave Mat another hug and danced across the kitchen floor and out the door, grabbing her satchel and paint kit on the way out the door. "You'll see!"

Mat heard the engine start on the psychedelic VW and the gravel crunch as Zorah drove out. *Mercurial and loyal. What have I done to deserve a friend like her?* She put the wine glasses in the sink and headed upstairs, her mind spinning with the possibilities for tomorrow.

Chapter 23

To her right, colorful afghans swirled in the wind, revealing then hiding the entrances to the caves in the mountain. To her left, a wide plain stretched to the horizon, a dusty but clearly marked trail leading to lush greenery in the distance. When she looked to the right, she felt unease tinged with terror but also with anticipation and the expectation of finding treasures beyond imagination. To the left, the treasures were somehow known, comforting, fulfilling, but also banal and dull. There was a path straight ahead, but it only stretched a short way into the distance. Lined up across all three images were the faces, old and new, of those she'd loved, hated, lost, and found. They glowed and dimmed in an ever-changing pattern. Slowly the visions were replaced by a single giant canvas with images appearing on the left and fading away to the right. Zorah stood to the right, clapping gleefully. The canvas began to glow bright red as an image of Dan Collins slowly took over the canvas, his wide grin growing bigger than his face, a ballot framing the wall behind him.

Mat woke with a start, disoriented and bathed in sweat. It was early morning, the sun not yet peeking over the horizon, but she was wide awake. Deciding it was no use to try to go back to sleep, she grabbed her robe and went down to the kitchen to start some coffee.

What have I agreed to? This is just like me, rushing in to try to save the day when I don't even know if it's salvageable. Why did I let Gilbert talk me into this? Okay, face it. It's because at least he has a plan. You know you weren't going to leave this alone, and he knew it too. You can be like putty in the right person's hands. This is just another example.

She poured herself a cup. She'd never been content to leave well enough alone, all depending, of course, on the topic. Playing a version of the knight in shining armor coming to the rescue was clearly one of these. *But who am I rescuing this time? And this time who or what is so important that I'm willing to put Zorah in danger again?* Her musings were interrupted by Zorah flying through the kitchen door after a night at her easels.

"Oh, Mat! You're up. I'm so excited. I got so many ideas for this mural, they just kept coming. Usually, I don't have to actually *choose* which ones to include. But this time there are just so many directions I could go in. I thought of making this the one for Lilah. Or maybe I'll do the one I started already and another one for the mall. I wonder if I have so many ideas because Lilah could be so creative. I can't think of how to reflect all of that in this mural without making it too chaotic. I'll just have to think of a way to get it to be more, you know, *together*. I know, maybe I'll create themes and do one theme for each mural. I could have murals all over that are connected by this theme idea." Zorah had been making herself a cup of herbal tea during this monologue, and she finally sat down, pausing for breath, her eyes bright and brimming with enthusiasm. "You're quiet this morning."

e-llegal code

Mat laughed. "I could hardly get a word in edgewise! That's not a criticism, truly," she added quickly at Zorah's look of dismay. "I love hearing about what you're doing at the studio. Please tell me more."

"Really?" At Mat's quick nod and smile, the grin returned to Zorah's face and she sipped the hot tea contently. "It was just so weird. The minute one thing occurred to me, another came along just behind it. I hardly had time to make a few sketches when I'd have to stop and work on another. It was exhausting keeping up!" The artist was beaming with satisfaction. "I hope I can sleep. If I don't, tonight might not be so great, but it was worth it."

How special it is that you find such satisfaction in your art. Mat hoped Zorah would have the career she dreamed of. After another cup of tea and coffee, they put dishes in the sink and went back upstairs to prepare for the day, each in her own way.

***

That afternoon, when she knew that most of the volunteers were gone and Dan would be working late, Mat pushed open the door to his campaign headquarters. She greeted the few remaining volunteers she recognized and passed through to the back unchallenged. *At least he didn't tell everyone I wasn't welcome here.* The light was on under the door to his inner sanctum in the back of the space. She entered without knocking. Dan was sitting in his chair on the phone and looked up as the door swung open. He stood up immediately, told the caller he'd get back shortly, and hung up.

"What the hell are you doing here? I told you to get lost and never come back! Are you deaf? Get out now!"

Mat closed the door gently behind her and walked across to his desk.

"I will as soon as you've heard what I have to say."

"I can't imagine you have anything to say that I'd want to hear. Turn around and get out now."

"You won't know until you hear it, and I think you'll want to hear it." Mat sat in one of the two chairs in front of his desk. "Go ahead, sit down, Dan. This has to do with the voter fraud you're planning."

Dan stared at her in stunned silence. He watched her warily.

"I'm not planning any voter fraud. Now get out."

"Oh, but you are. That disk we found on Kim pretty much proves it."

Dan's face lost all color, and he sat down as if punched in the gut. "That's crazy! I don't know anything about that. You can't prove I told anyone to write that code."

"Ah, but I can. He included a comment that says you asked him to write the code. It's an easy thing to audit the software on the machine and see if that code is on it."

"But I didn't! That kid had a grudge because I wasn't going to hire him after he graduated and he must have dreamed up this scheme to ruin me."

e-llegal code

"That may be, although I doubt it. But I have a plan to find out who's telling the truth."

"What's that? Wait, I don't care. Just get the hell out of here."

"I wrote a program to take votes from you and give them to your opponent. I'm planning to install it before the vote next month."

"You can't do that!"

"Sure I can. As easily as Kim did. You're not the only one who can hire a smart student who would think it fun to get around safeguards as a test and install some code to do that."

Mat let that sink in, watching Dan's eyes dart from one side of the room to the other.

"That's not all."

Dan switched his attention to her, alarm flickering quickly across his face before it settled into the benign expression familiar on so many posters.

"You mean there's more. I can't wait."

"I have proof you gave Lilah pennyroyal and it killed her."

Dan paled anew, sweat broke out on his brow, his benign expression switching to near panic before settling again into the picture on the posters.

"You're crazy. I didn't give her that. Where would I get it anyway?"

"You got it from Lilah's friend Steve. She told me you showed up and wanted a sample of the herb and instructions on how to extract oil from it."

"So what, that doesn't prove anything."

"I also found a letter in Lilah's apartment saying you gave her pennyroyal to help with her morning sickness. But that wasn't what you had in mind, was it?"

"That still doesn't prove anything. Even if I did give her some for her morning sickness, it doesn't mean I killed her with it."

"I think the autopsy results will show that's what killed her."

"It still doesn't mean I killed her." Dan got up abruptly and stormed around the side of the desk. "Now get out. I'm going to call Greene and have you arrested for harassment and for conspiracy to commit voter fraud. Get out now!"

Mat was on her feet and heading for the door by the time he got to the chair she had occupied. She looked back once and recoiled inwardly at the look of pure hatred on his face. When she had closed the door behind her, Dan picked up the phone and dialed a familiar number.

"Jim?" he barked into the phone. "We've got a problem."

***

Back in her car, Mat dialed Gilbert's number on her cell phone, once again marveling at the instrument in her hand. *This really is convenient.* It rang until the answering machine came on complete with reggae music and Gilbert's melodious voice asking the caller to leave a message. After leaving a message about her conversation with Dan, she drove through the streets deep in thought until she found herself at Candlewick. *I guess as long as I'm here I could stop in and thank Miranda for getting me in touch with Gilbert.* She climbed up to the top floor of the building. The space was becoming familiar and she found herself looking forward to the glimpses of color and styles she passed on her way to the area where Zorah had her studio. Her friend's space was strewn with paper sketches on the floor, tacked to the wall, lying on the desk, and taped to the easel. She certainly had been busy last night. She felt tinges of envy at the creative juices she felt flowing around her and chuckled to herself. Salee and Zorah would both understand. She continued on to Miranda's space but found it neat, tidy, and empty. *Hmmm, must be Miranda's day off.* She wandered back through the studio spaces, down the stairs, and back to her car. *Maybe Greg would like to get an update on my activities.* She dialed his number and heard him pick up on the third ring.

"Just when I thought my evening would be wasted, the love of my life calls to rescue me. How did you know I needed rescuing?"

Mat laughed. "Must be some sort of intuition. I did wonder if you'd like an update on my activities."

"Sounds intriguing but not like 'this is the night for that nice dinner.'"

"No, unfortunately, but I haven't forgotten."

"Good, because I'm really looking forward to it."

"So what sort of updates are you talking about? It hasn't even been twenty-four hours since we last discussed your activities."

"It's been a long day. Why don't we meet at that pub again?"

"It's becoming a habit but one I like. See you there in twenty minutes."

As can sometimes happen, they found themselves sitting at the same booth as the night before.

"You know, if we come in here tomorrow night and this booth is taken I'll be tempted to tell the occupants to move because this is ours," Mat said with a smile.

Greg seconded her feeling of ownership, "I might help you move them along." He ordered a beer and Mat a red wine.

"So what's happened to make this a long day?"

"I'm not sure where to start."

"Why not with you leaving my apartment and go from there."

Mat smiled and nodded in silent agreement. "Well, I went home and found Gilbert sitting at the kitchen table having coffee."

"So Miranda came through for you."

"Must have or Gilbert has another skill I didn't know about. Mind reading."

"And breaking and entering unless there's another explanation for finding him at your kitchen table with a cup of your coffee."

"No worries there, Zorah got home at about the same time. She left him in the kitchen, told him to make himself some coffee if he wanted it. She figured I'd be home soon to change clothes at least."

"Zorah is a very astute woman if you haven't noticed."

"I've noticed. She's priceless for sure."

"So what did Gilbert have to say for himself? Where has he been by the way?"

"He wouldn't tell me except that he's been on some assignment out of the country. He did say he got involved because a drug cartel is laundering money through Dan's campaign. Apparently, he approached Dan to see if he would work with them to trap these drug lords."

"What did Dan say?"

"He said he'd think about it. Gilbert was to check with him and get back to me on his answer."

"What happens if Dan doesn't want to help?"

"That's where I come in."

"You're kidding! Don't tell me Gilbert is dragging you into his mess?"

"Calm down, Greg. He's not *dragging* me into anything. I'm going along voluntarily."

Greg stared at Mat in disbelief. "Haven't you learned by now how dangerous that man can be?"

"Just listen to the whole story, please."

Greg sat back. "Just remember, Mat. That man is capable of anything. If you get in his way, there's no telling what he'll do."

"I know but this is important."

"Not as important as your life."

"Are you going to let me finish?"

"Go on." The impatience and irritation in Greg's voice were unmistakable. He began to drum his fingers on the table, disbelief hardening his features.

"If they are going to get him on the money laundering, they have to scare him into doing something rash."

"You mean, you have to scare him into doing something rash."

"You were going to let me finish."

"Go on."

"So I met with Dan a little while ago and told him I had the disk and knew what he asked Kim to do. I told him I was going to change the program to make sure his opponent would get fifty-one percent of the votes instead of him."

"I knew it! Mat, you are really stirring a hornet's nest."

"Maybe, maybe not. Gilbert and I agreed that if Dan was legit, he would call Greene and tell him what I was going to do."

"Oh, this gets better and better."

"Don't you see? If he does and Greene gets upset, Gilbert will defend me and say it was his idea. He'll explain the whole thing about the money laundering."

"And if he's not legit?"

"I admit it does make me a bit of a target, but Gilbert says he has a mole in Dan's organization to watch out for me and Gilbert will be close by too."

"How can he possibly think he and this mole can protect you 24/7?"

"Don't be so dramatic. We think whatever Dan does, it'll be obvious and there'll be plenty of time to see it coming."

"I think you're both delusional. You just put a neon sign around your neck saying 'come get me,

I'm the one you want.'" Greg took the last swallow of his beer and grabbed his jacket. "But it is why I think you'll be safer if you come back with me tonight instead of going back home. Zorah's out with her art, right? If anyone tries anything tonight, the house will be empty. Tomorrow we can worry about tomorrow."

"I also told him about Lilah's letters and that they proved he gave her pennyroyal." She had to squelch a laugh at Greg's look of horror.

"I'm speechless."

"Look, if he's legit, then the program business won't hurt him at all. But I'm still convinced he gave Lilah an overdose of pennyroyal and it killed her. There's only one way to bring that into the mix and that is to make it one of the accusations."

"Does Gilbert know you did that?"

"I tried to tell him, but he isn't answering his phone."

"Greene and Collins might not be the only ones firing you when you tell him."

"Well, it's done and now we see what the fallout is, if any. It may all be the delusional fantasies of two overly imaginative people as you say."

"I didn't say that."

"Close enough."

"If nothing else, I wouldn't be surprised if he sued you for defamation of character, especially if he thinks you're going to take this public."

"Can he do that if I don't?"

"I'll have to check. It's not my area of the law." Greg sighed in frustration. "Is there anything else I should know if I'm going to stay close to you?"

"Are you going to?"

"Going to what?"

"Stay close to me."

"Oh." Greg leaned forward with both arms on the table and took her hands in his. "Well, I may be delusional as well, but I'm going to try not to let you out of my sight until this is over."

"What about your work?"

"I'm sure there's a solution to that problem that will occur to me in the morning."

Mat smiled in response. He slid out of the booth, took her hand, and headed for the door and what they both hoped was the safety of his apartment.

Chapter 24

After Mat left, Zorah fixed a salad of lettuce, tomatoes, and feta cheese with oil and vinegar dressing, tore off a large chunk of artisan bread, and boiled water for tea. At moments, she was bouncing on her toes and, at others, feeling like she was dragging a ten-pound ball behind her. *Whew, my body is just all over the place. I'm wired and tired.* She put her plates in the sink and headed upstairs. *I know what I'll do! I'll take a night off! A bit of meditation, some herbal tea, some melatonin to settle me down even more for a good day's sleep with no alarms. Then a long soak in the tub when I get up, run some errands at that all-night shopping mall, have a leisurely dinner, another good day's sleep and back to work—that's the ticket. I've got notes and sketches all over the place, a night off will do me good and I won't lose a thought. And I just might sleep into the night the way I'm feeling.*

Shortly after 1:00 a.m. Zorah woke. She looked over at the clock. *One o'clock in the morning. Boy, I must have been tired!* She lay there luxuriating in the silence and groggy half-sleep brought on by meditation and a deep sleep. *I could lie here forever but that's not going to get my mural done.* She smiled at the thought of the ideas she had generated, feeling the energy coming back at the thought of the work ahead. With a happy sigh, she rolled over and slid her feet to the floor. *Guess I should start my day. Where did I leave the shopping list? Don't want to get to the studio tonight and have to turn around and come back for anything.*

She tiptoed down the hall and crept down the stairs, guided by the nightlight and fearful of waking Mat. At the bottom of the stairs, she froze, her senses on high alert. She heard it again, low but distinctive, the scraping of metal on metal. A pause, then it sounded again, insistent, determined. She looked around as if she could see where it was coming from, trying to focus on the direction of the sound. The back door. Fearful but too curious to resist, she crept toward the kitchen and the direction of the sound. The scraping was replaced by a series of clicks. She watched in fascination as the back door slowly opened, millimeter by millimeter. It cleared the door jamb and Zorah looked into the dark shape of a man silhouetted against the back porch light as a loud shriek pierced the night. She jumped at the sound, and the figure paused, then it moved in her direction. Above the din of the shrieking alarm, she heard a loud voice.

"Well, no matter. What I need to do will only take a second." The figure moved in her direction, impeded only momentarily by the kitchen table. Zorah turned without hesitation and fled up the stairs, down the hall, and into her room, slamming the door behind her. The alarm continued its piercing shriek and the phone started to ring. She looked desperately around for a place to hide. She knew he would look immediately in the obvious places: under the bed, in her closet, behind the curtains. She headed for the voluminous caftans she had hung by her bed, creating a waterfall of color and thick fabric framing her bed. She slipped behind one side,

e-llegal code

flattening herself against the wall. As the alarm wailed, the phone stopped ringing and she heard the intruder open Mat's bedroom door with such force it crashed against the wall. *OMG, Mat, didn't you hear anything? I should have warned you. OMG.* She started to cry silently, tears running down her cheeks as she tried to stifle her sobs. Somewhere the shrieking alarm was joined by another piercing sound. *Thank God, the police!* The sirens grew louder as they approached. With a *bam*, Zorah's door swung open. She watched in fascination through a gauze panel as the figure stood in her doorway. He hit the light switch and the room was flooded in the soft glow of the lamp on the dresser.

"Where are you?" bellowed the figure. He paused, head cocked, listening as if suddenly aware of the police siren. "Damn!" he yelled into the room. "Wherever you are, this isn't over." With that, he turned and fled down the hall. The alarm and siren continued their clashing cadences as if competing for the listener's attention.

Within seconds, the front door crashed open, and she heard voices downstairs. "Police!" and "clear" as the uniforms moved from room to room. The alarms stopped. Zorah crept out from the caftans and was at the head of the stairs when a policeman appeared on the bottom step both hands raised cradling a gun pointed at her.

"Halt, police! Put your hands in the air!"

Zorah raised her hands and immediately dropped to the floor in a dead faint.

***

"Zorah! Zorah!" Mat pushed the bottle of smelling salts closer to Zorah's nose. Almost immediately her friend came to with a start and recoiled from the acrid odor.

"What is that?" Zorah pushed the offending hand away and turned her head into the cushion.

"Thank heaven. Zorah! it's me, Mat."

The artist turned her head back and opened her eyes. "Oh Mat, I'm so glad you're here. I was so scared. Did you catch him? Why didn't you wake up? I thought you were dead."

"I'm so sorry. I stayed with Greg last night. He's here too. When I got a call from the alarm people I knew someone must have broken in. I figured you were at work and would have set the alarm before you left for work."

"I didn't go to work," Zorah explained. "I decided to take a day off and spend it on me. I actually slept late and got up to get some tea. I heard that guy doing something with the kitchen door lock. Next thing I knew, he was chasing me upstairs and there were loud sounds, sirens. It was horrible!" She burst into fresh tears.

"Can you talk to the police? They want to know what happened."

"Sure," Zorah said between sniffles.

Mat gestured to the policeman standing at the door. "I think she's alright to talk to you now." She got up and moved to the other side of the living room and sat by Greg.

"Guess I'll have to find another roommate after this," Mat mused to Greg.

"Why? She wasn't hurt."

"But she was frightened out of her wits. I would have been too. She made me promise this wouldn't happen again. Guess my assurances aren't worth much."

"You're making those assurances for someone else. If you are going to keep nosing around like this, you'll need a roommate with nerves of steel." He looked at her with a sly grin on his face. "I volunteer."

"Ms. Briscoe!"

Mat looked up to see Detective Greene crossing the living room to stand in front of her. "Please tell me this has nothing to do with the Collins investigation."

"I don't know what it has to do with. I wasn't here. I just know someone tried to break in and scared my roommate to death." She took a deep breath, grateful for a reason to avoid Greg's offer. "What are you doing here anyway?"

"We're short-staffed and it's my turn on the midnight shift. What do you think then? Burglary? More of your girlfriend's paintings?" He chuckled at the thought. "Not sure anyone would want those. They can't be worth much."

"That's unkind."

"That's the truth."

"Everyone has an opinion."

"One thing's for sure, you know how to get the cavalry out here. Second time in our short acquaintance, if I remember correctly."

"Have your folks found anything? I mean anything about the intruder? Zorah says he was wearing a mask and black clothing."

"We did find scratch marks on your back door lock. Looks like someone picked the lock. They're fresh, so must have happened recently. Course we can't tell when that happened. Either of you lost your keys and had to pick it to get in?"

"No." Mat glared in response.

"You?" Greene looked at Greg.

"No."

"I doubt your girlfriend would know how, so I'll skip her for the moment. We're dusting for prints, but if he's smart, we won't find any."

The policeman who had been questioning Zorah came over and tapped Greene on the shoulder. They conferred in whispers for a moment and Greene turned back to Mat. "He says your intruder left a parting shot before he ran out."

"What was that?"

"He said, 'Wherever you are, this isn't over yet.' Doesn't sound like a routine burglary to me."

Mat swallowed and she looked down at her hands.

"Who did he mean?" Greene went on. "Who is the 'you' in 'wherever you are' do you suppose? And why would he say that to . . . you, Mat?"

"Why do you think it wasn't Zorah?"

"Because," Greene threw back at her, "if I've ever seen a guilty look, it's on your face."

Mat studied her hands and refused to look him in the eye.

"What do you know about this?" Greene looked at Greg, who had been following this exchange with fascination.

"Me? I'm just an innocent bystander."

e-Ilegal code

"Innocent? *Hmmph*. I understand she"—he pointed to Mat—"spent the night with you and wasn't even here when all this occurred."

"True enough."

"Nothing else to say?"

"I wasn't here either, as you pointed out. I have no idea what's going on."

Greene turned on his heels and left the room, growling at one of the others to follow him as he passed.

In an hour, the print team had finished spreading dust all over the house and left. Mat went back to sit by Zorah who was still lying on the couch.

"I'm so sorry," she began.

Zorah turned tearful eyes on her friend. "I'm the one who's sorry. I didn't even try to warn you. I thought you were asleep and couldn't understand why you hadn't come out of your room. But if you had, you'd have run right into him and you'd be dead!"

"I thought you were at the studio. I'd decided to spend the night with Greg. What a mess this is. You could have been hurt or worse. I was so sure the alarm system would be the answer."

"It's not your fault. It really is a good system. The police came and nobody got hurt."

"I can't believe you're not mad at me and ready to move out."

"I won't say it didn't occur to me, but that was right when I came to. Before I realized I wasn't tied up or anything." The artist looked at her hands and shrugged, looking up at Mat. "Thing is, if they are always coming after you, then I might get in the way sometimes, but nothing really bad will ever happen to me. I know because Salee says it's my karma." She smiled at her friend. "You should have seen the way the others at the studio gathered around when I told them about the last time. I can't wait to see what they'll think of this!" Zorah's eyes danced at the idea.

Mat sat back and studied her friend. *Well, this is not the reaction I expected. But maybe I should have included it in the possibilities.*

"So, I don't have to look for another housemate after all?"

"Oh no. This will really spice up my work. I never told you, but I'm convinced the reason that fellow liked my mural and wants it in the shopping mall is because of the spirit it communicates, the hunger people have to connect, the fear that they won't. It's the fear I finally figured out how to get into my paintings." She turned to Mat and gave her a hug. "I got so much of that from you."

Mat hugged her back and stared after her as the artist got up and headed for the kitchen. "I'm going to make some tea. Would you like coffee?"

"Okay, thanks." Mat mulled over her friend's reaction and turned to look at Greg. His wry smile underscored his words as he replied, "Me too." He turned to look at Mat. "Guess you won't be needing a new housemate after all."

Mat shrugged and got up to go into the kitchen with Greg on her heels.

"What are we going to do about the front door? The police completely destroyed it when they rushed in," asked Zorah as they came in.

"The door is the only thing ruined," Greg commented. "I can go over to the hardware store and get another one and install it along with a new lock today. The sensor for the alarm is on the frame which is fine. I'll take its companion off the old door and put it on the new. You should be back in business tonight. And I'll spend tonight here just in case he decides to try again."

"You don't seriously think he will, do you?" asked Mat.

"If he's who I think he is, there's no telling what he might do."

"Who do you think he is?"

"I think he's Dan's chief of staff. The person who does his dirty work for him—from firing people to worse."

Mat's face paled as the reality of her predicament sank in. "I've really landed in it this time."

"What I think is that you need to contact Gilbert. You two wanted to rattle Dan's cage. Well, you did that. Gilbert needs to be updated, especially after last night."

They took the cups of the hot steaming beverages Zorah offered and gathered at the kitchen table.

"You're right. I'll do that and see what he wants to do next. We didn't get that far in our planning, and this wasn't exactly in the script."

"Wild animals don't use a script and that's the category Dan's sidekick belongs in. Dan, too, for that matter." Greg rose and put his empty cup down. "Thanks for the coffee, Zorah. I need to get over to the hardware store. If I can get the door, I can install it. Then I need to put a few hours in at the office. I'll get back here as soon as I can. Greene said they could have a patrol officer drive by at intervals for the next few days to keep an eye on the house. Not sure what good that will do, but anything is welcome."

"Thanks, Greg. Zorah, go run your errands. I'll stay here until Greg gets back. I really don't think whoever he is will be back this soon."

"Better yet, why don't you come with me. If he does, he'll find no one here."

"I guess you're right. Let's wait until Zorah leaves. That way we know the house will be empty if he comes back."

They waited fifteen minutes for Zorah to get a quick shower, dress, and come down the stairs with her shopping list and string bag. Mat and Greg left right behind her. Greg stopped to prop the broken front door against the opening as best he could to make it look like the door was still functional.

Mat waited and then they headed for his car. *Why do I feel so bad, so unsettled? It's not just the break-in, or maybe that's most of it. I wanted to rattle Dan's cage, but this is not what I thought he would do. Is all my bravado based on the condition that nothing really bad happens to me or anyone I care about? Am I so hungry to make an impression, to stand for something, that I'm ignoring reality?* They drove to the hardware store in silence, each lost in their own dark thoughts.

Chapter 25

When they got home, Gilbert was sitting on the front steps. He rose, dusted off the seat of his pants, and went over to meet them.

"Looks like you had some excitement here recently. What happened?"

"You must be able to read my mind or that contact number got to you faster than I would have thought possible," Mat answered.

He smiled. "So you just called."

"All of this"—Mat made a sweeping gesture with her hand that included the front door and whole house—"happened last night or, rather, early this morning. I'm surprised you didn't see the police leaving as you drove up."

"I did get approached by a cop who wanted to know what business I had with you. It took a phone call to keep from getting hauled off to jail." Gilbert pulled off his stocking cap and rubbed his forehead.

"I'm sorry about that, but it got crazy last night, and Greene thought it best to have a patrol on my house."

Gilbert watched as Greg began to unload the new door and lock from his truck. He turned briefly to Mat. "Go on in and I'll stay out here and work on the door with Greg. Then we can go over what happened last night."

"Sounds good. I'll make us some iced tea while you work."

An hour later they were all sitting around the kitchen table with coffee or tea, the new door and lock installed. Mat had given Gilbert a quick summary of the night's events.

"This had to be Dan warning me," she finished.

"I won't argue with you," Gilbert conceded. "This means our attempt to rattle Dan's cage worked, better and sooner than I expected. If the intruder was his chief of staff, that alarm system was a lifesaver, if not yours, then Zorah's."

"Please don't tell her that. She's just agreed not to move out. That might change her mind."

"Would you blame her, given the events surrounding you since I've known you?"

"That's a vote of confidence."

"Just facing facts."

"What is this plan of yours, exactly?" Greg interjected. He had been watching Mat and Gilbert's verbal sparring for several minutes.

Mat smiled at Gilbert. She enjoyed the rapport they had developed. Maybe Greg was envious, but, perversely, that only increased her enjoyment of the moment.

"To start, we rattled Dan's cage, as I said. He went into attack mode instead of calling the police on Mat. That means he's not the innocent he claims to be." Gilbert twirled his coffee cup around. "I'm assuming Mat was the target of both warnings and that they came from Dan. The question is what to do next." He pursed his lips, raised an eyebrow, and looked at Mat. "We didn't get past this point in our plan."

"That's because it depended on which way he went." She sipped her coffee and gazed into its depths. "Maybe we should think about what is going on from Dan's point of view. He's spooked, probably told his chief to take care of the problem—me—and now he knows it didn't work and he's having the same discussion we're having. It's just what to do next."

"So . . . we have to try mind reading as a strategy?" Greg asked them, obvious skepticism adding a sharpness to his words. "What I mean is, to understand what he'll do next, we need to know how he thinks. I haven't known him long enough for that. Have either of you?"

"Let's go at it this way," Gilbert said, avoiding a direct answer. "He's desperate to win this election and desperate to keep any hint of vote tampering out of the press."

"Not to mention desperate to keep his affair with Lilah under wraps."

"So, what does this triply desperate man do next?" Greg asked.

"Maybe just what the guy said, come back and try again."

"I agree." Gilbert summed up. "What I don't want to do is just sit back and wait for them to come to us. I'd rather go to them. But how and when?"

"Heaven, help me . . ." Greg raised both arms in an act of surrender. "I'd rather not aid and abet this craziness, but I think I have an idea." He leaned forward, arms on the kitchen table. "What if Mat calls him and says there's new evidence and she wants to meet and discuss it."

"What new evidence is this?" Gilbert and Mat looked at Greg, wide-eyed. "How did you get it?"

"That's just it, there really won't be any, but we tell him, 'W*hat if* we found a work log Kim had that documents everything he did for Dan, including the vote machine tampering.'"

"He'll just say it's still hearsay evidence, won't he?" Mat queried.

"Maybe, but even if it's still circumstantial, you can say it's piling up and the newspapers will have a field day with it."

"It just might work." Gilbert smiled.

"What good will that do, other than spinning him up some more?" asked Mat.

"I think he'll want this ended sooner rather than later and he'll do something rash. He won't see this coming." Greg sat back with satisfaction.

"So who delivers this message and meets with him?"

Greg and Gilbert's heads both turned to Mat.

"Me?" Mat looked from one to the other. "Why me? Why not Gilbert?"

"Because," Greg said, "he'll wonder why Gilbert, who is law enforcement, hasn't gone to the authorities already."

"Thanks for your support. I thought you wanted to keep me safe." Mat frowned at Greg.

He leaned forward and took her hand. "I do, and one way is to get rid of this son-of-a-bitch. Putting you in danger is the last thing I want, but you seem to be in his bull's-eye. I don't see how we can ignore the opportunity that gives us. If we do it my way, you'll never be alone with him."

She sat back, considering the proposal. She shut her eyes, opened them, then nodded, saying, "I have to agree, it just might work. He's so rattled now, it could send him over the deep end and get him to do something rash. At least we have a chance to be on top of it instead of just waiting around for him to strike."

"Give me a chance to get some backup in place and then make the call," Gilbert said. "You won't be in there alone. Greg, you're in it now and there's a role for you here. It shouldn't put you in a direct line of fire, but it will give us some extra eyes on the situation from another vantage point. Mat, you and I will go in together."

"I wouldn't miss this for the world," Greg said. "And since it was my idea, I want to be around to protect the investment I've made in Mat." He grinned at her.

"Okay. Let's get started before this gets too maudlin," Mat announced, and got up to make more coffee.

Chapter 26

At Dan's campaign headquarters, he and Jim were behind closed doors in the back office.

"What do you mean, you didn't know about the alarm? That's supposed to be your forte, scouting out locations to do whatever you need to do."

Jim's voice rose, keeping pace with Dan's, "It wasn't there when I checked two days ago. You had me running all over town with this campaign. I can't be everywhere."

"Maybe you need help cleaning up. Maybe you should include that artist friend of hers in your cleanup." Their voices continued to rise as if competing for airtime.

"I could, but aren't we stacking up the bodies a little high?"

"What do you care?" Dan growled. He began to prowl around the office like a nervous cat. "Just make sure nothing can be traced back to me."

Jim raised an eyebrow. "That can be arranged, but that kind of insurance takes money."

"No worries there." Dan stopped prowling and turned to Jim. "There's plenty of that to go around."

"There better be. My rate just went up."

Dan faced Jim, tilting his head, eyes wide and brow furled with growing anger.

"What does that mean? You're paid plenty for the work you do."

"Maybe for the work you hired me to do. That job description has expanded significantly. Time for a raise." Jim sat in one of the chairs in front of the desk. "That kickback you're getting from your friends up north is quite generous. You can share some of that."

Dan blinked, confusion and defiance flickering across his face. "How do you know about that?"

"C'mon, Dan. You hired me for my many abilities, one of which is intelligence gathering."

"Snooping, you mean."

"No need to call names. I just followed the money trail. And I know there's plenty to share." Jim leaned back, a smile forming at the sides of his mouth.

"Over my dead body," Dan snarled, then backed away, as if looking for a way out of his rash words.

"That can be arranged." The smile faded quickly from Jim's face. "But I doubt you really want this whole thing to end like that."

"I wasn't speaking literally." Dan glanced sideways at Jim. "Don't be hasty. We'll talk about it when this is all cleared up. I'm sure we can come to some arrangement."

The smile returned to Jim's face. "I'm looking forward to it." He stood and headed for the door. "Don't worry about Ms. Briscoe. It's going to look like a very tragic accident."

***

The sound of angry voices had been heard down the hall and in the open workspace where volunteers stuffed envelopes and discussed which neighborhoods to visit.

"Wonder what happened to make him so angry?" Sheila asked a volunteer sitting next to her.

"Who knows? He's got that nasty chief of staff in there with him. Someone's in trouble. Glad it's not me." Her friend rounded up the stack of envelopes and got up to put them in the mailbag on the other side of the room. "Anyway, it's better we don't know."

Thinking that this was just too juicy to pass up, Sheila picked up a plastic cup and headed to the back where a water fountain might allow her to hear what was being said. After a few minutes, she scurried back to her chair as the door to Dan's office swung open and crashed against the wall.

"Don't come back here until you can tell me it's done!" Dan's angry voice reverberated down the hall. Jim emerged, the muscles in his jaw working to clench and unclench his teeth, swallowing his anger and managing a thin smile as he passed Sheila and the others on his way out.

***

Dan slammed the door to his office shut as the phone rang. He picked it up and barked, "Who is it?" He listened, a slow smile appearing on his face. "Well, well, isn't this a voice from the past. You sound upset. What can I do for an old friend? Now? Of course I can make time for you. I'll be here for a few more hours at least. Just

e-llegal code

come on to the back. Anyone here can tell you where my office is." He hung up and sat down, mulling over the call and the problem of Mat and the voting code.

Half an hour later, he looked up as the door to his office swung open. Hector stormed in, walked up to the desk, and put her hands flat on the polished surface. She leaned over, getting as close to him as the expanse of desk allowed.

"I'm going to kill you!" she hissed at him as if spitting venom. "You son-of-a-bitch, you killed my baby!"

"Wait a minute—" Dan half rose from his seat. "I haven't killed anyone. What are you talking about?"

"My baby, my Minnie!"

"Minnie? What do you have to do with Minnie?"

"She's my baby, my girl, my daughter, my pride and joy." Hector paused to take a breath. "I knew you were trouble. I tried to tell her to stay away from Lilah and you, but she wouldn't listen, you son-of-a-bitch."

Dan sat down again and stared at Hector, incredulity robbing him of speech. "Minnie's your daughter. You can't be serious?!"

"Why not? Do you think because I'm not Miss America, no one would find me desirable?"

"No, no, it's not that, it's just . . ."

"You gave Lilah pennyroyal, I know you did. Enough to kill her! And when Minnie found out, you killed her too. You murderer!" Hector was screaming now, and Dan hurried around the desk to close the door. Hector turned to keep him in her sights.

"You're crazy!" he hissed after closing the door. "I was in love with Lilah. Why would I kill her?"

"Because she was pregnant. With your child. You didn't want that to get out. Wouldn't be good for your campaign image, would it?"

Dan approached her, hands spread wide, trying to inject calm into their exchange. "Now, Hector, we can discuss this friendly-like, can't we? Exactly what proof do you have that I gave Lilah pennyroyal?"

"Detective Greene told me that she left a bunch of letters, her diary actually. She said you gave her pennyroyal to help her morning sickness. How nice of you." Hector's sarcasm was not lost on Dan.

"What if I did?"

"Toxicologists can find out how much she took. If they can prove you gave it to her, you're looking at a whole bunch of charges, or at least at a ruined political career once I get done with the newspapers."

"How did you find out about those . . . did you say, letters, anyway? Who told you about them? Where were they?"

"None of your business. But Minnie knew about them. They'll be public knowledge soon and you'll be done."

"Now wait a minute, Dr. High and Mighty." Dan glared down at Hector. "You might want to think twice once I remind you of what I can tell the press about you."

e-llegal code

"What are you talking about?" Hector eyed Dan suspiciously. "You don't have anything on me."

"Oh, I don't do I? Lilah told me about the RU486 that was being smuggled into that abortion clinic where you volunteer."

"RU486?"

"That's right. I know what that is. It's legal in France as an abortion medicine, but illegal here, at least at the moment. But that clinic has a steady supply."

"I didn't know." Hector's tone changed as she gathered her thoughts. "Anyway, even if it's true, I don't have anything to do with that."

"No one's going to believe that after I get through with you. A medical examiner volunteering at an abortion clinic that gets a regular supply of RU486? It's only logical that you know about it. It's a short leap to insinuate that you supplied it."

"That's not true, it's a lie."

"Maybe, maybe not. Doesn't matter in the end. Your reputation will be shot. Could be you'll lose your job."

"You wouldn't!"

"Only if you ruin me." Dan sat back with a smug look on his face. "Looks like we're at an impasse."

Chapter 27

"Hello, Dan Collins Campaign," Dan answered the phone, satisfied with the results of the morning's verbal exchanges with Hector and Jim.

"It's Mat. Don't hang up."

"Why shouldn't I?" he growled, irritation and annoyance sharpening his voice. "You've caused me enough trouble. Time to end it."

"I assume you've put your pit bull on my trail?"

Dan didn't reply.

"I'll take that as a yes. You should consider calling him off until you hear what I have to tell you. Believe me, you'll want to hear it."

"What makes you think that?"

"Just call him off and I'll be at your office in an hour." Mat slammed the phone down, her heart pounding. *Here's hoping I live long enough to get to his office. Why do I do these things?*

An hour later, Mat walked through the front door of Dan's campaign headquarters with Gilbert and Greg. Showing him the display of literature on Dan, she told Greg to wait by the front door. He could act like he was a new fan if anyone asked. She and Gilbert headed to Dan's office in the back.

"Let me go in first," she said to Gilbert in a low voice.

"That wasn't the plan," he hissed back. "He could take you out and there'd be no one to help."

"I'll leave the door cracked open." Without waiting for a reply, she opened the door without knocking to find Dan on the phone with his back to her.

"Yes, that was the message I left . . . yes, just for a while. She's coming here with more information, and I need to know what that is. Then she's all yours. Stay close, we'll know where she is once she arrives."

"*Ahemmm.*"

Dan turned around abruptly to see Mat standing just inside the door. She stepped in, leaving the door ajar.

Dan cocked his head, a slow smile growing on his face. "Don't you know how to knock?"

"I don't feel like being polite." She crossed the room and sat at one of the chairs in front of Dan's desk. "Ready to talk?"

"Depends on the topic. What's this new information you claim to have?"

"What if I were to tell you we found a work log that Kim, the kid you murdered—"

"I didn't murder that kid, or anyone!" The smile fled from Dan's face. "It's a slanderous lie. Get out!" Dan blurted, the color rising on his face along with his voice. He glared at Mat who stayed in her seat.

"I'm not so sure. As I was saying, what if we found his work log? Say it has all the details of the tasks you gave him." She leaned forward, pinning Dan to his spot with her eyes. "Including your request to alter the vote counting code to give you the higher percentage, no matter what."

"He couldn't have because I never told him to do that." Dan sneered. "Get. Out. Now."

"What he said and what he did seem to have been two different things." Mat didn't budge. "Do you want to take the chance he lied to you? You can, but I think Greene and the public certainly will find this non-existent log compelling."

"You're lying, threatening me like you did with the code you said you would insert into the Votomatic to swing the vote to my opponent. Why should I believe you?"

"Because I wasn't lying then and I'm not lying now. I want you to confess that you conspired to commit voter fraud," Mat continued, pushing him relentlessly. "You arranged to have Kim killed and sent your buddy to break into my house and threaten me."

"You're crazy. Get out before I call the police and have you thrown out."

"No, you won't. The stink this would raise, true or not, would put a black spot on your reputation that you wouldn't be able to erase any time soon. You'll withdraw from the race citing personal reasons, resign from your company, again, citing personal reasons. If you cooperate, maybe Greene can get some leniency and you'll have a future, albeit years from now."

"This is ludicrous. What's to keep me from killing you on the spot? That would really keep me out of the papers except for my coming victory in the election." He got up and went around to the door. "You know what? I've had enough of this." He shoved the door closed and approached Mat. He leaned over and picked up the phone. As he began to dial, Mat aimed a knee at his groin. She rushed for the door as Dan bent over groaning and coughing from the pain. It was already open. Standing in the doorway was Jim, Dan's chief of staff, a rope in one hand and the other arm around Gilbert's neck. He stood like a statue while Gilbert tried desperately to grapple his arm from his neck. At the same time, Sheila came barreling down the hall, a stack of posters in her hand.

"Hi Jim," she said, cheerily pushing past him, "I just need to speak to Dan quickly. She pulled up short seeing Mat standing, arms akimbo facing Jim. "What are you doing here? I thought you quit. Never mind, this'll only take a second." She pushed past Mat and went over to Dan who was still bent over gasping in pain.

"Mr. Collins, what's wrong? Shall I call an ambulance?" She reached over for the phone and picked up the handset.

"No!" Dan grabbed her hand and straightened up as much as he could. "I don't need an ambulance."

"But you're ill! You should see a doctor. You can't get sick now, the election is only a week away," Sheila cried, attempting to wrest the phone from Dan. He grabbed it and shoved her against the desk.

"I don't need a doctor. Just leave, now."

Sheila turned to see Jim holding Mat by the arm and the rope in his other hand. Gilbert lay crumpled on the floor where Jim had dropped him after using a choke hold to immobilize him.

"What's going on? Why do you have that rope? What are you doing?" Sheila stared wide-eyed at the chief of staff, taking in Mat's terrified expression and Jim's hand on her arm.

Dan stood up with a groan. "Your timing has never been great, Sheila. I'm afraid it's going to get you in a lot of trouble this time."

"What do you mean?" Sheila turned to look at Dan, hurt and bewilderment written all over her face.

"Did you get my message? Is that why you're here?" Dan asked his chief of staff. "Never mind, it doesn't matter why you're here."

"Yeah, I got your message, but that's not why I'm here."

"Oh?"

"I'm not waiting until this little issue is taken care of to discuss my increase in pay."

Dan stared at him, disbelief leaving him momentarily speechless. "You really want to do that in front of this audience?"

"Why not, they'll soon be dead. But I get your point. We can wait until this is over, not a minute longer."

"Agreed. Let's get them out of here. I don't want any more volunteers wandering back here to see this."

Jim looked down at Gilbert. "He'll be out for a while."

"You take Gilbert out back and do whatever you want with him. I can handle getting these two women into my trunk." Dan pulled a handgun out of the top drawer of his desk, checked to see that it was loaded while Jim held both women in

e-llegal code

an iron grip. Mat watched in fascination as Dan put the gun in a shoulder holster. Sheila began to cry uncontrollably.

"Shut up!" Dan hissed at Sheila. "If either of you yells, I'll shoot the other one, got it?"

Sheila stopped blubbering and she nodded along with Mat.

They exited the office but instead of attempting to walk them through the front, Dan turned them toward the back and around a corner to a door that opened into the back parking lot. *Damn! Now Greg won't know what's happened.* Mat fought panic as she and Sheila were bustled over to Dan's limo. They were shoved into the trunk and the lid was slammed shut.

They heard Dan's voice outside the trunk, "You can yell all you want. Yell yourselves hoarse. We're taking back roads out of here and no one will hear you with the traffic anyway. Mat felt tears welling up and blinked them away as best she could. She swore and pounded the lid of the trunk. *How did I get here? Locked in a trunk with a ditzy, middle-aged housewife who's falling apart beside me. OMG, it's only going to get worse. She took a deep breath and said to herself, "I will not cry."* She repeated the mantra over and over as the car lurched out of the parking lot and sped into the street, only slowly realizing Sheila was quiet beside her. "Sheila," she whispered. *Please* tell me you haven't passed out."

***

In the lengthening shadows of early evening, Greg watched Dan shove both women into the trunk, glad he had made the decision to leave the office and watch the front and side of the building from across the street. He saw Jim go to his car with Gilbert over his shoulder and drive off. As Dan's big limousine pulled out of the parking lot, there was no question who he would follow. He sprinted to his car, started the engine, picked up his cell, and dialed Greene's number.

Chapter 28

Slowly consciousness returned. Gilbert struggled to sit up, blinking his eyes, trying to see through a filmy darkness. Tight ropes bound his wrists and feet. He breathed deep, trying to clear his head of the last bits of fog.

"Good timing."

Gilbert turned toward the voice.

"Who are you? Where am I?" Gilbert's voice croaked.

"Don't worry. Your voice will return to normal eventually." The shadow moved under the single lightbulb illuminating the top of a head, putting the face in a shadowy light. Gilbert saw the edge of a small table next to the shadow. He recognized Dan's campaign manager. "You're Jim something or other, right?"

"Jim will do. We go a long way back, you and me. We were even buds for a while, went different directions in the end. I have a proposal for you."

"What's that?" Disoriented, Gilbert fought to clear his mind.

"I spent some time in Croatia a couple of years ago, as a mercenary I think it's called, in their little war of independence."

"Yeah?"

"Great place to make a quick buck if you follow me."

"Not sure I do. Anyway, what does it have to do with me?" Gilbert was finally able to shift to a sitting position, his back against a cold concrete wall. He looked up to see small windows at the top of the opposite wall, lit by the glow of street lighting. *I'm in a basement somewhere.*

Jim squatted down and looked straight at Gilbert. "I need something done for me and, lucky me, you're one of a few people who can do it."

"What makes you think I'd do anything for you?" Gilbert croaked.

"Because I know who you care about and where she lives. Believe me, I won't hesitate to make my presence known if you refuse to cooperate." He stood, pulled a single chair over in front of Gilbert, and sat.

"One other thing. Those yahoos you set up to follow us are wandering around the neighborhood looking for you. They'll never find us. So if you refuse to help me, you won't be able to help your daughter because you won't leave this building alive."

Gilbert raised his head until he could look Jim in the eye. "If you harm a hair on her head . . ."

"You'll do what? Kill me? How quaint. Let me assure you, that won't happen. But I will just as surely kill you and your daughter if we have to discuss this much longer."

Gilbert stared silently at Jim, then sagged against the wall. "What do you want?"

"There's a little problem of a pending investigation involving drug smuggling that I may have been involved in."

"Ahhh."

"Indeed. I need it to go away."

"What makes you think I can do that." Gilbert managed a sneer. "Make a pending investigation go away?"

"Because I know where you are in the pecking order of this investigation. You're the one who brought the charges. You can make them go away. I'll give you three minutes to consider any other options you think you have before I kill you and go after your daughter." He pulled out his cell phone and dialed a number.

"While you are thinking, I've got another issue to clear up."

***

In the limo, Dan picked up his cell phone and called Hector.

"Hello, Doc."

"What do you want," growled Hector.

"Now that's no way to greet an old friend. I have a proposal for you concerning the subject we spoke about earlier."

"I'm busy."

"Believe me, you want to take time to relax a little and hear my proposal. I'm almost to your building. I'll pick you up out front." He hung up and drove the few miles to the morgue, obeying the speed limits, stop signs, and red lights to the letter. Hector was waiting outside on the curb, pacing impatiently. Dan drove up beside her and unlocked the door.

***

Inside the trunk, Mat noted the stop and voices. *Maybe this isn't a stoplight. Should I yell?* With a lurch, the car moved on. Mat concentrated on the turns and odd sounds she could pick up from the trunk but soon lost track as they sped down the streets. Voices from inside the car were a low murmur, at times louder, at others quiet. It was impossible to make out the words. She thought about punching out one of the taillights. Sheila stirred beside her. *She can help. Maybe a cop will see it.*

Chapter 29

Half an hour later the car drove over rough terrain and then over gravel and came to an abrupt stop. Dan pulled his gun from a shoulder holster and pointed it at Hector.

"We're getting out of the car now. If you try to run, two people in the trunk are dead!"

Dan got out of the car and went around the front to the passenger seat. He opened the door.

"Out!" he ordered, stepping back from the door.

Hector stepped out. The car had stopped in the middle of a large clearing in an old lumber yard. It was deserted now except for stacks of unmilled wood and a ramshackle building. A few spotlights were coming on as the darkness descended.

"Where are we?" asked Hector. She swallowed in an attempt to control a growing panic. She looked around, eyes darting left to right.

"Used to be a thriving lumber mill but the owner fell on hard times. Had to sell. Guess the new guy wasn't into lumber that much. He sold most of the inventory and is looking for an investor. Probably going to turn this into an apartment complex or something."

"Why are we here?" Hector's voice almost broke in her fear. Her eyes locked on Dan's, pleading. She kept talking, trying to distract him. "What's going on? Please tell me," she finished with urgency in her voice, growing desperate to know what she faced.

"Well, I'm not planning to kill you. Not if you do what I say."

"What is that?" Hector gulped. She took a deep breath to squelch a rising hysteria.

"You're going to help me dispose of a couple of bodies."

"What?! Bodies? No, I'm not! I could have told you that back at the morgue!"

"Yes you will, or you'll lose everything you've worked for all your life. It's not a big deal anyway. You just happen to work at a convenient place for hiding them."

Hector stared at Dan, her eyes wide in horror.

"No, I can't. I won't. I won't do it!" She backed up a step or two, trying to put some distance between herself and the images he conjured.

Dan turned murderous, unhinged eyes on Hector. He seemed to grow in stature, hovering over her, a giant in front of a helpless child. He stepped forward, closing the gap she'd tried to create between them.

"Tell you what. I won't kill Sheila if you do what I want." His smile chilled her. "How does it feel to have a life in your hands instead of a dead body?"

Hector's panic began to overwhelm her. Her voice shook. "You said two people are in the trunk. Who is the other one?"

"That snoopy computer dame. Thought she'd put one over on me with a software fix." He chuckled. "Well, I can fix her fix once she's out of the picture. Then she came here tonight with some notion of a work log that stupid kid was keeping. It's time to clean all of this up and you're going to help me."

"No!" Hector blanched at the full import of Dan's words.

"Aww." Dan's tone changed to sarcasm. "Don't say 'no' to me." He cocked his gun and pointed it at the trunk. "All I have to do is unload this clip into the trunk and if both of them aren't dead, they'll be in a world of hurt."

"No, no. Don't, please. I'll do it," Hector pleaded with pain-filled eyes. "Don't shoot. Just please tell me one thing."

She watched in horror as a slow smile grew on Dan's face. His calm in the midst of her desperation sent fear spiraling upward. "What do you want to know?"

"My daughter. What happened to my daughter?" Hector pleaded, her voice breaking with emotion. She crumbled onto the ground, shrinking into herself, begging him. "Just tell me! What happened to her . . .?" her voice trailed off, lost in overwhelming sobs.

He cocked his head, running his eyes over Hector as if observing an interesting specimen in a lab. "All right. But only because I'm feeling generous. If you want to blame anyone, blame Lilah. If she hadn't gotten herself pregnant none of this would have happened. But she did and she expected me to be happy about it!" His voice rose in amazement. "Me! A political candidate with an election coming up. She kept saying she didn't care if we weren't married. All that stuff didn't matter to her." Dan's posture grew belligerent. "Well, it matters to my voters for sure! So, yes, I gave her pennyroyal. I thought it'd make her lose the baby. What else could I do? I couldn't have that getting out." He dropped his eyes to the ground in a moment of reflection. "Outside of that, she was a lot of fun and someone attractive to take to parties." His tone grew harsher as he continued, "She ruined it all by getting pregnant. How was I to know she'd take so much and kill herself?"

"What about my Minnie?" Hector whimpered. "Why did you have to kill my Minnie?"

"Ah, Minnie. If she hadn't come to see me I wouldn't have had to get rid of her. But she did. She came to my campaign headquarters and accused me of killing Lilah." He glared at Hector, his expression radiating bewilderment. "As if that was *my* fault!" He marveled at how the world had turned against him. "And you! You're no better than those two."

"What do you mean?"

Suddenly the screech of tires interrupted them. A small tan sedan threw up rocks as it sped into the lumberyard and came to a stop beside Dan's limo. The driver's door opened, and a woman stepped out.

"What the hell are you doing here?" demanded Dan, his strident voice reflecting consternation and confusion.

"I'm trying to save your ass and your campaign. And my career."

"What do you mean? How can you save my campaign? It's not . . . it's fine. What's going on!" Dan demanded.

"I need you to win this election and you're ruining it all."

"I am not! There are just a couple of loose ends to take care of. It's all under control."

"I doubt that. I'm here to make sure you take care of those loose ends, Dan. I've got too much tied up in this. I told you, you've got to win this election or I'm going to lose everything."

"How are you going to lose everything? You can just stay in your ivory tower with the other over-educated, privileged airheads who can't find their way out of a paper bag without help."

"Is that so? It's not that simple. I'd have to start over at another college, one without the reputation this one has. My life's work would never be noticed. I'd be finished where it matters." Dr. Peterson paused to draw breath. "I can't let that happen. I was even going to guarantee your win with that routine in the code for the Votomatic machines."

Dan's mouth dropped open as he stared at her. "I thought that bitch—" He pointed to the trunk of his car. "I thought she was making that up."

"She wasn't. Now you're in for another surprise. I sent Jim to your campaign. He's been keeping an eye on you from the start."

Dan continued to stare at her. "But why?"

"I told you. I need for you to win and go on to bigger things. I let you do things your way, but now it's my turn. I know you're laundering money for the guys up north. Your cleanup guy works for me. Once we knew the code would work, we needed to get rid of the kid who broke into the vote counting headquarters. Unfortunately, he forgot to get the disk and I had to send him back to find it. Trouble was, he chose a couple of idiots to break into the morgue who wouldn't have known what they were looking at even if they found it."

Dan continued to stare at her, speechless.

"Before you think about turning on me, let me assure you all the evidence points to you. After all, you're the one everyone thinks has the most to lose. I'm just an over-educated, airhead who couldn't possibly dream up something like this. I also have evidence of your money laundering to use if necessary." She walked over to stand on the other side of Hector.

"We do have a problem now, don't we?"

"We?"

"Yes, tie her up and let's get it over with."

"What about the two in the trunk?"

"What two?"

"Some computer bitch and a stupid volunteer from my office."

"You idiot! Why did you bring them?"

"That bitch said she was going to rig the vote against me. The other woman just walked in at the wrong time."

Professor Peterson said in exasperation, "Heaven help us. Well, no way around it now." She pointed at the trunk. "Once we have them taken care of, we can figure out how to get rid of the bodies. Tie up that one." She pointed to Hector. "Get the others out of the trunk. Go on, do it now!"

e-llegal code

Dan grabbed Hector, hauled her to her feet and spun her around, capturing both wrists in one hand while he pulled a two-handled cord from his pocket. "Good thing I brought two of these." He wound the cord around Hector's wrists, tied them, and shoved her to her knees. "Stay there or I'll take care of you first."

***

As soon as the trunk lid opened, Mat raised up on one elbow, her eyes blinking rapidly at the sudden light that was fading fast as the night approached. She could make out Dan, and Hector kneeling on the ground to his left with her hands behind her back.

"Out!" Dan ordered, staying a couple of feet away from the trunk.

Mat crawled out of the trunk, hanging onto the side of the fender to get her balance. She looked around, then stopped, staring in surprise at the woman beside Hector who stared back, equally surprised.

"Professor Peterson! What are you doing here?"

Lynn recovered first. "Oh my God!" She turned to Dan. "Why was she in your trunk?"

"I told you. She's the computer bitch who said she was going to rig the voting machines."

"I heard you." She turned back to Mat. "I just never dreamed it would be you! Why do you always turn up in the wrong place at the wrong time?"

"But Lynn," Mat began, "why are you here? What is going on?"

"I told you Dan had to win so I could continue with the research that would clinch a tenure-track position for me. I'm just ensuring that happens. I'm sorry you got caught up in our plans." She turned back to Dan. "Let's move this along. Who's the other person?"

Dan peered at Sheila who had not moved. He turned to Mat. "What's with her?"

"I think you've scared her to death. She passed out, hasn't said a word since you shoved her into the trunk."

"Well, isn't that convenient? Still, what she doesn't know won't hurt me." He turned his attention to Mat. Before he could take a step toward her, a car careened into the yard. They both turned toward the sound, momentarily blinded by its headlights. It ground to a halt and Jim stepped out, leaving the headlights on to brighten the scene.

"What the hell are you doing here?" bellowed Dan.

"Helping you, although it seems that isn't necessary."

"What about that DEA agent? Are you done with him already?"

"I let him go."

"You what? I told you to get rid of him!" Dan shouted, his eyes shifting rapidly from Mat to Jim to Lynn and back.

"He and I have an agreement. I can always get rid of him after he does a little job for me." Jim leaned against the car, thumbs in his belt. "I'll get

e-llegal code

rid of him the way I got rid of that student for Dr. Peterson and that girl for you."

"So it was you who killed that student?"

"Don't be so surprised. Dr. Peterson hired me for all kinds of tasks. Turns out you've benefited from my skills as well."

"You mean this skill?" Dan holstered the gun, reached into his jacket pocket, and pulled out a short cord with handles at either end. Mat's eyes widened as she stared at it. Dan chuckled at her expression.

"Never seen a garrote? I'm willing to bet you've never had one around your neck either." He laughed. "Well, there's a first time for everything. But I'll give you a chance to skip this experience. Answer this question and maybe I'll let you live. Did you rig the voting machine code like you said?"

Lynn turned to focus her attention on Mat. "Well, did you?"

A slow smile accompanied Mat's response. "You'll know when the votes come in." She watched a mix of emotions run across Dan's face, first surprise, then confusion followed by anger at the implications of her words.

"It doesn't matter." Lynn turned to reassure Dan, "I can get another student to break in and check before the election."

"Then your death is on you," Dan growled, heading for Mat.

Mat turned to run but Dan was surprisingly quick. He got an iron grip on her arm, and she couldn't wrench herself free. In one swift movement, he got the garrote around her neck and started twisting the handles, quickly tightening the cord and keeping her from getting her fingers under it. Mat heard Hector screaming and Dan's hot breath next to her ear. He tightened the noose, slowly enjoying the terror he knew it brought his victim. "Jim showed me how to use this. It's ironic, really. When they find your body they'll even think he did it."

Mat struggled to draw breath, fighting the terror of the tightening cord with every bit of her strength.

"It's no use, you know. I can take my time, but the ending will be the same."

Mat clawed at the rope, feeling her consciousness slipping away, black spots growing larger and larger as she struggled for breath. She could hear Hector crying for him to stop and Jim laughing in the distance. Gathering her strength for one last attempt to escape, she tried to aim a hard backward kick to his knee when she heard a loud *crack* followed by another and the cord went limp. She fell to her knees, gasping for breath.

Through roaring ears, Mat heard sirens, and Sheila's voice mixed with Greg and Detective Greene's. She breathed deeply, trying to clear her head and catch her breath. She felt hands on her shoulders and stronger ones pulling her to her feet. Then she was looking into warm hazel eyes flecked with gold and slumped into Greg's arms.

Chapter 30

It didn't take long for the area to be lit up by the headlights of police cars and ambulances. A fire truck arrived given the threat of fire in the old lumber yard. Mat sat in the back of an ambulance while the medic checked her vitals with Greg beside her. Sheila was in the other, protesting that she was fine.

"Why is Sheila here?" Greg asked.

"You won't believe it, but she's the mole Gilbert told me about. She barged into Dan's office on purpose when she saw us go in. She told me while we were in the trunk that she is DEA. She said she was going to act like she'd passed out in the hopes that Dan would ignore her. That's exactly what he did."

"I believe it. Greene and I came running when we saw Dan put that garrote around your neck. We were over by the stack of lumber and couldn't hear anything. Sheila says she recorded the whole thing on a microcassette. Then she put a bullet in him and Jim from the trunk."

"Glad she finally got around to it. I thought she'd forgotten about me." Mat rubbed her neck. "So Dan's dead?"

"'Fraid so."

"What about Lynn?"

"Who?"

"Dr. Peterson. The woman who was standing by Dan and Jim."

"Oh. She wasn't armed and we caught her trying to drive off in the confusion. According to Sheila and Hector, who is fine by the way, Jim confessed to killing Kim and Minnie. Dan told Hector he gave Lilah the pennyroyal."

"What is Hector doing here anyway?" Mat asked.

"Dan called her. He wanted her to help him hide the bodies in the morgue when he had taken care of you and Sheila. He was blackmailing her."

"What could he possibly know about Hector to blackmail her with?"

"She won't say and now we'll never know." Greg shrugged. "Probably just as well."

Mat looked up at Greg, panic fresh in her eyes. "Where's Gilbert? Dan's tough guy left with him. He was supposed to get rid of him."

"Gilbert had a couple of his DEA buddies keeping an eye on us. When they split up, one of his buddies followed Jim and Gilbert." Greg pointed them out next to Sheila. "Apparently, Jim worked some deal with Gilbert, choked him unconscious, then left. The agents spotted Jim when he came out of one of the buildings they had targeted. One of the agents found Gilbert in the basement. The other one followed you and Sheila. He was with us by the pile of lumber. We couldn't tell what was going on."

"How did you know where we'd gone?"

"I didn't stay inside the campaign headquarters. I got nervous and wanted to be where I could see both entrances and the parking lot if possible. I was across the street when Dan put you and Sheila in the trunk. I followed you and called Greene on the way."

Mat's expression shifted from understanding to puzzlement. "One thing I don't understand is why Sheila, if she's such a hotshot DEA agent, didn't take care of Dan before we got shoved in the trunk."

"I asked her that. She said then the charge would only have been attempted kidnapping. She was going to try to get him to confess to money laundering through the drug lords. Then Hector got him talking. Now all our questions have answers."

"Except one." Mat looked over at the police cars and ambulance clustered together on the other side of Dan's limousine.

"What's that?"

"Lynn. Dr. Peterson. I'd never have thought she'd go to such lengths to make sure her research was good enough for that position she wanted. It's hard to believe she's changed that much from the person I knew in college."

"Maybe you never really knew her back then."

Mat pursed her lips. "I guess."

Greg looked at the medic who nodded that Mat was good to go. "You'll need to give the police a statement, but Greene said that could wait until tomorrow first thing." He put his arms around Mat, who was still wrapped in the light blanket the medic had given her, and they walked slowly to his car.

***

"Mat, you're up early." Zorah hauled her bag of painting supplies and fabrics through the front door. "I just brought these home to go through them and get rid of some stuff. What are you doing up so early? Sorry, I already said that."

She paused, sitting down in the chair opposite Mat who was curled up on the sofa, an afghan wrapped around her. She sat up at Zorah's entrance. "Sooo, why *are* you down here? Couldn't sleep? Stay there"—she motioned to Mat to lean back into the sofa again—"I'm going to get us a cup of tea."

She went to the kitchen, turned on the kettle, and searched for tea and mugs while continuing to talk. She returned to the sofa, handing Mat one of the mugs. "I know! You want me to guess," she said with a big grin. "This'll be fun. Let's see, you had a nightmare, you were wishing you were with Greg instead of here, you—"

"No, no," Mat interrupted her, laughing at her nonstop chatter.

"Greg brought me home late last night to get some sleep. He thought I might sleep better if he wasn't here. But I couldn't settle down. After what happened, I don't think I'll sleep for a week."

"Oh Mat, you mean something happened last night?"

"In spades." Mat summarized the day and evening's events and sat back. She still felt a little blindsided by it all.

"Ohmigod." Zorah stared at Mat with a mixture of fascination and horror, her hands around a steaming cup of tea.

e-Ilegal code

"Honestly, Zorah, until Sheila told me who she was in the trunk of that car, I had no idea she wasn't just another infatuated fan with a crush on Dan. She played her part so convincingly. Dan never suspected. She sure fooled me too." She paused to take another sip of tea. "But the person who really shocked me was Lynn. I just never would have guessed she was so obsessed with getting that position at the university that she'd do what she did." Mat studied Zorah's expression for a moment. "If this means everything you said before is moot and you'll be leaving, I'll understand. I sure don't want you to stay here if it upsets you. There must be someone else out there to share this house, although I'm sure she, or he, won't be nearly as interesting as you!" *Or as compatible, fun, caring, etc.*

Zorah smiled shyly at Mat. "A while ago I'd have thought the same thing. After getting kidnapped, I was ready to pack my bags. But I really like it here. I reminded myself that I wasn't going to let my fears keep me from doing the things I love. That includes living where I want to and being friends with who I want to. It's hard to remember that decision sometimes, but I have to or I'll just go backward. And I'm not going to do that."

Mat returned her smile in earnest. "I couldn't have told you before how glad I am that you're staying. When I first thought you'd leave, I told myself finding another roommate would be easy. I mean, who wouldn't want to live here? But when that thug broke in and I realized I really might need to do that, it put me in the worst mood."

"I'm glad too. I'm not easy to live with. Not many people can give me space to sleep when I want, and they don't want to listen to me talk about my art or friends at the studio. You seemed so interested from the start. There's only one thing you have to promise me you'll do."

"What's that?"

"You absolutely have to let Salee come over and do her Xtreme Xorcism."

"Her what?"

"Xtreme Xorcism. And the sooner the better." Zorah's expression and tone had turned deadly serious. "You have no idea how strong the negative emanations coming from you are. They are following you around from your experience last night and if we don't do it soon, they'll find a home here and we'll have a devil of a time, pardon the expression, getting them out of here. Then I would have to seriously think about moving. It would get into my art, and all kinds of negative things would happen to my inspiration."

"Well, we can't have that." Mat smiled, then added, "Seriously," to assure Zorah she wasn't making fun. "You know, I'm starting to feel some of those emanations you talk about. Not much, but it's there."

Zorah smiled back. "It's a start. Now you need to try to sleep. I'm going to try a new meditation chant that Salee told me about. It's supposed to help bring on a long, deep sleep. If it works after this conversation, then it's the real deal. And I'm going to need it to get the new commission

e-llegal code

finished in time. Mat, I really think I'm on my way!" She got up, put her cup in the sink, and went to grab her bag of fabrics and paints.

"If it works, please tell me about it," Mat's voice followed her out of the kitchen. She sat going over the events of the past several days, wondering more than once at the close calls she'd had. *One thing's for certain, this consulting gig isn't the boring grunt work I thought it might be. Sure there are moments, but, frankly, they are a welcome respite when other things are going on, kidnappings, illegal commerce, voter fraud, murders . . .* After another cup of tea, Mat checked the doors and windows and headed upstairs. *I think I could sleep all day and night,* she thought, snuggling under the covers.

***

It was the end of the road. Mat looked behind herself trying to see how she'd gotten there, but she couldn't tell. Trails led from the mouths of caves with well-trod paths between them, all leading to where she stood. In front of her was a giant canvas, its images growing and fading in the bright light of a new morning. She tried to see around it, to what lay ahead, but the blinding light made it impossible to see. Then she began to float, hovering over the scene below. To her left was a large billboard with the words "New Slate" over pictures of four people whose features were blurred, each one looking like the others. She looked to the right: the mural she'd seen before had grown larger. It was centered in the middle of a crowd of cheering people, all raising champagne glasses in a salute to the artist who stood on a platform beside the mural. The artist's face was turned away as she looked at her mural. Beside her was an easel. A bucket filled with paint brushes, each dipped in a different color of paint, was on the floor. As Mat watched, the paint brushes rose up one after another and swept across the canvas, slowly obscuring the entire scene with soothing tones of blue and green.

If you liked this book, please consider leaving a review.

Thank you!

Free Short Story!

Sign up for the author's mailing list and get a free copy of ***Johnny and Jake***.

A chance encounter ramps up a long-standing feud between two brothers.

In Johnny's mind, his life seems to careen down a one-way street of lost opportunities, ones that favor his brother Jake.

How long can one endure a life spent watching your brother have it all?

When feelings run this deep, tragedy is waiting in the wings.

Click here to get started: cvalba.com

About the Author

C.V. Alba is the author of action-packed mystery novels set in the urban environment of 1990s Washington D.C. These gripping crime thrillers are rooted in the years she spent in the business world of high-tech.

There she encountered dishonesty, cover-ups, half-truths and outright lies—even murder and crime as thrilling as any murder mystery. From those experiences she developed her strong female protagonist. Her mystery stories provide fast-paced action and adventure mixed with romance and strong friendships.

C.V. Alba grew up in Europe and the United States. She loves detective and murder mysteries solved by strong, assertive but vulnerable women. She also enjoys walking, music, and most of all, her family. She resides in Virginia with her husband.

C.V. Alba's work has been published in the Blue Ridge Writers Journal and the Journal of the Virginia Writers Project.

Acknowledgements

Who to thank first? Certainly, John Nicolay former editor of Blue Ridge Writers and current editor of Virginia Writers Project who published my short stories.

Krysta Winsheimer, my editor who gave me constructive advice and wonderful suggestions along with encouragement and wisdom. She is incomparable.

Members of the Virginia Writers Project, my Beta readers, and numerous others who read early versions and helped shape this book.

Last, but not least, Jerry for his love, patience and encouragement while I worked on this book, and Peter who supports me, laughs with me and is the other great joy of my life.

Made in the USA
Middletown, DE
06 June 2024